The Sugar Sands

Lyle Garford

Dedication

This one is for Richard and Tracey and Shadow

Except where actual historical events and characters are being described for the storyline of this novel, all situations in this publication are fictitious and any resemblance to living persons is purely coincidental.

Copyright © 2021 by Lyle Garford

All rights reserved. No part of this book may be reproduced or transmitted in any form or by any means, electronic or mechanical, including photocopying, recording, or by an information storage and retrieval system, without permission in writing from the publisher.

Published by:
Lyle Garford
Vancouver, Canada
Contact: lyle@lylegarford.com

ISBN 978-1-7772783-5-9

Cover photo by Dmitry Bruskov/Shutterstock.com

Book Design by Lyle Garford
www.lylegarford.com

First Edition 2021
Print Edition available on Amazon and other retailers.

Chapter One
Barbados
May/June 1772

The young British Royal Navy officer was standing at ease, staring out at the tranquil Caribbean waters of the broad sweep of Carlisle Bay, Barbados as it shimmered in the unseasonable heat of a late May afternoon. The deck of *HMS Wiltshire*, the small 28-gun Royal Navy frigate he was standing on, was rocking slightly from the light chop of the gentle waves rippling the surface of the bay, making a host of other Navy and merchant ships at anchor in the harbour do the same. In the distance he could make out tiny figures going about their business along the broad waterfront docks of Bridgetown, the capital of Barbados.

With little else to occupy him as he stood waiting, the officer's mind drifted to focus on the ongoing problem he faced in dealing with a pair of the more truculent members of his regular watch. The two men, Ralston and Hodges, were the newest and rawest members of the crew and neither of them wanted to be where they were. The Second Officer of *HMS Wiltshire* gave the barest shrug of acknowledgment when asked about their history.

"Not sure, Mr. Spence," said the officer. "I think they were given a choice of sweating in whatever stinking jail they were in here in Barbados or joining us. In any case, they are in the Navy now."

"I guessed as much, sir," said Lieutenant Owen Spence, the twenty-year-old Third Officer of *HMS Wiltshire*. "They don't seem to have any experience with the sea, but I wanted to make sure of it. Well, we needed more men, and we take what we get. They will learn soon enough."

How to go about teaching them what they needed to know was the issue. An all too easy solution was to simply beat both submission and knowledge into them, whether they wanted it or not. Both men had already tasted the bosun's starter, a thick and stiff piece of rope with a chunk of lead embedded inside the tip to give added weight. The bosun's usual practice was to whip it hard across whatever part of their bodies were to hand and several occasions to do so arose in the week since these new men joined the ship.

The two men had already also witnessed far worse punishment delivered by the same bosun as he applied the lash to the back of another miscreant strung up on a grating. The minimum twelve lashes delivered created a cross hatched pattern of deep, painful stripes on the sailor's back. Both newcomers had watched the punishment in glowering silence.

None of this was new to Owen, for his family had sent him to sea when he was barely fourteen years old to serve in the Royal Navy as a midshipman. Having since served with a variety of different Royal Navy Officers above him, Owen long ago learned not everyone had the same style of leading their men. Many took the simple approach of using harsh discipline, even before any sign of trouble. On the opposite end of the spectrum a few actually strove to lead them willingly before resorting to the lash.

Owen thought of the latter approach as being

both firm and fair in his dealings with the men and he preferred it. This usually meant finding a way to reach an understanding with them, helping them to realize he really was trying to be fair and their own best interests lay in cooperating with him.

More than a few sailors in past made the mistake of viewing this as a sign of weakness, but they soon learned what a lack of compliance would bring, for Owen had no qualms about showing how firm he could be. He preferred minor punishments such as stopping a sailor's grog ration for a day, but the lash was always waiting to be used. Several of the more obstinate ones over the years ended up being flogged as punishment because Owen put them on report.

Owen knew he was fortunate many of the senior officers on the three different ships he served on since joining the Navy leaned toward using the firm but fair approach to varying degrees. Owen learned over time by watching how they handled a host of different situations the best approach was to take slow but firm steps toward reaching an understanding with raw newcomers to the ship. His dedication to learning the skills necessary to sail any ship afloat combined with the growing confidence he could truly lead the men under him led to passing his examination for Lieutenant six months ago.

With his future seeming bright and boundless, the mundane reality of dealing yet again with two more raw recruits was not about to faze him. He well knew he would find a way through to these two men, sooner or later. The hardest part was to make the initial gain of mutual understanding, however small it might be.

But as he mused over how to do it with these two in particular, a slow trickle of sweat was running down the middle of his back from the warmth of the day and the heavy dress uniform coat he was wearing. The combination made him drowsy and it difficult to focus on how best to reach these two men. The distant thump of a ship's boat touching the side of the frigate brought him wide awake from his reverie, for the reason he was wearing his dress uniform was about to board the ship.

Both the old Captain and the First Officer of *HMS Wiltshire* were already gone, shifted to serve on other ships by the Admiral in Barbados in charge of The Leeward Islands Station, while the new ones were coming to take command. Owen was well aware new senior officers would have their own ways of commanding the men, but he was fully confident he would adapt to whatever those ways were. Both he and the Second Officer were frustrated no one had bothered to tell them who was coming to join the ship, but it no longer mattered, for the wait was now over.

Owen took one last, sweeping look about to ensure the sailors manning the side were at attention as the Second Officer had commanded and fully ready to welcome the new Captain to the ship with due honours. As the Captain's hat appeared at the railing the bosun immediately began to pipe him aboard, while the Second Officer ordered the salute. Following right behind the Captain was another Officer and a young, teenage midshipman.

Owen stared at the three new arrivals, feeling a mild sense of foreboding steal over him without understanding why. The Captain had a fleshy, slightly overweight look to his face which matched the rest of his body. Combined with his greying hair the overall picture was of someone who had long since given up on exercise in any form. Owen judged him to be perhaps in his mid to late forties, while the First Officer standing beside him was half his age at best. In a flash of insight Owen saw the clear resemblance between the two men. A quick glance at the young midshipman joining them confirmed his own resemblance with the two more senior officers, making it obvious all three were from the same family.

To find a midshipman related to a ship's Captain was in no way unusual, for to be sponsored by a family member was a convenient way to find a career for second or third sons who weren't expected to inherit a title or relatives from an officer's extended family in a similar situation. Having a First Officer with a familial connection was much more uncommon and enough to raise eyebrows, but not unheard of. With the nation not at war, openings on warships were at a premium, and Owen knew it was all too likely the Captain had been granted a favour.

The growing sense of unease remained. As Owen focused on it, he realized what he was feeling was due to the odd sense the Captain himself was somehow familiar. The realization of who the new Captain was finally struck home hard as the Second Officer stepped forward to greet the man and introduce himself. The shock was enough to rock Owen back slightly on his feet before recovering himself. The surprise of the man's appearance here and now was an icy stab to the heart, for Owen had not seen him for over eight years. The Captain glanced briefly at Owen on seeing the unexpected movement, but he turned his attention back to the Second Officer now speaking to him.

"Captain, permit me to welcome you and your First Officer aboard *HMS Wiltshire*. I am Second Officer Lieutenant George Strand. You have the better of us as to who you are, as all we received was word our new Captain and a new First Officer would be coming today."

The Captain shook the proffered hand of the Second Officer perfunctorily before speaking.

"I am Captain John Smithe. This is your new First Officer, Lieutenant Harold Smithe and, yes, he is one of my sons. The midshipman with us is my nephew, Francis Smithe."

"I am honoured to meet you, sirs. Permit me also to introduce our Third Officer Lieutenant Owen Spence, Captain."

Owen saluted and stepped forward, offering his hand in welcome also.

"Captain, I am honoured as well. Welcome aboard, sirs."

The Captain glanced briefly down at the extended hand before looking up with an icy, frigid stare at Owen's face without saying anything. Owen left his hand outstretched for an awkward moment before pulling it back with a sinking feeling in his heart, for he was certain Captain Smithe now realized who he was.

"Lieutenant Owen Spence, is it? That would be Owen Spence, one of the younger sons of Richard Spence of Torquay, wouldn't it? Yes, of course you are. I can see the family resemblance. I was not aware you were aboard. I trust you understand your presence here wouldn't have been my choice, but no matter. You are here now."

The Captain turned back to the Second Officer, who was standing in open-mouthed surprise at the affront the Captain had given to Owen and was clearly still trying to digest the implications of what had occurred. The Captain scowled as he spoke.

"Well? Let's be about it, shall we?"

"Uh, sir?" said the Second Lieutenant, still looking confused and not understanding his meaning.

"Good Lord," said the Captain, turning for a brief aside to his First Officer. "You've got some work to do with this lot."

Shaking his head, the Captain turned again to the Second Officer, speaking with slow emphasis as if he were talking to an errant child.

"Mr. Strand, I live in hope somewhere in your head is the knowledge of what a Captain does when first joining a new ship?"

The Second Officer stiffened at the obvious rebuke as he responded.

"Sir, yes, sir. You need to read yourself in. I shall muster the men."

Close to ten minutes later the entire crew had finally made their way from wherever they were to the waist of the ship and been assembled into something resembling a state of order to hear the Captain read his orders aloud from the quarterdeck. Aside from the standard language of all such orders to assume command of a ship the only real point of interest to the crew and the officers was the news *HMS Wiltshire* was being transferred to the command of the Admiral of Jamaica Station for active duty. The Captain was ordered to take on sufficient stores for the journey and to shepherd a small convoy of British merchant ships to Kingston when they were ready to depart.

As he finished reading his orders the Captain folded them up and returned them to his pocket. Now officially in full command, every man aboard knew the Captain wielded absolute power over all aspects of their lives. The critical question now was how he would go about it. He glared about at the sea of faces with an ominous, dark look on his visage before speaking.

"Right. All of you need to understand I expect obedience to myself and my officers above all. The Articles of War are there for a reason. You ignore them at your peril. I will not hesitate to order discipline when I deem it necessary. I also expect efficiency and, I must tell you, I am not impressed with what I have already seen. When you are ordered to do something, you do it instantly and not when you bloody feel like it. I simply cannot believe how long it took you all to gather to hear me read myself in. This will improve or the bosun will be paying attention to you with his starter more than you would like. Or worse. The choice is yours."

The Captain fell silent for a moment, glaring

about as if daring anyone to speak. No one did, for even newcomers to the ship like Ralston and Hodges were well aware of the power conveyed to the Captain by The Articles of War, a stringent set of rules covering a host of behaviours forbidden to those serving on Royal Navy warships. Little room for forgiveness or mercy was in them.

"So, you have been told. I want this to be the most orderly, efficient, well run ship in the entire Royal Navy and it shall be. You are dismissed."

As the men shuffled back to their duties the Captain called to Owen and the Second Officer to remain where they were as he stalked over to stand in front of them. The First Officer and their new midshipman came to stand behind the Captain.

"Gentlemen, that was bloody appalling. I cannot believe how lax they were in following orders. This speaks directly to the kind of leadership you two display. Or perhaps it is the obvious lack of leadership. Lieutenant Smithe, I will be in my cabin. I want this ship set to rights immediately and I want to be underway to Jamaica by the first week of June. I leave the task and these two for you to deal with."

As the Captain turned and marched aft toward his new cabin the First Officer stepped forward, but he looked first at the new midshipman still standing to the side.

"Francis, go muster a party to have our kit brought aboard. Make sure the Captain's belongings are first. He is already disappointed, and it won't do to make it worse."

After watching him salute and leave, the First

Officer returned his attention to the two officers.

"Well, you heard him. He has high expectations and so do I. Mr. Strand, you will now give me a tour of the entire ship. Along the way you can introduce me to the warrant officers. What is our complement of Marines, sir?"

"Lieutenant, we have a dozen Marines and one Sergeant. I will introduce you to him on the tour."

"Very good. Mr. Spence, while we are doing this you will gather the ship's logs for the past three months for inspection. You will also prepare a detailed inventory of all stores, including ordnance for my review. I also want an understanding of how your watches are organized and who is doing what. The tour will not take long, so have this ready within the hour. You are dismissed."

"Sir," said Owen, saluting before he turned to go. As soon as he was free, he went as fast as he could to find the gunner and the purser, for he knew he would have to rely on their intimate knowledge to meet the demands placed on him. He swore to himself as he went, for the trickle of sweat running down his back had turned to a river and it wasn't because he was left with no time to get out of his heavy dress uniform.

***

Three days later Owen was supervising a group of men loading more stores into the hold in the stifling heat of the afternoon. Ralston and Hodges were in the party, as they were the rawest members of the crew fit for little other than heavy, physical work such as this. As they finished wrestling yet another barrel over to be slung into the hold, they both wiped their brows and went across the deck toward a small, open cask of water with a dipper attached for drinking. Owen was bent over peering into the hold at the men below and hadn't seen them leave until he straightened up. He scowled when he saw them.

"Ralston! Hodges! Get back here. Now, damn you!"

"Sir, we are thirsty," said Ralston, as Hodges took a quick gulp from the cask before handing the dipper to Ralston. He quickly did the same and both men returned at the double back to their positions.

"You bloody fools. You don't do anything unless I tell you to. Everyone is thirsty, but we get the job done first. In future you wait your turn."

"It's only because it's so hot, sir," said Hodges, a resentful look on his face.

Owen rolled his eyes. "You think I don't know this, you jackass? You don't see the other men wandering off doing whatever they want whenever they feel like it, do you? For God's sake, just shut up and get back to work. We'll have no more of this or you'll both be facing punishment, you hear?"

As Owen turned back to the task at hand, he saw the new midshipman Francis Smithe had appeared and was standing nearby. The young man had obviously watched the scene and now wore an odd look on his face. Owen glared at him in response.

"Well? Do you need me for something or are you just dawdling about?"

The young man stiffened and saluted as he responded, an aggrieved look on his face.

"No sir, I am on my way to see the First Officer

with a report he wanted."

Owen couldn't help scowling. "So why are you standing here? Get on with it."

Owen's work party had finished the job an hour later and he was dismissing the men when the First Officer came looking for him. As the men dispersed Lieutenant Smithe drew him to the side, folding his arms as he glared at Owen.

"Mr. Spence. I have a report some of the men were straying from their duties and then arguing with you about it. What do you have to say for yourself?"

"Sir?"

Lieutenant Smithe sighed in an obvious display his patience was being tried and shook his head.

"Midshipman Smithe reports two of your men were derelict and gave you back talk today. I want to know what happened and what you did about it. Now, sir."

Owen groaned inwardly as he explained the situation and tried for a hopeful conclusion.

"Lieutenant Spence, these men are the rawest of our recent recruits and know little of our ways. Between the bosun with his starter and myself, we have made progress. I am confident we will have them in line in future, sir. I made it clear to them any more such displays will bring swift punishment."

He was hoping the way he had dealt with the men would meet with approval as he finished speaking, but the icy look on the First Officer's face dashed the notion.

"Really, Mr. Spence? I think we had better see if

the Captain has confidence your approach is best for all concerned."

***

The sickening, meaty sounding slash of the latest stroke of the cat across the sailor's back was different than the first few already delivered. These had seemed like a quick, sharp cracking sound to Owen, but as the red stripes continued appearing, etching deeper and deeper into the man's flesh, the sound became a muffled, wet slap muted by the blood now being spattered widely across the deck. The bosun's hands were red with gore as he applied the last few lashes to the second of the two men receiving punishment.

Little time was wasted to summon the crew to hear The Articles of War read aloud and for the Captain to announce his decision. Both Ralston and Hodges were sentenced by the Captain to twenty-four lashes each. Hodges's muffled screams ceased as he went limp and lost consciousness soon after the first twelve were delivered, but Ralston had borne the punishment better. Even so, he was groaning aloud in agony by time the last few strokes were applied.

Owen supervised the working party tasked with cleaning up after the crew was dismissed. Ralston gave him a frozen look of mute anger mixed with pain as he was cut down from the grating he was tied to and a sailor stepped forward to offer him help to go below. Owen made certain none of the other officers were close enough to hear him as he spoke under his breath to the man.

"You can't say I didn't warn you."

Ralston gave him one last quick glance conveying a mixture of both despair and hatred at the same time, before he winced and began moving on. Midshipman Smithe came over and saluted as the blood was rinsed away over the side and a party of men began holystoning the deck to clean the stains.

"The Captain wants to see you, sir. I am to assume charge of the working party."

Owen glared at him in silence for a few long moments before turning away. The temptation to ask if he was satisfied with the outcome of what he had done was strong, but Owen knew it would only land him in yet more trouble. The Marine standing guard outside the Captain's cabin saluted and announced him as a visitor. From within came the muffled order to enter.

Owen resisted the urge to look about as he came in, for this was the first time he had come aft to see the Captain. In itself, this was unusual, for most new Captains always hosted a dinner for the officers of the ship soon after taking command as a way to know them better. Captain Smithe had extended invitations to his son and his nephew every night since joining the ship, but none to either Owen or the Second Officer Strand. Owen saluted and focused on the Captain seated at his desk, with the First Officer standing off to the side. The Captain wasted no time, frowning as he spoke.

"Mr. Spence. I am sorely disappointed in you. I expect you believe the punishment I ordered today was excessive, as it was more than the usual minimum punishment. As far as I am concerned, the men need a clear understanding I mean what I say. As for you, I am sad to say there are many more like you out there who believe in coddling the men. Well, I made myself clear when I came aboard, did I not? I simply won't have any of it. The Navy is built on discipline, sir. You will change your ways in dealing with the men or you will suffer the consequences, sir. The Articles of War apply to you, too. I told you what I wanted and as far as I am concerned, you have disobeyed me. I will be generous this time and merely offer you a warning."

The Captain sat back in his chair and stared at Owen for a long moment.

"Well, have you anything to say?"

"I understand, Captain. I appreciate your generosity, sir."

"Do you, now? I expect you are wondering why I am even being generous given our history, aren't you? No, don't answer that. You know I am being magnanimous. Your father deserved everything which happened, and I regret nothing. But I am not such an ogre I would hold his son to account, too. As I told you when you came aboard, this situation is not my choice. But make no mistake, if you are going to serve me you will do so on my terms or not at all. There is nothing further to say. You are dismissed."

"Sir," said Owen, saluting as he turned and left. His once seemingly bright and boundless future was now shrouded in darkness. Worse, the ship around him felt like a cage.

***

In the short space of less than two weeks the

atmosphere of *HMS Wiltshire* changed from being a normal Royal Navy ship to one far more muted and fearful. No one could be heard laughing, even when off duty. The men had simply hunkered down to wait for the situation to change, which inevitably it would. The problem was the day when it might happen was nowhere in sight and likely wouldn't be for a very long time. Fortunately, the small convoy the Wiltshire was to shepherd to Jamaica was finally ready to depart, muting the growing frustration of the Captain at their delays. The crew could forget their problems with the work at hand.

Second Officer Strand finally found time to talk to Owen without others to listen in two days out on the journey. The Captain was unhappy with the way the ship was sailing and sent both of them to look at the contents of the hold to see if anything could be shifted to improve the situation. Strand looked all directions to make doubly sure no one was nearby before he spoke.

"Mr. Spence, we find ourselves in an interesting situation, don't you think?"

Owen eyed the man warily, before glancing about himself and responding. While the two men had served together for over five months now, Owen couldn't claim to know him well.

"I expect one could describe it this way, sir."

"Indeed. Mr. Spence, I confess I am rather taken aback at how the Captain is dealing with us, and you in particular. Can I rely on your discretion here, sir?"

"Sir, you can."

"Understanding our situation a little better might

help both of us, although I don't know there is much either of us can do about it. You obviously have some history with him. What can you share with me?"

Owen sighed. "Sir, it is a long story, but I will try to condense it. In case you are not aware, the Smithe family is large and very wealthy. The family has several sugar plantations of various sizes throughout the Caribbean and several properties back home. The Captain's uncle is in the House of Lords. I think the Captain himself has plantations out here, but where my family comes into the picture is with his properties in England. My father was involved with him in some small land transactions together and the relationship soured. I met the Captain long ago when I was barely twelve years old, before it all went wrong. I don't know much of the details, since I was just a child. What was relevant to me, you see, was my family nowhere near as wealthy or connected and this is still the case."

"I do see. Go on."

Owen shrugged. "My father reached a point where he understood he was being undercut and he was in clear danger of losing everything. I didn't know at the time, of course. Being as young as I was, I only knew my parents were very worried. The problem the family faced is my father was an honest man. I think once he became involved, he realized there were some elements of very questionable dealings going on and he was not happy about it. He couldn't disentangle himself, and it became so acrimonious he called Captain Smithe out and challenged him. The Captain refused, preferring to settle the matter in court. As I said, they have far more resources than us."

"And your father lost everything."

"Most everything. He was crushed, sir. With what little influence he had left he found me a posting as a midshipman and here I am. I received word some months after sailing I would never see him again. He was found at the base of a cliff, smashed on the rocks. I was told the official story is he was out walking, likely slipped, and fell. I think the truth is he fell into depression at being unable to provide for the family. My mother was equally crushed by this. She had health problems and, I think, simply lost heart and the will to live. She is gone, too."

"And now you have no family left?"

"My younger sister was sent to live with a distant aunt and uncle. I have an older brother in the Army somewhere. I do have other aunts and uncles out there, but I have not seen any of them in years. The Navy has become my family."

"I see. Well, the Captain seems to be bent on maintaining a harsher discipline than either you or I are used to, sir. And his son appears to be of the same mind. No surprise, I guess. I will think on it and your situation in particular, but I see no easy answers to changing this. I don't know, Mr. Spence. Right now, the only way out I can see is to request a transfer or to somehow be invalided off the ship. Both of those courses of action are fraught with obvious problems. Who do you think the Admiral on station is going to listen to, us or the Captain?

You could maybe feign an illness, but when would you get another posting? In any case, thank you for your confidence. Of course, this conversation never happened, you understand."

"I understand, sir, and I appreciate your concern."

"Right. Let's get back to business."

***

When he came off watch later in the evening Owen ate his dinner with little enthusiasm. The Marine Sergeant in the officer's wardroom, a gregarious man named Thomas Dawes, tried engaging him in conversation, but let the attempt go on seeing Owen had no interest in being social. The fact the midshipmen at the table included the Captain's nephew was an inhibiting element for everyone.

Owen had deliberately minimized his interactions with him since the incident with Ralston and Hodges. The young midshipman responded by walking a fine line, offering a knowing smile whenever they did interact which could be interpreted in different ways. He was careful not to give obvious offence, but Owen had little doubt the younger Smithe was all too ready to use his relationship with the Captain and the First Officer to maximum advantage.

The rest of the officers and crew quickly learned the same lesson. Despite being junior to the three other midshipmen the ship was carrying Smithe soon began ruling them with an iron fist. One had already been caned severely by the bosun for a minor misdemeanour while another was mastheaded by the First Officer as punishment for a similar offence. Both punishments were the direct result of Midshipman Smithe bringing the transgressions to the attention of the First Officer.

Owen relented and apologized to the Sergeant, feigning being tired before retiring to the miniscule quarters set aside for him alone. This consisted of a small bunk bed with space underneath for his duffel bag, a tiny desk with a chair and a lockable drawer to keep the little money he had on hand safe, and a hook on the wall to hang his uniforms on. The space was framed by thin wooden screens on either end which could be removed if needed. A sheet pulled across the length of his quarters gave a small measure of privacy. As small as it was, it seemed a welcome refuge where he could let his guard down and be himself.

The problem was he felt as wooden in his small haven as he had come to feel every time he was on duty. The simple joy of being young and proud of having achieved the skills to sail and command a massive Royal Navy frigate was gone. Being forced to constantly present a bland, stiff face to the others on the ship without ever being able to let his guard down was completely foreign.

The worst part was he could do nothing about it and his earlier conversation with Lieutenant Strand had sent him even further to the depths of despair. As he had told the Lieutenant, the Navy was his family and, in fact, his life. He had no one at hand to fall back on if he was forced to leave, and he had few resources to see him through if he did.

His parents gave him a small sum to see him off

in his new life when he left home for the Navy, but he had no room for luxuries. Little was left of his meagre pay as a Lieutenant after paying his regular wardroom expenses. Even purchasing new uniforms on being promoted Lieutenant had dwindled his resources alarmingly. As the nation was at peace, he had no prospect of earning more by sharing in the reward of captured enemy ships bought by the prize courts into the Navy.

Owen gave a small sigh as he lay stretched out on his bunk. Realizing how tense he felt he deliberately focused on trying to let it drain away. He knew nothing could be done for now and his only remedy was to stay the course, hoping for a change in fortune. The release he sought from the tension took a long time to come.

***

"Lieutenant Smithe, what in God's name are they doing on that bloody scow?" said the Captain, an angry look etched on his face as he focused his glass on the last of the six merchant ships following well behind HMS Wiltshire. The Captain had ordered the frigate to tack on hearing a hail from their lookout advising one of their charges was slipping well behind the others.

The First Officer was doing the same as his father, except he was wearing a confused frown on his face. He finally brought his own glass down and turned to Lieutenant Strand. A frustrated tone was obvious in his voice as he spoke.

"Lieutenant, signal those bastards they are to make more sail immediately. Have the gunner fire a gun to make sure they are paying attention. Captain,

I don't know what to make of this. I could understand having issues maybe once or twice, but this is the third time today."

Aware of how unhappy the senior officers were, the Second Lieutenant ensured the orders were swiftly carried out. The Captain grunted his approval, but a scowl remained on his face as he replied to his son.

"Well, if they don't get going there won't be a fourth time, because we will fall back and put a shot through their sails to show them who is in charge here."

The bark of the signal gun firing made both men raise their glasses once again, straining to see if their message had any effect. Lieutenant Strand and Owen were standing nearby on the deck and both followed suit. Silence descended for a moment as everyone focused on the scene, before Owen called out a warning.

"Captain! There was puff of smoke mid ship just now. I think someone on the ship fired a swivel gun."

"Yes, I believe he is right," said the First Officer. "I—good God, what is happening on that bloody ship?"

All of the officers stood open-mouthed in shock as the merchant ship fell away from the little convoy in complete disarray, her sails shivering badly. Two of the yards were unable to bear the strain and snapped off, bringing a tangle of rigging crashing to the deck. The Captain let loose a stream of angry curses as he snapped his telescope shut. Finally mastering himself, he turned to the First

Officer.

"Bloody lubberly idiots. Lieutenant Smithe, bring us about. Signal the rest of the convoy to heave to while we run down and sort this mess out. So much for making good time to Jamaica. Lieutenant Spence, take Midshipman Smithe and find out what these incompetent bastards are doing. Take Sergeant Dawes and a party of his Marines with you as well. If they are busy shooting at each other, you may need to bash some heads. I'll be in my cabin."

The Captain turned and stalked away toward his cabin before stopping near the entrance. He turned back to glare at Owen.

"And Lieutenant Spence? When I say bash heads, I do mean you will bash heads. I am talking about the first sign of obstinance. I'll have none of your mollycoddling these fools and I don't care about the fact they are civilians. I want this convoy back underway immediately, you hear?"

"I understand, sir," said Owen, but the Captain was already marching back to his cabin.

Ten minutes later the Wiltshire was stationed a hundred yards off the starboard side of the badly wallowing merchant ship. Wary of what they might find, Owen made certain the boarding party was heavily armed and ready for anything. As they rowed closer Owen was able to study the ship better, having had little time to do so before the convoy sailed.

The ship was named *The Perfect Lady*, but up close she failed miserably at living up to her name. Even at a distance Owen was sceptical about how well maintained this shabby looking old ship was. She was in dire need of fresh paint and, in Owen's experience, this was almost always a tell-tale sign of other problems to be found. Reaching the ship's side, Owen grabbed the rope ladder of the floundering ship with some difficulty. Once he had a firm grip, he barked out orders before he began making his way up the side.

"Right. Marines to follow me smartly. Everyone at the ready, please. God knows what we are going to find here."

Owen couldn't believe the scene before him once he made his way over the railing and steadied himself. The entire main deck was a muddled shamble of tangled rigging, broken spars, and torn sails. In the waist of the ship Owen could see four dead sailors lying in pools of their own blood, undoubtedly the result of a blast from the swivel gun set on a railing at the top of the stairs leading to the quarterdeck. Yet more dead men were strewn about on the quarterdeck itself.

The only living men in sight were sitting clustered around the mainmast. One of them eyed him with a bleary look as Owen approached. With effort he attempted to struggle to his feet. The sailor almost fell on his face as he did, as he was unwilling to let go of the half empty bottle of rum in one of his hands. Blood stained his clothes in several spots, but none of it appeared to be his own. A cutlass dark with drying blood on the blade lay near where he had been sitting. He looked down at the others lying on the deck.

"Avast, lads, thank God, for the Royal Navy is

here to save us. Get on your feet."

Finally steadying himself with one hand on the mast he took a quick swig from the bottle before turning to look at Owen, grinning innocently and slurring out a further few words.

"Aye, we've had a right bad time of it, Captain."

"You are drunk. Put the bottle down and listen to me. I am Lieutenant Spence of *HMS Wiltshire*. Who are you and what in God's name is going on here?"

While Owen was speaking a second man struggled to his feet and tried to take the bottle from the sailor Owen was talking to. Owen intervened, grasping the bottle himself and hurling it overboard. An outraged look appeared on the second sailor's face and he made to throw a punch at Owen, which was easily dodged. Owen kicked him hard in the groin and the sailor fell to the deck, vomiting profusely where he lay. With him out of the way Owen reached out and grabbed the first sailor by his shirt to pull him closer. The reek of sweat, stale breath, and the overpowering scent of cheap rum almost made Owen gag.

"Answer me, damn you, or you will be puking on the deck like him."

The sailor's eyes bulged in fear as he stammered out a response.

"Sir, I am able seaman John James. The Captain and the First Mate tried to murder us all, I swear it. You see for yourself the swivel gun set on the quarterdeck, right? They used it on those dead men over there. We had no choice but to defend ourselves. Sir, they were tyrants. This ship has been a living hell."

Owen was silent for a moment before shaking his head in dismay.

"You imbecile. You have just condemned yourself, because what you are talking about is called mutiny."

Owen shoved the sailor away from him and he stumbled as he fell back, landing hard on the deck with a shocked look on his face. Owen turned to the men waiting behind him, focusing on the Marine Sergeant first.

"Sergeant Dawes, detail a couple of men to guard these fools. If they can find some chains to load them down with then by all means use them. The Captain will decide what to do with this lot. You and the rest of your men are to search the rest of the ship in case there are more of them. If you find more, bring them here and load them down with chains too. Mr. Smithe, have Midshipman Green in the cutter waiting below row back to the ship. He is to request the Captain send our carpenter and a working party to clean this mess up so we can get the ship underway. He can also tell him this appears to be a mutiny and we are still actively investigating. When you have done this you will join me in searching the Captain and First Mate's quarters to see if we can learn more."

As he was finishing speaking the sailor John James struggled back to his feet and made to grab his Owen's shoulder to talk to him again.

"Sir, it wasn't like that, I—"

One of the Marines saw him coming and smashed the butt of his weapon into the man's midriff to stop him. The sailor crumpled and fell to the deck clutching his middle with a groan of agony. The men around Owen began dispersing in all directions. Owen gave the prisoners no more thought and strode over to mount the stairs to the small quarterdeck. He found yet more bloody carnage, as four additional dead bodies were strewn about the deck. All of them bore vicious slash wounds from cutlasses, although one had been run through by a much finer, bloodied sword still in the hand of the man Owen presumed was the dead Captain.

Owen sighed and looked back at the swivel gun pointing into the waist of the ship. These small, portable weapons could easily be mounted anywhere on a railing of a ship and their normal use was against external threats. Because this one was obviously placed to defend against an internal threat spoke volumes, but it changed nothing. Mutiny was mutiny. Midshipman Smithe came up and saluted as Owen was searching the pockets of the dead Captain. He found what he was looking for in the form of a small chain around the man's neck with a key.

"Mr. Green is on way back to the ship, Lieutenant. Orders?"

"Nothing we can do but try and learn more. I expect what this sailor told me will be enough to damn them all, but we must be thorough and do our job, Mr. Smithe. We need to search the cabins and see if we can find a log or a journal to tell us more. I am thinking this key may help. Let's go."

Going below they soon found what was clearly the First Mate's sparse quarters, while Owen was certain the next cabin aft had to belong to the Captain. After a quick look around, he ordered Smithe to do a thorough search of the First Mate's quarters and then join him as he went onward.

Owen frowned when he found the Captain's cabin to be as bereft of belongings as the First Mate's, but he realized this would be in keeping with the poor condition of the ship itself. Owen surmised this was a man living on a knife edge, perhaps only a few steps away from life in a debtor's prison. A ship in such poor condition would be an obvious sign to all but the most desperate men the Captain would pay little, thus attracting the kind of men for the crew who would need harsh discipline to keep them in line.

Finding little of consequence in the man's few belongings Owen turned his attention to the small desk. Most of the drawers held nothing more than normal writing supplies, but the key unlocked one holding what Owen was looking for. He reached in and pulled out a book Owen was certain would be the ship's log, a second small notebook, and a small but heavy bag clinking with the sound of coins. Midshipman Smithe came in as Owen was studying the small notebook.

"Sir, there was nothing of consequence in the First Mate's cabin."

"Right, well, this is what the key unlocked for us. Have a look at the log to see if you can find anything while I deal with this."

"Is that a bag of coins, sir?" said Smithe as he began leafing through the log.

"Hmm? Oh, yes. I doubt there is much in it. This

notebook seems to be a personal diary, but he is a man of few words. I don't see anything in here raising alarm. Anything of interest in the log, Mr. Smithe?"

"No, sir," said Smithe, quickly leafing through the pages. "This looks to be just the usual navigational notes one would expect. No mention of problems with the crew or even punishment."

"Strange. Right, let's be off."

As he finished speaking a Marine stuck his head in the door.

"Lieutenant? The Sergeant is still below finishing the search, but he is almost done. I am to report a few other men were found below. They were passed out from the drink. They have been brought on deck with the others."

"Thank you. You can tell him I will meet on deck shortly if you see him."

"Shall we bring all of this with us, sir?" said Smithe as the Marine left.

Owen mulled it over for a brief moment. "No, we put it all back in the drawer. The Captain will want to decide what we are going to do."

Owen locked it all back in the drawer, leaving the key in the lock. As they left the cabin Owen looked at Smithe.

"Right. I'm going back on deck to sort this mess out. Find the Sergeant and have him post a Marine to guard the cabin, then report to me on deck."

"Sir," said Smithe, saluting as Owen carried on down the corridor and up the steps to the open deck.

By the time Owen made his way back to the deck the working party from the ship was climbing aboard. Lieutenant Strand had joined the party at the Captain's request, a sign of unhappiness over what was being reported to him. The two officers were soon deep in discussion with the carpenter over what he was seeing. Almost thirty minutes later Lieutenant Strand shook his head and turned to Owen.

"Well, there's nothing for it. This is a bloody mess and I think it will take far too much time to make effective repairs at sea. We will have to take it in tow. You've done enough over here Mr. Spence. Take Mr. Smithe back with you and report to the Captain. I will stay here and supervise with Midshipman Green. It's going to be a slow voyage to Jamaica."

A half hour later Owen was standing in the Captain's cabin making his report. As he finished the Captain slammed a fist on the desk in frustration.

"My God, civilians. You are certain we have no choice but to take them in tow, Lieutenant?"

"Sir, both myself and Lieutenant Strand agree with the carpenter's thinking. The merchant ship has no spare supplies. We would have to use our own stores to make temporary repairs. Even if we did, she would be limping along."

"Damn, damn, damn. Well, I shall make it clear to the Admiral where the fault lies for the delay in our arrival. And the bloody mutineers?"

"They are now in chains in the hold and awaiting your decision, sir."

"Much as I would love to string them up on what is left of their yards, we will leave it for the civilians to decide. You are dismissed."

With *HMS Wiltshire* a hive of activity taking *The Perfect Lady* in tow, Owen had little time to focus on anything but the task at hand. He was about to go off watch for some much-needed rest after the job was done when the First Officer appeared beside him. Owen had come to recognize when the man was angered, and he sensed it immediately from the frozen look on his face.

"Mr. Spence. I have a disturbing report about you."

"Sir?"

"I confess I am having difficulty believing this about a Royal Navy officer, but I trust you understand when I am told an officer has stolen something which does not belong to him, I will investigate."

Owen's jaw dropped. "Stolen something? Sir, I have no idea what this is about."

"Mr. Spence, I am told there was a bag of coins in the Captain's cabin on that ship. It was in a small brown coin pouch with a draw string. I am further told you were observed pocketing this. Where is this bag and why did you not report it?"

Owen was shocked, but with effort recovered himself.

"Sir, it is true there was a small bag of coins in the drawer where the Captain kept his log and his diary, which I told the Captain I had examined. I mentioned to him we left everything where it was found. A Marine was posted to guard the cabin. I swear to you I did not take the money."

"Really. Well, if this is the case then you will not

object to a search of your belongings."

"Of course, sir. Please, let's proceed."

After making their way below Owen gestured at his meagre belongings in his bunk and stood to the side as Lieutenant Smithe worked his way through it all. The Lieutenant briefly examined the money in Owen's locked desk, but he soon left it for Owen's money was in a dark green bag. The last item he chose to search was the duffel bag. The Lieutenant stiffened as he reached the bottom and turned to look at Owen before pulling a bag out, holding it up for inspection. Owen stared open-mouthed, not believing what he saw, for this was the same bag from *The Perfect Lady*.

"Let's go, Mr. Spence. We will discuss this with the Captain."

Owen followed the First Officer aft and saw Midshipman Smithe standing off to the side on the quarterdeck, wearing the same knowing smile Owen had come to loathe. Owen was thinking furiously as they went and in a flash it all became clear. Unable to resist he stalked over to him, steaming with anger. In a grating, low voice Owen made certain only the Midshipman would hear him.

"You evil little shit. This is your doing. I swear to God, you will pay for this."

"Mr. Spence! Get back here this instant." barked Lieutenant Smithe, after suddenly realizing Owen was no longer behind him. "Now, sir!"

***

An hour later the breadth of the plot against Owen was laid bare. Midshipman Smithe testified to the Captain he saw Owen surreptitiously pocket the bag before leaving the cabin without knowing he was being observed. The Marine who poked his head in the door confirmed the bag now sitting on the centre of the Captain's desk was the same one he had seen on *The Perfect Lady*. Midshipman Green affirmed he was off duty in the officer's quarters and thought he saw Owen dash in briefly to rummage in his belongings after returning from the merchant ship.

Owen had stared hard at Midshipman Green as he spoke, but the young man refused to look at him. Owen understood why, for he was the youngest and most timid of the midshipmen on board. A scenario where Midshipman Smithe had either bribed or more likely threatened him into saying what he did was all too possible to imagine. Even as young as he was, Midshipman Green knew well where the power lay on board *HMS Wiltshire*. All Owen could do was to testify to what he knew was the truth, but it wasn't good enough for the Captain.

"Well, Mr. Spence. I have heard all I need to here. I believe I pointed out to you once before The Articles of War apply to you. This kind of behaviour is a breach of so many of them I hardly know which one to apply first. But as you are an officer, this requires a court martial. We will undoubtedly find sufficient Captains in Jamaica to convene one. I cannot have you continuing to serve until this is resolved. Lieutenant Spence will have a separate space prepared for you, as I'll not have your taint in the wardroom any longer. You will confine yourself to whatever space is prepared for you until we reach Jamaica. Now get out of my sight and await the Lieutenant on deck."

"Sir," said Owen, saluting perfunctorily before turning to leave. As he did, he saw Midshipman Smithe standing behind the two senior officers where they couldn't see him. The young man openly smirked with glee at Owen for the barest moment. And as Owen walked out of the cabin, he heard the Captain speaking once again.

"Harold, we have a gap to fill because of this. I will make Francis here acting Lieutenant to help out until we reach Jamaica. With any luck the Admiral will see fit to find a ship for your own and we can make Francis's acting permanent."

Chapter Two
Jamaica
July 1772

Three days after reaching Jamaica and dropping anchor in Kingston Harbour, Owen was peremptorily summoned from what was effectively the temporary prison he had been confined to below deck. The Marine who appeared told him he was ordered to bring all his belongings and follow him to the deck. Owen was brought straight to the First Officer, blinking in the sunlight he had not seen in days as he stopped and saluted. Lieutenant Smithe was blunt.

"Lieutenant Spence, the Captain has ordered you off the ship. You are to find quarters for yourself ashore and to advise us of your whereabouts. You will be summoned in due course for your court martial."

Owen was shocked, shaking his head briefly before replying.

"Sir, I am still an Officer in the Royal Navy. Am I not entitled to my berth on the ship?"

Lieutenant Smithe scowled. "Are you deaf or just stupid? You are in fact still an Officer in the Navy, which is why when you are ordered to do something, you bloody do it. How much longer you are an Officer remains to be seen."

"Sir, may I at least submit a chit to the purser for my expenses?"

"I think it most unlikely the Captain will authorize it, but I will ask him. Now take your kit and get off this ship. The men are waiting to row you ashore to Port Royal."

Owen stood staring at the man for a long moment, before looking around. Everyone in sight seemed to be deliberately looking away, but Owen was certain they all knew exactly what was happening. Owen turned back to the Lieutenant, gave him a perfunctory salute, grabbed his duffel bag, and made his way to the side of the ship. A sailor lowered his duffel bag down to the small ship's boat as Owen climbed down to where a midshipman and two sailors waited.

Five minutes later the boat left him to set foot on the shore of the historic Pallisadoes, the winding, thin isthmus forming the outer barrier of Kingston Harbour. The sudden shock of going from a dark, smelly, and dank makeshift prison cell to the fresh air and sunshine was a surreal sensation. Adding to the strange numbness Owen felt was an ominous foreboding over what had happened. Owen could see no logical reason for it, but without doubt one was somewhere in the Captain's mind.

Adding to the turmoil he felt inside was the new reality of where he now was. Owen had never been there before, but he well knew the history of this place, which was in reality little more than a long sandbar built up naturally over time. While his inner confusion and circumstances put a damper on it, he still couldn't help feeling curious about what was arguably one of the most famous ports in the Caribbean.

The Pallisadoes was once far larger than now. In the late fifteenth century the Spanish occupied the island of Jamaica and established what would eventually become the town of Port Royal on it, but the Spanish presence was never very large. In 1655 the British forces of Oliver Cromwell's regime needed a victory and after casting about for a target they ousted the Spanish from the island. Although Spanish Town was the official capital of Jamaica, Port Royal soon became the dominant economic centre of the island because of the port and a key decision made by the Governor at the time. This dominance soon made it the largest centre of power in the entire Caribbean.

Wary of a Spanish attempt to retake the island, the Governor of the period invited The Brethren of the Coast, descendants of the pirate buccaneers, to make Jamaica their home base. This motley group of pirates was composed mainly of English, Dutch, and French sailors making a living preying on the merchants of nearby Spanish islands and those on the entire coast of the Spanish Main itself. The English government in Jamaica legitimized their activities by offering them letters of marque from the Crown as privateers. With a secure base to resupply their ships, strength in numbers, and their new veneer of legitimacy, the privateers were motivated to succeed.

The ensuing flood of riches from ships and their cargos being brought into Port Royal to be condemned in the prize courts was enormous. With their shares of this massive new wealth the crews naturally wanted to celebrate, and Port Royal soon became known for far more than being a major economic centre, to the utter dismay of the more upright, religious citizens of the island.

A host of taverns, inns, and brothels soon appeared to fuel all manner of drunkenness and debauchery. At peak the town was rumoured to have one tavern for every ten citizens living in it. A host of merchant shops and warehouses along with Royal Navy facilities were also crammed onto The Pallisadoes, making it a warren of narrow and all too often highly dangerous streets for the unwary.

A massive earthquake in June of 1692 brought it all to an end as two thirds of the town disappeared beneath the waves, with the resulting tsunami destroying what hadn't already sunk below the water. Although Fort Charles at the entrance to the Harbour survived, along with parts of the Royal Navy Dockyard, attempts to rebuild the town to its former state saw little success. Combined with the growth of the importance of sugar plantations, the days of the privateers were numbered. Across the Harbour the town of Kingston grew in response and Port Royal never regained its former prominence.

Owen had long felt one of the benefits of being in the Royal Navy was the opportunity to actually see the far distant shores which the dry pages of books he read long ago in school spoke of. Despite Owen's natural inclination to explore it all, he brushed it aside to face his far more immediate concerns. Lodging prices seemed exorbitant at the few inns he could find. On seeing the dismayed look on his face one of the innkeepers took pity on him.

"As much as I would like to have you paying me for one of my rooms, I sense you are concerned about the prices. They are indeed high here, as establishments such as mine are few on The Pallisadoes. We have numerous merchants, Navy officers waiting new postings, and people staying here to await passage to England or somewhere else. May I suggest you hire a boat to ferry you across to Kingston, sir? You will find a much wider range of prices and establishments there. I am sure one of them will meet your needs."

Owen thanked the man profusely and did as he suggested. Several small boats waiting for customers like him lined the waterfront, while a swarming host of others jostled for position around the numerous anchored warships. Everything from coconuts filled with rum to fresh fruit to whores were on offer to those aboard. Some of the brisk business being conducted was with the approval of their officers, but much was not, for the officers couldn't be everywhere at once. He stared wistfully at the various other Royal Navy ships in the Harbour as he was rowed past, wondering if he would ever find himself aboard one as a serving officer again. A large seventy-four-gun ship of the line dominated them all, undoubtedly the flagship of the Jamaica Station Admiral.

Standing on the main docks of Kingston Harbour was a far different experience. While Port Royal had what seemed a fair bustle of activity about it, the contrast with Kingston was stark. These docks were crammed with merchant ships in virtually every available space in the process of loading or unloading all manner of cargo. A host of warehouses, shops, taverns, and inns lined the broad sweep of the street set back from the docks following the curve of the bay. Everywhere Owen looked people were bustling about their business with purpose. A large proportion of mostly black men Owen knew could only be slaves were doing the hardest and most physical work in the blazing hot sun.

Owen soon realized inland beyond the docks yet more taverns and inns could be found. As the prices for a small room seemed high along the waterfront he ventured deeper into Kingston warily, but the further he went the more questionable and seedier it became. The tension he felt over the whole situation seemed unbearable and he had no way to lift his spirits. Hot and thirsty from trudging about with his duffel bag, he finally stopped in one of the taverns for a drink and to get himself out of the blazing mid-day sun.

As he gratefully sipped at the ale brought by a young black serving girl, the turmoil he felt inside slowly changed to an unfamiliar lassitude over what to do next. In the well-ordered life of a Royal Navy officer something always needed to be done, leaving little time to think of anything else. His only real need now was to find lodging which was clean, inexpensive, and would meet his simple requirements. With nothing to do beyond this and as it was still mid-afternoon, he knew he had plenty of time to find something suitable.

Although this tavern also had an inn with rooms above it, in looking closer at his surroundings he wasn't certain this would meet his standards. The few other customers in the tavern appeared as unsavoury as the tavern itself. The entire place seemed poorly maintained, but he stayed where he was and ordered yet another drink when his mug was almost empty. If nothing else, the bored serving girl was pretty enough, and she seemed more than willing to engage him in conversation to pass the time.

***

Owen awoke late the next morning to the sun streaming into the room past the rough, makeshift curtains covering the one window in the room. The light stabbed his eyes as he opened them and he groaned as he moved his head, instantly regretting making a sudden movement. He held his head in his hand with eyes closed again, struggling to find a memory to explain what was happening. The stale, sour taste of ale in his mouth soon answered at least one of the questions in his mind.

A vague memory came of ordering yet more to drink and deciding to remain where he was. The girl was eventually replaced by another server and once she was off duty, she joined him at the table. He remembered her arranging for the two of them to take a room upstairs at some nebulous point further in the evening. With a start, Owen realized he was likely not alone in the creaking, old bed he was in, but after cracking open one eye and turning slightly, he saw no one was with him. Despite this, the girl had obviously spent time in it at some point, for he could smell her scent on the bed sheets and could see someone had lain there.

Owen checked his money and saw his funds were rather more depleted than he wanted them to be. As he counted it out the memory of paying the girl her fee came back to him. Feeling depressed and ashamed of his weakness, Owen nonetheless made an effort to clean himself up by using the nearby washbasin and towel he assumed the girl must have brought for him. He looked around the dingy, poorly maintained room and decided there had to be somewhere better than this to stay.

He stopped to have breakfast in the tavern before setting about with his bag to find a different inn. After checking with a few more places, he found one not far from the waterfront which held promise. The exterior seemed little different than the others, but the interior was another matter.

At first, he couldn't place why The Spanish Rose Inn was this way, as the few customers drinking in the tavern which occupied the ground floor were certainly no different than any of the others he had seen. In a flash of insight, he realized what made it stand out was how the subtle touch of a woman was obviously at work in how the place was decorated. This tavern had plants, pictures, and the occasional dish of flowers to soften the feel of what was otherwise merely another place to drink or sleep. The walls were also painted in bright, soft colours, whereas all the other taverns Owen had stopped at were done in various dark shades. A small check in counter near the staircase leading up to the rooms above was decorated in the same way.

The answer as to who was responsible for it all soon came when he enquired of the tavern serving girl about lodging. A slim, petite woman with ink black, softly curling hair barely reaching to her shoulders appeared from the back to deal with him and she introduced herself as the proprietor of the Inn. Owen was taken aback for a moment, but even as despondent as he felt he had to smile on seeing her. She looked up at him and smiled in turn, giving him an appraising look.

Despite himself, Owen couldn't help feeling an immediate attraction to her. She was perhaps a few inches over five feet tall, with dark eyes matching the colour of her hair and a cheerful, pleasing face. She wore a loose, shapeless dress which failed to hide the fact her breasts seemed proportionately a little larger than what he would have expected for her small frame. Fine lines around the corners of her eyes betrayed the reality she was perhaps in her early to mid-thirties in age.

Owen sensed the same level of interest from her. He knew his six feet of height, slim and strong frame, and his youth would be attractive. The few women he had occasion to be over the years with had confessed his dark brown hair and weathered, strong face presented a compelling picture overall. Despite his best efforts not to let it show, her price for a room was a little higher than he wanted. She seemed to sense it and without him asking she lowered her price substantially when she learned he might be there for more than one night. The relief on Owen's face was obvious.

"I thank you, madam," said Owen. "I confess this is much more within my means. In truth, I am not certain how long I will be here. I am happy to pay you for a week to start and perhaps we can go from there?"

"Wonderful, sir," she replied, with only a small

hint of a Spanish accent to her voice. "My name is Isabella Martinez. I don't often have guests staying so long. I am sure we can work something out if you need to stay longer. If you are taking your meals here too, I will be happy to take this into account as well."

"Very good, madam. My name is Owen Spence and I thank you for your kindness."

She shook his hand to seal the bargain and Owen marvelled at how soft it seemed, before bringing out his coin pouch to pay the fee. As he counted out the coins, he could see she took note of how small it was, but instead of commenting on it she smiled up at him when he finished.

"There is one rule here I must insist on, Mr. Spence. You must stop calling me 'madam'. It makes me feel as if I am old enough to be your mother. Well, perhaps I am, but I'm not ready to admit it. Please call me Isabella."

Owen laughed. "I like your name, Isabella. I shall willingly do so if you agree to call me Owen."

Isabella smiled to settle their pact and took him upstairs to show him his room so he could settle in. He couldn't help but hope meeting her was somehow a sign of changing fortunes.

***

Owen stared out of the begrimed window of his room to find out what the day before him would be like, but he wondered why he was bothering even as he did it anyway. He well knew the day would likely be much the same as the day before. He was proved right as the sky was the brilliant, cloudless blue he expected it to be. By afternoon puffy, white clouds would appear on the horizon spread about by a gentle breeze, but it would be rare for one to actually block the sun for anything more than a few brief seconds.

The other constant he was growing accustomed to was stifling, sticky heat. By afternoon he would be forced outside, unable to stay in the rather hot, tiny sleeping quarters he was paying for. Even with the only window open, the breeze was insufficient to move any of the air noticeably in the one room he occupied. Leaving the window open at night was of debatable benefit, for while it cooled off enough to give at least some comfort it also allowed the mosquitos in. Owen adapted by building himself a makeshift mosquito net to cover his small bed.

Despite all this he knew his lodgings were pleasant enough and a big improvement from the first inn he stayed at. While still tiny, the space he was now calling home was far larger than what he was used to being given on a warship. A closet to actually hang all and not just some of his clothes, a desk and chair with plenty of room to write on it, and a large dressing table with a mirror and wash basin to shave and clean himself were all luxuries he was unaccustomed to. As part of his fee the room was cleaned every day and well maintained, aside from the window which needed cleaning from the outside.

Owen had kept mostly to himself in the almost two weeks since he had left the ship. He sent word to the ship of his whereabouts along with a written request for funds to cover his lodging soon after he settled into The Spanish Rose. A Marine appeared a few days later with a terse response acknowledging his letter. To his surprise, a bag of coins came with it. The Marine confirmed the funds were to cover his lodging, but he had no word of when he was to expect a summons. Owen decided to take it as a hopeful sign. Isabella watched the whole interaction with the Marine with curiosity, but she said nothing.

During the day Owen had little else to do but explore his surroundings and he soon found his first impressions of Kingston were correct. The town had clearly surpassed The Pallisadoes as the main centre of commerce and was growing at what appeared to be a constant rate. On the fringes of the town new shops and homes were being added everywhere, but the waterfront was where the town was bustling. Merchant ships from everywhere were in port, along with sailors from a host of different nations speaking all manner of languages.

What really captured Owen's interest was the lush landscape beyond the town limits. The dense foliage everywhere was a deep, dark green colour, which to Owen somehow seemed subtly different than anything he had seen elsewhere. In his mind he compared it to the pleasant green fields and forests of home, but the depth of the colour here was simply not the same.

Even more interesting were the rolling, dark green hills surrounding most of the town and in particular a mountain range he could see in the distance to the north and east. At certain times of the day a strange blue mist seemed to wreath the summit, giving them a surreal look. He felt a longing to explore it all, but knew he had to stay close to the Inn and be available for when the inevitable summons would come.

In the evenings Owen took his meals in the tavern before retiring to his room. Despite the temptation to stay and keep drinking, he knew he had to be wary of spending too much of his limited resources. He mingled little with the other customers in the tavern, but slowly came to know Isabella a little better during brief conversations when she was free from what seemed the constant demands of running her business. Her curiosity about the Marine's visit him led to his confession he was a Lieutenant in the Royal Navy, but he gave no clue as to why he was staying with her. The attraction he felt for her didn't go away and if anything seemed to grow even more with each interaction as they came to know each other better.

The summons finally came a little over two weeks after his departure from the ship. Owen was in the tavern finishing his breakfast when a Marine he recognized was from *HMS Wiltshire* walked in the door. Owen realized at once he was wearing his dress uniform. The man came over and saluted when he saw Owen rising to greet him and do the same.

"Lieutenant Spence. I am commanded to escort you to the ship. We are expected within the hour."

"It's today, is it?"

Owen waved to a chair at the table the Marine nodded agreement.

"Please have a seat. I must dress appropriately. This won't take long."

Owen struggled with mixed feelings as he

changed into his dress uniform and strapped on his sword in his room. On one hand he felt almost wooden with fear his career in the Navy could be over this day, while another part of him was simply glad the interminable waiting was finally over. He stared at himself distractedly one last time in the mirror and steeled himself for what was to come. As he marched downstairs to join the waiting Marine, he encountered Isabella near the counter at the foot of the stairs. Owen sensed someone had alerted her something was happening, and she was waiting for him to appear.

She stepped forward as he reached the bottom and stood before him, a curious look on her face. Sensing her interest, he stopped and waited for her to speak. She slowly looked him up and down, not giving away her thoughts. After a long moment she finally spoke.

"So, whatever it is you have been waiting for, it is today, is it?"

"It is."

"What will become of you? Will I see you again?"

"It remains to be seen, Isabella," said Owen, finally allowing a wry smile to crease his face. "If I am leaving, I must return to settle my accounts with you and collect the rest of my belongings. You can be assured I will do so."

"Of course you will. You are an officer and therefore a man of honour."

"Well, sadly, I can't in honesty stand here and tell you all officers in fact meet this description. But I assure you, I strive to always be a man of honour, and I sleep well at night knowing I am. I will be back."

Isabella searched his face for a moment before speaking.

"You know, you are a very handsome man, and you are even more so in a uniform."

She put a soft hand out to brush away a small piece of lint he had missed. Looking up at him once again she placed her hand on his shoulder and to his utter surprise used it as leverage to reach up and kiss him on the cheek.

"Well, Lieutenant Spence. I hope whatever is going on works out for you. I look forward to seeing you again."

Owen nodded his thanks, giving her a brief bow of gratitude, before turning to the Marine. "Let's go."

***

As he finished climbing the side of *HMS Wiltshire* and found himself standing once again on her deck, Owen already felt it a foreign, surreal sensation to be back. The two weeks ashore was the longest such period he had been off any ship since joining the Royal Navy years before and without doubt this contributed to it, but the familiar faces who were once again doing everything but look directly at him made the feeling even stronger.

Lieutenant Strand was the one exception who was looking at him and after they saluted each other wordlessly he motioned for Owen to follow him. They stopped on the quarterdeck as the Marine went aft to announce Owen's arrival. After looking about to ensure they weren't being overheard, Lieutenant

Strand muttered in a low voice to Owen.

"Mr. Spence, we don't have much time. I have volunteered to be your advocate for this. There are three Post Captains awaiting us inside. The bad news is the other two Captains are junior to our own Captain. Because of this, my plan is to introduce as much doubt as possible into the other two Captain's minds at every opportunity. The key witness in this is Midshipman Smithe, who as it happens is now Acting Lieutenant Smithe. I strongly suggest we keep this simple. Our position is he is somehow mistaken in believing you took the money. Were the others not junior to our Captain I would suggest we be more direct about the fact he is lying."

"I see. Mr. Strand, before we go further, I want to thank you for this. I expect taking this on is not putting you in favour with the Captain."

"I couldn't stand by and watch this without making the effort, Owen. These people have no honour whatsoever. Well, I can't say the same about all of them. I suspect our former First Officer Smithe, who is now Captain of his own ship, was honourable enough in his own way. I believe we are getting a new First Officer soon. But I've come to understand this bastard nephew of the Captain is a born liar. You, on the other hand, are not. We can't claim to know each other well, but I've seen enough to be certain of it."

"Well, once again, thank you. I know you are a man of honour, too. I agree with your strategy, sir."

"Call me George, Owen. We are friends, are we not?"

"We are, George," said Owen, reaching out to

shake the other man's hand. "Tell me, for I am curious about something. Do you know why the Captain sent me off the ship?"

"Not precisely, but I have my suspicions. I overheard him talking to the First Officer about having been to see the Admiral and he let slip the fact the two other Captains would be junior to him. Damn me for thinking these things, but I believe he must have enough sway with the Admiral to engineer a situation like this. I think he is confident of the outcome and he wanted to clear the way for his nephew. Once he had it organized to his liking, he made his move. I believe it no coincidence it was the next day he sent you off the ship."

Owen's heart sank, for this was exactly his own fear and he sighed.

"The Captain and his family are powerful people, George. I shouldn't be surprised at this."

Lieutenant Strand heard his sigh, and as the Marine reappeared on the quarterdeck and beckoned them to enter, the Lieutenant spoke one last time.

"I will do my best for you, Owen. I am not afraid for myself. And even if things don't go our way today, be assured I will spend every waking day trying to find the means to make this young bastard pay for what he has done. Now let's go have at them."

The Marine stopped them at the entrance and looked at Owen.

"Sir, I am commanded to ask if you know what to do upon entering."

"I do," said Owen. "Lead on."

Inside Owen found the Captain's dining space

rearranged to accommodate the court martial. Three Captains were seated on one side of Captain Smithe's long dinner table, now pulled close against one wall of the cabin to give more space. A small table with two chairs was set off to one side, with a single chair and table on the opposite side of the room in which sat a Lieutenant Owen didn't know. In the middle was an empty single chair facing the three Captains.

The two officers and the Marine all saluted. Owen stepped forward, pulling his sword from its scabbard, and placing it lengthwise on the table before the senior officers as custom dictated. He knew when the proceedings were over what the three Captains did with the placement of the sword would tell the outcome. If the hilt of the sword was turned to face him, he would be acquitted, but if the Captains turned the sword's point to face him, his career would be over. Captain Smithe pointed to the table with two chairs and the two Lieutenants wordlessly took their places as the Marine who had escorted them in stationed himself by the door.

"Lieutenant Spence, these gentlemen with me are Captains Walter and Turner. You are charged with numerous breaches of The Articles of War, but at heart the issue before us is whether you are guilty of the charge of theft. Lieutenant Harold Smithe, who is actually now a Captain assigned to another ship, would normally be the one to bring the case forward against you. As it happens, I can today introduce our new First Officer Lieutenant Worsley and he is willing to take on this task. As you are aware, Lieutenant Strand has agreed to advocate on your behalf. Witnesses will be called and both officers will have opportunity to question them. So, let's be about it. Lieutenant Worsley, the proceedings begin with you."

The Lieutenant rose from his chair and began a detailed summary of the events of the day the officers of *HMS Wiltshire* were forced to board *The Perfect Lady*, using notes already prepared for him. At the end he brought out a witnessed deposition from the former First Officer as to his own role in discovering the money hidden in Owen's bag of belongings and went through what it said. Before Lieutenant Worsley could call his first witness Captain Walter interrupted him.

"I have a question before you go further, sir," he said, turning to look at Owen. "You were present when the former First Officer searched your belongings. Is what he said in this deposition the truth?"

"Sir, it is, but I have no idea how—"

"I didn't ask that," said Captain Walter, a sharp tone to his voice. "What I want to know are the facts. Do you agree with the fact he found this bag of money in your belongings?"

"Sir, I agree his account is factual."

"Thank you. Please proceed, Lieutenant Worsley."

The Captain's nephew was brought in and took a seat in the witness chair. After finishing his testimony both Lieutenants Strand and Worsley took turns grilling him on the details. Lieutenant Strand used every opportunity to find a gap in his story, pressing him to admit he could have been mistaken. After ten minutes of back and forth the Captain's son was looking distinctly nervous, chewing his lip, and hesitating before answering each question. When a bead of sweat finally appeared at his hairline and began rolling down one side of his face Captain Smithe intervened.

"Lieutenant Strand, you are going over the same ground this officer has already attested to. I fail to see the purpose in having him repeat himself."

"Captain, with respect, a man's honour and career are on the line here. I know you understand I am merely doing my duty to ensure justice is served here. It is imperative we establish whether or not the witness recognizes any possibility he could be mistaken."

The Captain glared at Lieutenant Strand. "I am well aware of what is at stake here. As far as I'm concerned, the witness is simply repeating himself. I suggest you move on."

"Sir, I have no further questions," said Lieutenant Strand.

The Marine who had seen the two men and the money together in the Captain's cabin on *The Perfect Lady* was next to give testimony, but he was done in less than five minutes. Midshipman Green was brought in to attest to believing he saw Owen dash in and out of the officer's quarters, but he made a point of being so uncertain and nervous in his testimony the Captain soon dismissed him too, despite the protestations of Lieutenant Strand.

Owen now took the witness chair to give his own version of what had transpired. Both Lieutenants quizzed him on various points, but he stuck to providing the simple facts of what he knew. As he finished Captain Walter frowned and sat forward.

"I have a question for you, sir. It is obvious you believe you had no role in this money appearing in your belongings. So, how do you think this money got there?"

Both Captain Smithe and Lieutenant Worsley tried to interrupt, but the Lieutenant deferred to Captain Smithe who was now glaring at his colleague.

"Captain Walter, you are asking the witness to speculate. We are here to rule based on facts. I don't believe the question was appropriate."

Captain Walter shrugged. "Perhaps not, but if what this officer says is true and he did not take the money, then it begs the question of who did? If he knows who did, it needs to come out."

Captain Smithe stared hard at him for a moment longer, before turning to face Owen.

"Well? Answer the bloody question. But I strongly suggest you stick to facts you know."

Owen was already sweating inside his uniform and now the question he feared was before him, he knew he was faced with a hard choice. He could openly accuse the Captain's nephew, but he had no proof he was guilty and accusing another officer of such a crime without hard evidence would guarantee an unfavourable outcome. With an inward sigh, he made his decision.

"Sir, the only fact I know is I did not take this money. I do not know how this happened nor do I know for certain who did take it. It is a fact I believe this is an attempt to besmirch my reputation.

It is also a fact I am certain Acting Lieutenant Smithe is mistaken."

Captain Smithe scowled, and a burning look of obvious anger appeared on his face.

"Lieutenant Spence, are you accusing the Acting Lieutenant of theft? Think hard about what you are saying."

"I never said that, Captain. I do say he is mistaken."

A lingering silence descended on the room as Owen finished speaking. Captain Smithe gave an audible sniff, obviously conveying his disgust as he carried on.

"Well? Has anyone else got anything to say? Lieutenant Worsley? Lieutenant Strand?"

The new First Officer replied he did not, but Lieutenant Strand stepped forward.

"Sirs, I have one last thing. I wish to give a personal testament to the character of Lieutenant Spence. We have served together for several months now and I think it fair to say I have come to know him reasonably well. An act such as he is accused of is something simply not in his character to do. I have found him to be a man of honour and the kind of officer anyone would want to serve with."

"Yes, yes, thank you for this, Lieutenant," said the Captain, a dry tone to his voice. "I shall provide my own thoughts on the point to my colleagues. Right, we need to discuss what we have heard. All of you shall wait outside until summoned."

***

The call to return came less than thirty minutes afterwards. Owen looked at Lieutenant Strand, who clapped him on the shoulder in encouragement, but Owen noted his new friend wore a stony look on his face. With the Marine guard leading they made their way back into the Captain's cabin. As the Marine stepped to the side Owen had a clear view before him.

To his utter dismay, the point of the sword was turned toward him.

The rest of the proceedings seemed a blur, but they were mercifully short. The Captain read a brief prepared statement confirming the decision to withdraw his commission as an officer and dismiss him from the Royal Navy. The other two Captains stared down at the table without looking up, although Captain Walter gave what seemed a tiny shake of his head as Captain Smithe finished reading. Owen was given a brief set of orders to report to the Admiral's administrative offices in the Dockyard three days hence to collect the remainder of his pay. After his sword was returned to Owen, Lieutenant Strand was ordered to escort him off the ship.

Once again no one would look at him as Owen marched woodenly over to the railing to climb down to an already waiting boat to row him to shore. Lieutenant Strand shook his hand once again.

"I am sorry, Owen. I wish you all the best."

"I know, George. I wish you the same. You will need to watch your back, sir."

***

An hour later he was back at The Spanish Rose Inn. Isabella wasn't in sight as he came in and went straight up to his room. The wooden sensation he felt on seeing the sword pointed his direction was not gone and if anything had intensified. As he stripped off his uniform, knowing this was the last time he would wear it, he struggled to keep from crying aloud in pain.

When he finished dressing himself in the few civilian clothes he owned, he sat staring about his tiny room and wondered what to do next. With the room already growing hot and sticky from the heat, he opted to go to the tavern for a drink. He knew he would have to focus and face the future at some point, but the same lassitude which had overcome him when he was first sent away from the ship returned with what seemed tenfold strength.

Owen found a few customers were already in the tavern, sheltering from the heat of the day. He slumped into a chair and signalled to the serving girl to bring an ale. Bare moments after she dropped the mug on the table in front of him Isabella slid into the chair across from him. She stared at him in silence, a questioning look on her face. Owen downed a large portion of the ale and tried to think of something to tell her, but simply couldn't find any words. As the silence continued the look on her face turned to one of obvious concern and she reached across the table to grasp his hand.

Her touch was the catalyst for the single tear which soon turned to a flood creating multiple trails down his face. Isabella only gripped his hand harder as she pulled a handkerchief from her pocket and began to dab it on his face. Owen let her do so for a few moments before taking it from her and pulling his hand away to finish the job as he strove to master himself. She finally spoke as he did.

"So, it is obvious whatever is going on here did not go well. Owen, I don't know what to say, but I am willing to help you if I can. It is not my business, but if you are willing to tell me about it, I am willing to listen."

Owen was silent for several long moments as he finished drying his eyes. He took another deep drink from his mug before finally speaking. As he began telling her the whole story, the words initially came out slowly, but soon enough they came in a flood. She interrupted him only once, when he mentioned the Captain's name.

"Smithe?" said Isabella, a sharp tone to her voice. "Is his name Captain John Smithe, by chance?"

"It is. How did you know?"

"I am familiar with the name. I was not aware he is back in Jamaica. Please do continue, I will explain later."

Owen carried on with his tale despite being puzzled. As he finished, this time he was the one to reach out and take her hand.

"Isabella, I swear to you, on my honour. I am not a thief, and I did not do what I was accused of. I cannot be certain, but I am almost positive it was the bastard nephew of the Captain who set this all up. Please believe me."

Isabella gripped his hand hard once again. "Oh, I believe you, Owen. We are all too familiar with the Smithe family on this island and this man in particular. He is very powerful here and has ruined more than a few people. He was on leave from the

Navy to attend to his businesses in Jamaica and elsewhere in the Caribbean a few years ago. My husband and I had a small plantation here at the time, but we were forced to sell it to him against our will at a price nowhere near its true value. If I had a way to pay him back in kind, I would do so without hesitation. But what will you do now?"

Owen shrugged and explained his personal circumstances as he ordered yet another drink be brought.

"So you see, I have nowhere to go and no one to turn to. I will have to give thought to my future. For today, I can only mourn what I have lost."

Isabella nodded. "I understand. I must go help in the kitchen to prepare for the dinner hour, but I will be back."

***

Owen cracked open one eye the next morning and groaned the second he did as sunlight streaming into the room stabbed into his brain. He lay where he was for a long time to let the mild throbbing in his head from having drank too much once again subside. After slowly making himself presentable he made his way to the tavern. The serving girl took one look at him and soon had a piping hot cup of coffee on the table in front of him. Once again, Isabella appeared and slipped into the chair across from him. She smiled as she spoke.

"Yes, I know, you need some time to recover. You did drink rather a lot last night, which is understandable. But while you are coming to grips with a new day, you can give thought to spending it with me. I think you need a break, and actually, I need a day off too. We can take some food and drink and a cart and spend the day away from all this. I know of a beautiful, secluded beach with plenty of shade an hour or so outside of Kingston we can go to. Does this sound good?"

Owen had downed enough coffee to mostly digest what she was saying, but he was surprised and a little confused. She saw his hesitation.

"What is it, Owen?"

"Um, Isabella, somewhere in the fog of last night I think you told me you are married. I appreciate your concern for me, but don't you think—"

She laughed and grasped his hand, interrupting him before he could finish.

"I am sorry, I wasn't clear. Yes, I had a husband once. He is gone. Perhaps I can explain it to you at the beach?"

Owen smiled for the first time as he rubbed his face and downed more coffee.

"Yes. Yes, I would like this."

***

The beach she took him to was as secluded as she promised. Had Owen been alone he never would have spotted the small break in the foliage alongside the cart path following the curve of the land around the various small coves they passed. The dense, dark green undergrowth masked what proved to be a much smaller path leading down to the small cove which was their destination.

After tying the horse and buggy to a tree, Owen carried the package of food and drink she had prepared the rest of the way down to the treeline where the soft, dark earth under his feet gradually began mingling with the light golden sand of the beach. Isabella had brought a large blanket she spread in an open area beneath a big tree with flowers which were dark orange and almost red in colour. She looked around and spread her arms wide.

"Well, what do you think?"

Owen was silent for a moment. "I think this is all beautiful and so are you."

She grinned as she slipped off her shoes, but she didn't stop there. Reaching down she grasped the folds of her dress and in one swift movement pulled it over her head. To Owen's utter surprise, she wore nothing underneath. She laughed as she saw the look on his face.

"This is my favourite spot to go swimming. You may have guessed no one ever comes down here except me."

Turning, she walked serenely across the sand and into the shallow water of the cove. When she was far enough out, she plunged all the way in, diving below the water to come up shaking her head and splash about. Owen finally recovered himself and almost ripped his clothes taking them off before joining her as she laughed at his haste. They met together in the water and he crushed her to him as they kissed long and hard. She finally pulled a little back and grinned at him again.

"Why, Owen, I think you like my favourite spot."

"Oh, I like more than that," said Owen, kissing her hard once again.

"Yes, I get the impression you do," she laughed

again, reaching under the water to grasp him in her hand. "Perhaps we should go back to the beach and dry off."

"What a good idea," said Owen, picking her up and carrying her back up to the blanket.

Because the sand was so soft and sugary, he was at the point of losing his balance by the time he got her to the blanket. They both laughed as they fell onto the blanket and didn't get up from where they lay again for a long time. After making love twice she lay with an arm and a leg draped across him as he lay on his back, cupping one of her breasts in his hand.

"My God, I wanted you," she said.

"I did too."

"As much as I would like more, I am realizing this took a lot of energy and I'm not so young anymore. I am starving, in fact. Let's eat."

In between bites of cold, spiced chicken with bread and fruit for their meal, they sipped from sealed mugs of ale she had prepared for them. Owen took the opportunity to finally ask about her story. Isabella shrugged.

"There is not much to tell, Owen. I was born here, as was my husband, because our families never left when the English invaded all those years ago. They would have lost everything had they left. The family had a small plantation, but as I mentioned, when the bastard Smithe came along he wanted it added to his holdings. Suffice to say, being Spanish on this island means you are second class when it comes to everything. We knew what would happen if we didn't sell to him, at the price he wanted. My husband and I opened The Spanish Rose with what little we got. He got sick and died four years ago. At least he got the chance to see our daughter Maria, which I guess I haven't told you about yet. She is seven years old now. She lives with my mother in her home on the outskirts of Spanish Town, because Kingston is no place to raise a child and I, of course, have no choice but to keep running the Inn. I know no other life."

"You couldn't sell and start a new business in Spanish Town?"

"I could, but I would not do anywhere near as much business as here. Spanish Town is the capital of Jamaica, but Kingston is where all the money is. It is also a dangerous place."

"I see. It can't be an easy life."

She shrugged. "This is my home and I make the best of it. As must you, of course. Oh, not necessarily make it your home, but you cannot change what has happened. You must look to the future."

Owen reached out and grasped a handful of the incredibly soft sand his feet were buried in and let it run through his fingers as he thought about his response.

"You know, I've never seen anything like this sand. I suppose it's no surprise since this is the first time I've spent any amount of time on a beach for the simple pleasure of it. But this sand seems amazingly soft."

"It is. Beaches like this have what we call the sugar sands, because it's so fine and powdery. Of course, on this island fine, powdery sugar is everywhere and so are these sand beaches. I suppose whoever started calling it this might have made a link in their mind between the two. I sometimes think the staggering amounts of money made from sugar could rival the amount of sand on these beaches, Owen. Anyway, if you decide to stay on this island, whatever you end up doing will likely revolve around sugar."

Owen let another handful of sand run through his fingers.

"Well, I can only hope I'll be able to hold onto any money I make easier than this sand," said Owen, turning to look at her. "I hope I can hold onto you, too."

Isabella reached over to caress his cheek with a soft touch.

"For a time, perhaps. Sooner or later this sand slips through your hands, as does money, and everything else in life. Owen, I am thirty-six years old and soon to be thirty-seven. I needed someone and you appeared. How old are you?"

"Twenty."

"Owen, you have a future ahead of you, whatever it may be. And I was right, you know? I am old enough I could be your mother. Jamaica is my home and I assure you I will never leave it. I can feel it in my heart. I don't want to leave it. Plus, my daughter and my mother are here. I will never leave them, either. You, on the other hand, are a sailor. Sailors need ships and they sail away."

Owen looked into his heart and felt what she said was true. He could only nod mutely in response.

"Yes. So, for a time we are together, Owen. I

will give your situation some thought. I do not do enough business to employ you, but there may be some options. There is work available, but it can be hard to find. It's all very fluid. We shall see. But for today, why don't we just enjoy our day together? We can go for a little walk on the sand or maybe a swim. Or perhaps now we are refreshed there is something else we could do?"

Owen laughed and pulled her closer.

Chapter Three
Jamaica
July 1772 to November 1772

Three days later Owen climbed ashore from the rowboat to step on the main dock of The Pallisadoes. He was once again carrying his duffel bag, now considerably lighter than before. After paying for his ride across the harbour he made his way down the street past the waterfront taverns already serving their first customers of the day, heading for the shop he remembered seeing the day he was ordered off the ship three weeks before. He recognized the intersecting street and plunged into a much narrower passageway, soon finding the small shop he wanted.

The shop was mercifully empty except for a grizzled, grey bearded man standing behind the counter. This suited Owen perfectly, for he had come to sell his uniforms and was hoping he wouldn't encounter anyone he knew while doing so. Owen walked over to the counter with his bag and explained what he wanted to do. The old man's eyes widened slightly on hearing what was on offer and he stared for a long moment at Owen with much more interest than he had shown when he walked in the door. Owen sensed the unspoken question in the man's mind, but it never came. The old man gestured instead at the bag.

"Let's see what you have."

Owen pulled out his one dress uniform and his two day-to-day working uniforms and spread them on the counter. The old man began carefully examining each for flaws or stains which likely wouldn't come out. After five minutes he finished his examination, put them down, and stepped back a little to rub his chin in thought for a moment.

"Right. The dress uniform is in very good shape. Hasn't seen much use, has it? And not too old, either. The working uniforms have seen their share of duty, but I'd say they are in decent shape. I think I can sell these without much difficulty, but you have a choice. One option is you can leave them with me on consignment and hope someone needing them comes in soon. We settle on a price range we are both happy with and see what happens. This will likely make you more money, but it may take more time than you want. If you don't want to wait, the other option is you can sell them to me, but you might not like the price I am offering you."

Knowing how limited his resources were, Owen saw little choice and asked him to make his offer to buy them outright. The sum the old man named wasn't as low as Owen thought it might be, but it was nowhere near what he had actually hoped for. Owen let his disappointment show and decided to try bargaining.

"Well, it isn't what I had in mind, for I need funds to buy more civilian clothes for myself, sir."

The old man shrugged. "Hmm, why don't you look around the shop? I have plenty of items on hand which might meet your needs and if you are going to help me move some of my product, I can take this into account. We can talk more when you are ready."

An hour later Owen walked out of the shop

pleased with himself, for his duffel bag was now a little fuller than when he walked in and it held a whole new set of clothing for himself. He knew a market existed for used uniforms which could be adjusted easily to fit a newly appointed officer cheaper than the price for a new one. Owen had also correctly reasoned the best marketplace for this was The Pallisadoes, where Navy personnel came and went all the time. While he hadn't left with as much coin as he wanted, he knew he would have had to spend it on more clothes for himself regardless. The hard bartering with the old man wasn't something he was used to, but Owen felt both of them had come away happy with the outcome.

His other reason for coming to The Pallisadoes was to visit the Dockyard to collect his remaining pay. After presenting himself to the guard post at the entrance he was given directions to the Pay Master's office off in a corner of the facility. The Dockyard seemed a hive of activity, which was no surprise to Owen. July marked the advent every year of the start of hurricane season in the Caribbean and few ships would venture to sea unless they had an excellent reason to do so. While September was always the most active month for these destructive, massive storms, they were known to sometimes appear as early as July and as late as November each year.

As every Navy warship always had some repairs which needed attention, the Captain of each ship in harbour wanted it all to happen while their ships were idle. Owen saw numerous parties from the ships working side by side with the Dockyard personnel. Pitch and tar, copper and lumber, and cordage and canvas were all in heavy demand. A swarm of carpenters were hard at work in the saw pit, shaping the raw wood to whatever was in need.

Owen saw several sailors off *HMS Wiltshire*, but he steered clear of them as much as possible and thankfully no one recognized him in his civilian clothes. A half dozen clerks were in the Pay Master's office marking their ledgers under the direction of an older man who came over to examine Owen's papers. He grunted acknowledgment and directed Owen to sit in the small waiting room, shuffling off into a back room.

Owen was glad no one had recognized him or commented on his situation. Since the day at the beach with Isabella, Owen had spent a lot of time thinking about his situation. He knew he had to break with a past he could not change and focus on building a new life for himself. He was unashamed of his situation, for he knew it wasn't of his making, but he simply wanted to move on without any reminders of the past.

A half hour later he walked out of the Pay office and made his way back to the dock. Stepping off the shore of The Pallisadoes and onto the small rowboat to go back to Kingston it felt like he was finally making the break he needed. He resisted the urge to look back one last time, despite knowing he would likely never have need to return.

Back at The Spanish Rose he made his way to his room to put his new clothes away. After combining the remainder of his pay with what he already had on hand, he considered how long he could make his money last. Owen knew if he was careful, he could pay for his room and feed himself for three or perhaps four months, but this was all. He was wrestling with the anxiety which came unbidden when Isabella knocked on his door and came in.

"I just heard you were back. Owen, I have someone I want you to meet. He may be able to find you work."

Owen's heart soared on hearing this and he stood up from his chair to pull her close.

"My God, you are an angel. Aside from meeting you, this is the best thing to happen to me in weeks."

Her eyes flashed and she smiled up at him as she returned his grasp with equal desire.

"I'll think of some way you can reward me later. But Owen, I must warn you. This man is hard and not the most pleasant customer I have ever had. He works as an overseer on one of the plantations. He wants me, which is why he keeps coming to drink here when he is in town, but I have kept him at bay. The thing is he pays good money, so I talk to him. It is unusual for him to be in Kingston in July, because this is a very busy time on the plantations, so I asked him why he was in town. Owen, he is here looking for a sailor. Someone who can navigate and command a ship."

Owen nodded. "A hard case, eh? It won't be the first time I've dealt with someone who fits the description. Let's go meet him."

The tough looking, heavily muscled man nursing a mug of heady smelling rum in the tavern appeared even rougher than Isabella had characterized him, but Owen was unfazed, for the man could easily have traded places with any of the common seamen on board a Royal Navy ship. Owen judged him to be in his early forties, darkly tanned from obviously being outside constantly. An evil looking scar ran down the side of his face and his arms were heavily tattooed. Isabella introduced him as Samuel Butcher. He didn't offer a hand to shake and neither did Owen, but the man eyed him appraisingly before finally speaking.

"Isabella says you are a sailor. Tell me about yourself."

Owen decided to be truthful about his situation, so in as few words as possible he told his story. Owen tried to finish by telling of the court martial and emphasizing his innocence, but Samuel cut him off.

"Yes, yes, I don't give a shit about that. You're ex-Navy, which means you can sail and navigate, and you are here needing work. Well, you timed this right, because I came here looking for someone to do this and couldn't find anyone till now."

"All right, what is the work and what is the pay?"

"The pay you will have to talk to the owner about, if you meet with his approval. The work is to command his sloop based out of Old Harbour. Ferry people and goods back and forth around the island. If you want this, you'll have to come with me tomorrow to the plantation to meet him. I'll bring you back if for some reason he rejects you, but I can't imagine why he would, since he needs you. So, you in?"

Owen didn't hesitate. "I'm in."

The overseer finished his drink, rose from his chair, and threw some money on the table to pay for the rum.

"I'll pick you up here a half hour after dawn tomorrow. It's too bloody hot out there to travel inland later in the day."

As he stalked out Owen and Isabella turned to each other as one.

"Well, what do you think?" she said.

"I still think you are an angel, and I don't know how to thank you. I also don't know if this will work out, but I will give it my best effort. I can't believe this will be my last night here. I must settle my account with you."

Isabella grinned. "You certainly must. I think I'll come to your room later to do that."

Owen laughed. "What a fine idea."

***

The overseer was true to his word. Knowing they had to be up early, both Owen and Isabella made a point of retiring to his room after dinner and exhausted themselves to a point where both slept soundly until woken by Isabella's kitchen helper. By the time he had washed up and downed a quick breakfast the man appeared in the doorway to the Inn. Isabella gave him a big hug before watching him climb onto the waiting cart with his duffel bag. The overseer smirked and got the cart underway as Owen waved goodbye.

"Found your way into her bed, did you? Congratulations, you are doing better than me. I suppose I shouldn't be surprised. The women can't resist those bloody uniforms."

Owen grinned and shifted to make himself more comfortable. "How long is the ride to the plantation?

Samuel shrugged and cracked his whip. "Maybe four or five hours, depending on how fast I can get this old nag to move. It's twenty-seven miles inland, which isn't really all that far. The problem is there is a section where it is two thousand feet uphill with no way around it, unless you want to take days and not hours getting there. We'll have to change horses a few times. We'll trade this old beast we have now for something a lot younger once we get out of Kingston."

Owen tried engaging the man in more conversation a few times, but as the day grew warmer the overseer seemed to become more taciturn, so Owen gave up trying. They passed through several areas of the sprawling town which even at this time of the day seemed unsafe. Most of the people they saw were black, and no one was smiling. Numerous ramshackle shops and taverns already had customers, who eyed the two men warily. Many of them stepped out into the road and stood near the cart as it passed by, begging for food or money. Owen realized most were older and several were missing limbs or had other deformities. Several had scars from being horribly burned in the past. A few women lingered in some of the doorways, calling out to offer their services.

To Owen's shock, a blind beggar with a cane to guide him was almost crushed under the cart as he came out from his hut to beg for alms. The overseer saw what was about to happen and swung the cart out of the way in time with an oath. As the cart went by the overseer reached out with his whip and slashed the beggar across the chest. The man cried out and stumbled back, falling into a nearby pile of reeking garbage.

"I say, weren't you a bit harsh?" said Owen, still stunned at what had happened. "The man was clearly blind."

Samuel looked askance at Owen, before grunting and turning back to stare at the road ahead.

"So what? The stupid bastard was getting in our way. If you think it was harsh, think again. Wait till you get to the plantation. You'll see. But it's time to forget about it. Get your sword out and keep it visible. We're coming to a part of town where anything can happen. I normally avoid this if I'm on my own, but coming this way is a lot shorter. Because there are two of us, they likely won't try an attack. We'll be through it soon enough."

Owen quickly realized the overseer had not understated the need for vigilance. Owen was forced to brandish his sword and threaten three men carrying clubs and knives who rushed out from behind a shack they were passing, trying to block the cart. The overseer alternated slashing at two of the men on one side and driving the horse hard right through them without stopping, while Owen aimed a cut with his sword at the third man. His victim fell hard to the ground with a wound to his arm and didn't get up.

As the decrepit shacks finally began thinning out Owen knew they were at the outskirts of town, and he breathed a sigh of relief. Soon after the road began to slope gently up and with every step the now tired horse slowed ever more. The overseer cursed and cracked his whip on an almost constant basis.

Owen was surprised the horse responded and made more effort, but he soon learned the real reason it did so was the beast knew its job would soon be over. Once past the edge of town they came to a small clearing beside the road with a dark green canopy of dense foliage and undergrowth on all sides. Owen realized this was the way station the horse was happy to see, with a small barn and a tiny shack attached to it. A slave came out to unharness the horse and lead a fresh animal from the barn. As the overseer predicted, this horse was much younger.

Two hours later they finally reached the summit of the hill. The rough road upwards was lined with the dense, thick green foliage Owen was now accustomed to seeing, a seeming canyon carved through the canopy of forest offering little to see on most of the journey. In a few steeper sections it deviated from the simple straight uphill path and wound back and forth in a series of switchbacks, affording periodic, short glimpses of the broader landscape ahead of them. Owen saw ranges of rolling, low green hills in the far distance which ultimately touched the distant shoreline of the sea. Dotting the vista before him were large patches of obviously cultivated lands too numerous to count. At the top was yet another way station where their final fresh horse was obtained.

The route down was a much gentler slope leading to the broad plain before them. Signs of human activity were appearing everywhere, beginning with the terraces filled by rows of plants. When Owen asked about them Samuel told him they were coffee plants. As they finally reached more level terrain the terraces gave way to seemingly endless fields of sugarcane, some of which had already been harvested.

Occasional parties of slaves crossed their path from one field to another on their way to yet more tasks. Large empty carts pulled by either mules or oxen followed behind the slave gangs, while those already filled to the brim with cut cane stalks went the opposite direction. As more and more large carts joined them on the road going the same direction as the two men, Owen realized they were all going to the same place.

After rounding a bend in the road Owen saw they had undoubtedly reached their destination. Several buildings clustered to one side of the road were obviously the heart of the plantation's operations. On the opposite side a wide, manicured lawn with numerous flowering plants and trees led to a white manor house gleaming in the sunshine on a small rise in the distance. Further past the barns and other buildings could be seen a large number of small huts and shacks interspersed with small garden plots. A host of slaves with white overseers were at work everywhere. Surprised at the sheer scale of activity, Owen frowned and turned to the overseer.

"Samuel, this is a huge operation. I recall Isabella said something to me about this being a busy time of year. I can see she wasn't wrong."

The overseer grimaced. "It's not supposed to be quite this busy right now. Normally, the main harvest of the cane is done in May and June. It's the driest part of the year. Doing it then means the sugar can be on its way no later than July. The problem is insurance rates start going crazy by late July because of hurricane season, right? Plus, the owners need the cash to stay afloat. They've had to pay plenty for supplies and to keep people like me at work."

"I see. He can't wait until maybe October or November when it's safer?"

This time Samuel shrugged. "He can if he has the resources, but by the fall prices will likely be lower because everyone else has gotten their crop to market."

"This all means there were problems this year?"

"Yeah. It was rainier than normal. A shortage of people didn't help. Prices for slaves are up this year. The owner hedged his bets he could get by with purchasing fewer than we wanted to meet our gaps, but he was wrong, as I knew he would be. He's a stubborn bastard when it comes to money."

The overseer pulled up outside one of the barns as he finished speaking and gave the reins to a slave who appeared from within to deal with the horse and cart. Telling Owen to bring his bag the two men walked over to a building which proved to be quarters for the various white overseers on the plantation. Owen was given a tiny room and told to meet Samuel outside after stowing his belongings. Owen found the man in conversation with another white man on leaving the building. The overseer didn't bother introducing Owen before the man nodded to Samuel and left. Samuel turned back to Owen.

"You'll have to meet Mr. Westfall in the morning. He is away on the far side of the plantation and isn't going to be back until late tonight."

"I see. Is there anything I should do in the meantime?"

Samuel shrugged. "After we get something to eat, I suppose you can follow me while I check on how matters stand here. It couldn't hurt for you to learn a bit about the operation."

One of the buildings turned out to be a massive kitchen dedicated to feeding the large numbers of workers. Owen and Samuel sat at a table in a separate area marked off for whites only to use. The food on offer was remarkably good. A tasty fish soup with fresh bread was provided to start, followed by grilled chicken and local vegetables Owen couldn't identify. Owen commented on the quality as they ate.

"Mr. Westfall makes sure we are fed well. The slaves don't get anything quite this good, of course. Salt fish for them, plus whatever else is cheap and filling."

After lunch the two men headed out and made their way into the heart of the operation. Samuel stopped several people to get reports from them. Owen listened with interest to each and soon realized everyone was behaving in a deferential manner to the man. After yet another such conversation Owen asked him about it. The overseer gave him a sharp look.

"Perhaps I didn't make it clear to you. Yes, I am one of several overseers here, but I am also the lead overseer for all of the owner's operations. They all report to me and I report to the owner. In other words, yes, I will be your boss if the owner decides to hire you."

As the afternoon wore on Owen followed the overseer about, learning what the plantation did while they went. The piles of raw sugarcane coming from the fields went to a mill where it was fed into a series of huge rollers powered by oxen which squeezed juice from the cane. Some of the juice went straight into fermentation vats which after the distillation process would produce rum, while the rest was subjected to a process of boiling and skimming away impurities.

The refining process resulted in molasses which was collected into sugar moulds and hogsheads of muscovado sugar. Owen could see the entire process was dangerous and demanding. He was glad to be standing in shade as he watched it, for he could feel the enormous heat radiating from the boiling vats even standing well out of the way as he was. He remembered the men with horrific burns they had seen on their journey to the plantation, and he surmised their injuries were likely accidents involving this process. With the sticky humidity of the afternoon Owen was amazed the slaves could tolerate the blazing heat and he mentioned it to the overseer. Samuel merely grunted with indifference.

"God gave them thicker skins than white people

so they could do things like this. The owners tried long ago to use indentured whites to do the job and they didn't last long enough to make the investment in them worthwhile. But these blacks are just beasts, you know, and are perfectly suited for this. You need to treat them as such. You would do well to remember it if you are going to work with us."

Although he knew such blatant racism existed, Owen had never been confronted with it so directly before. During his time in the Navy Owen had served with a few black sailors recruited to fill never ending gaps in the ranks of the ships. In his experience the black sailors were as capable as anyone else on the ship and what really mattered to most officers and their shipmates was they did their job. Owen knew some Royal Navy officers felt the same as the overseer, but most either did not or kept their opinions to themselves. Samuel's thinking made no sense to Owen as a result, but he was forced to stay silent. He needed the job.

As they moved to the next series of buildings Owen was surprised to find all manner of different crops were being harvested for sale by the plantation. Small amounts of cocoa, tobacco, pimento, ginger, and indigo was being processed in addition to a larger amount of coffee from the terraces they had passed on their journey. Owen found a huge, sloped glacis platform occupied another spot nearby where an enormous quantity of coffee beans was laid out to dry and cure in the sun before being cleaned.

"I'm surprised at the number of alternative crops you are growing, Samuel. I thought most of the plantations had switched to sugar alone."

"Most have, because this is where the real money is. Mr. Westfall has some lands more suited to other crops, though. If it makes him money, he is happy."

On a different route back to their quarters at the end of the day Owen was shocked to find a young, naked black man chained to a large post sunk into the ground. Heavy manacles around his neck, wrists, and ankles held him in place. He was slumped against the post in a pool of his own reeking urine and faeces. Owen could see the manacles had chafed his skin raw in several places. As they came nearer to the slave another overseer going the opposite direction aimed a kick at the man as he went by. The slave scowled and roused himself, grabbing a handful of his excrement. Stretching the limit of the manacles around his wrists, he flung it at the overseer who had kicked him.

Enraged at being splattered with it, the overseer immediately pulled a small whip out of his belt and began beating the slave. Owen couldn't believe what he was seeing and was even more surprised at the indifference Samuel showed to it as they walked on past the scene. Owen couldn't stop himself from commenting on it.

"My God, Samuel. I know you said I would have to get used to this, but what did he do to deserve being chained to this pole?"

Samuel shrugged. "Who knows? He undoubtedly did something. He is one of the newest slaves on the plantation. It takes a while to break some of them in, especially the young males. We have to show them who is in charge here. Don't lose any sleep over it."

"But how long will he be chained there?"

"As long as it takes. Two or three days without food or water while the bugs feast on him will change his attitude."

Owen lapsed into silence as he contemplated the scene now behind them. He was used to harsh and sometimes arbitrary discipline in the Navy, but this was taking punishment to a whole new horrible level. Owen was appalled, but once again his desperate need for the work forestalled him and he spoke no more. As the two men neared their quarters a group of young female slaves crossed their path on their way to another building. They showed no interest in the two men, but Samuel stopped to scrutinize them as they went by. When the last of them were past he turned to Owen.

"Well, what do you think? There are some new ones in the bunch and a couple you could almost call comely. I think I'll sample one of them tonight. Hey, you want one, too?"

"Uh, what do you mean?"

"Don't be dense, man. I'm talking about bedding one of them tonight. It costs you nothing, if this is what you are wondering, and they aren't in a position to say no. Think of it as a perk of the job."

"I see. Uh, Isabella kept me up late last night, so I think I'll pass. Thanks for the offer."

"A young studhorse like you needs to recharge? Isabella is that good, is she?"

The overseer laughed as he slapped Owen on the shoulder without waiting for an answer.

"Suit yourself. Let's get some dinner."
***

Owen was on edge the next day as he followed Samuel into a rear entrance of the manor house, knowing how important the coming interview with the owner was. Inside the manor was an entirely different world. Even though Owen knew they were coming in via the servant's entrance, he was stunned at the sudden opulence on display.

The well-organized, spotless kitchen was the first area they passed, a sure sign of more wealth than Owen had ever seen. He had a glimpse of the manor's parlour with immaculate furniture, hardwood floors, panelled walls, and crown mouldings as they passed it in a hallway to the owner's office at the rear of the building. Owen sensed this owner was enjoying far more wealth than he had imagined, and he resolved not to sell his services cheaply.

As the two men entered the owner simply pointed to the two chairs in front of his desk, without bothering to get up to greet them. He made them wait as he finished making some entries in a journal, before finally closing it and looking at Samuel.

"Well? What have you got for me?"

Samuel introduced Owen and explained why he was here. The owner raised an eyebrow at mention Owen was now an ex-Royal Navy officer.

"Tell me your story, Mr. Spence."

When he finished Owen emphasized he was not guilty of the offence he was accused of, as he had done when he first told his story to Samuel. The owner cut him off in mid-sentence with a brusque wave of his hand.

"Don't waste my time, Mr. Spence. Everyone says they are innocent. Look, you aren't going to be the first thief I've ended up employing. What you need to understand is if you are caught stealing from me you won't just be sent packing with a slap on your wrist, like in the Navy. You'll be beaten to within a hair's breadth of your life, you hear? And only then will you be shoved out the door."

"I understand, sir."

"Right, you were an officer, so this means you can sail and navigate. I'm sure Samuel here told you I have a sloop to ferry goods about the island. The crew are slaves and will need discipline, far more than whatever the Navy might hand out. We'll see how you do. The only thing left then is to sort out your pay."

The owner eyed Owen speculatively for a moment before naming a monthly sum. Owen kept his face bland as he quickly thought about the offer, which was slightly better than the minimum he was hoping for. The problem was the sum was also little more than what a Navy Lieutenant made. Owen calculated the owner knew the Navy rates of pay and was counting on it to satisfy Owen. What the owner had not expected was Owen had already made up his mind not to settle for the minimum, recalling Samuel had inadvertently given a hint when they first met of facing trouble finding someone for the job.

As bad as he needed the work, Owen reasoned he had little to lose. Deliberately letting a dismayed look appear on his face, Owen slowly shook his head and politely told the owner he was expecting better. The owner folded his arms, scowled, and rolled his eyes.

"Mr. Spence, do you know what the costs are to run a plantation? They are enormous, and I make minimal profit. If I paid outrageous wages like you want to all of my men, I wouldn't be in business for very long."

Owen briefly looked around the room at the fine furnishings it held. An expensive crystal decanter with glasses sat on a side table nearby. The beautiful crown mouldings he saw in the parlour were also in the owner's office, while the desk the man was sitting at had without doubt cost a fortune. Owen said nothing about it all, letting his look around the room speak for itself.

"I understand, sir. I am certain you have many challenges, but so do I. I must look to my own interests, just as you do. If necessary, I will return to Kingston and seek employment elsewhere."

The owner groaned and got up from his desk to go pour himself a drink, staying silent as he did. At first Owen was afraid he had gone too far, but the longer the silence stretched the more certain Owen was he had correctly judged the man's need. The owner finally sat back down in his chair and named another sum, higher than the first. He gave Owen what was obviously intended to be a stern look as he did.

"This is the best I am prepared to offer right now. Consider yourself on probation if you accept it. If you serve me well, we will speak again six months from now. I can be a generous man to those who meet my needs. Well, make a decision, Mr. Spence."

"Six months," said Owen, rubbing his chin to pretend he was still thinking about the offer, when in reality he was elated. "All right, I can prove my worth by then. I accept."

"Excellent. There is no time to waste. You and Samuel will depart today for Old Harbour. I have far too much product stacked in my warehouse waiting to be moved to Kingston and you need to get it there fast. Samuel knows what to do. Good day, sirs."

As they left the manor house and made their way to their quarters to get their belongings Owen watched Samuel look around in all directions, obviously ensuring no one was either watching or listening to them. With a satisfied look the overseer turned to Owen and let a huge grin slowly appear on his face.

"Congratulations, I didn't think you had it in you. You played him well. You are going to need those negotiating skills from time to time. You probably don't want to know you maybe could have demanded even more, but I think you came out of this all right."

"Even more? Is he really so desperate?"

"I would say so. Even I don't know the whole picture, but it is true he needs to get product to market and do it fast or his profits won't be anywhere near as fat as he wants them. If I were you, I wouldn't pay too much attention to his complaints of poverty. His goal is to return to

England in less than five years from now, taking a ship full of money with him. He won't be the first owner to pull it off around here. He'll put me in full charge of the operation before he leaves, and I'll be set for life. So be useful to both of us and you too could be set for life."

"I see. I'll think about it."

***

The journey to Old Harbour was on a winding road snaking further west around the high hills they traversed on the trip from Kingston. While not as steep, they still needed several fresh horses at way stations along the route to complete the journey, for this time they were accompanied by other larger carts hauling casks filled with all manner of produce from the plantation. They made good time as most of the journey was downhill to the coast and the last third of the route was along a flat plain leading to the town.

Old Harbour proved to be perhaps a third the size of Kingston, but the distant glimpse Owen had of the port itself as they rode into town gave him the sense of being as busy as its larger rival. Numerous warehouses lined the wharves of the town blocking his view of the harbour, but he knew a host of ships of various sizes would be tied up and in the process of loading or unloading all manner of cargoes. The overseers worked the slaves hard to store everything away by the end of the day. Owen was impressed at the size of the Westfall plantation's warehouse near the dock, which was indeed filled almost to capacity when the latest shipment was added.

Leaving the others to finish the work the two

men walked the short distance to the docks where Owen was expecting to see his new ship. What he found instead was a host of shallow draught barges tethered to the shore and he looked at Samuel with puzzlement. The overseer grinned and pointed out to sea, where further out in the bay lay numerous larger ships at anchor.

"She's out there with all the rest. The good thing about this harbour is it is relatively close to Kingston, where most of the shipping comes and goes from. The bad thing is the shallow water close inshore, which means using these barges to get everything to and from the ship. It's a pain in the arse, but what can you do? This is the fastest route to get the product to market. We'll get out to the ship first thing in the morning. But enough of this, let's go get a drink."

***

Owen thought he would be bunking for the night in a local inn, but instead found himself staying in quarters in the warehouse itself, where separate spaces for both the slaves and the overseers who worked there were built. The warehouse even held a small kitchen facility to feed everyone, who were all up at dawn and soon back at work.

Owen and Samuel caught a ride on the first barge laden with barrels of sugar out to the ship. He couldn't help laughing aloud as they drew near enough to *The Fair Mermaid* he could make out details of her appearance, for she was nowhere close to living up to the name. Samuel grinned and seemed to know exactly what he was thinking.

"I hope you weren't expecting better. She's a

right shabby old bitch, but she gets the job done."

After having scoured every area of the ship two hours later Owen found himself agreeing with the overseer. No sailor would be attracted to the overall appearance of this ship, but maintenance where needed was done. The ship was a fore and aft gaff rigged sloop which Owen judged to be 70 tons and almost fifty feet in length with only one mast. He frowned when Samuel told him his crew numbered just twenty men, but his needs would depend on what he was expected to do, so he didn't pursue the question further. In the end he had only one real concern.

"Samuel, what do we do if we have to defend ourselves? I've not seen any weapons."

"You run if you are in trouble. You won't be sailing anywhere other than along the coast of the island, so the odds someone might come after you are slim. Any real problems you might have are more likely to come from the crew, which is why there are a couple of swivel guns and other weapons stored in a locker in your cabin."

By the end of a day involving a blur of endless details to learn and decisions to be made, the ship was fully loaded and ready to sail. Learning who had what skills among his crew was the most important task. All the men crewing the ship with him were black slaves, except for a white overseer named John, who had numerous roles. The most important of these was to serve as his bosun to maintain discipline. Owen looked at the crew with a wary eye, in much the same way as they appeared to be doing to him. They would all learn about each other soon enough.

With the cargo finally secured Owen began issuing a series of orders to raise the anchor, loosen the sails, and get the ship underway. Owen stood by the helmsman to gauge how the ship responded and was soon satisfied the overseer was correct, for *The Fair Mermaid* would indeed serve. As they steered out to sea Samuel came over wearing a puzzled look on his face.

"Owen? Aren't you going the wrong direction?" he said, pausing to point. "Kingston is over there."

"I know. Don't worry, we will get there."

"Uh, most of the previous Captains of this ship, including the last one, always hugged the coastline."

Owen shrugged. "I'm not the previous Captain. Until I've had time to study the charts, this ship isn't going anywhere near the coast other than to sail into a harbour. You wouldn't want the bottom ripped out from under us, would you? Besides, it would take forever to get to Kingston staying inshore and following the coast. I don't know why the last Captain would do that, unless he was someone who had no confidence in his navigation skills. But mark my words, we are going to pick up a nice offshore wind very soon which will have us at our destination a lot faster than we would if we just hugged the coastline. We will tack as soon as we catch it."

"I see. Well, finding you seems a bit of good luck. The last Captain was a drunkard."

"Oh? You had to let him go?"

"He drowned. He was so drunk he fell overboard. By the time they got the ship back to him he was gone."

Samuel told Owen how impressed he was when, as Owen predicted, they arrived in early afternoon after having made excellent time to Kingston Harbour. The product was quickly offloaded straight into yet another waterfront warehouse. As soon as space on the ship came free provisions for the plantation stored in the warehouse were brought out, but the other overseers supervised it all. Owen spent his time in port following Samuel about as he connected with other merchants in port to negotiate sales of the product. Owen was soon bewildered at the prices and the nuances of the negotiation process, but he followed as best he could. As the day ended Samuel took his leave of Owen.

"Right, I am staying and will be here for a few days. Keep bringing the product here just as you did today. Don't worry much about the negotiation process as it is really my job, but I will authorize you to conduct some yourself once you have a better idea of how it all works. The overseers in the warehouses know what to do anyway even if I am not around. All you need concern yourself with for now is to get the ship back and forth."

"Just one question, Samuel. Is this all there is to it, sailing back and forth between here and Old Harbour?"

The overseer shrugged. "Most of the time. The only other place you will go periodically is Black River, as a fair number of ships pick up cargo there, too. It's further away, but if it is where we have to take the product to sell it, then we will."

Owen spent the night on the ship itself. One of

the crew doubled as cook for the men and he served up a basic meal which made up in quantity for what it lacked in quality. His sleep was fitful as he was unused to the strange new quarters he was in, but he woke with the dawn and the rest of the crew. After a quick breakfast they were on their way within an hour.

Two hours into the return trip John was below checking on the cargo when Owen noticed one of the lines used to tether the ship to the dock when in port was not stowed properly. He ordered one of the sailors to deal with it and went back to paying attention to ensuring the helmsman was staying on course. A few minutes later he looked back and realized the job was still undone.

Owen stalked over to the man, who was standing near the mast talking with two other sailors. As the sailor turned with a quizzical look to face him Owen drove his fist hard into the man's midsection, crumpling him to the deck. Owen hauled him back to his feet still clutching his stomach in pain as the other two sailors stood back looking shocked. Owen looked briefly at the others as he pulled the man close.

"Right, you all need to understand something. I will be firm and fair with you. When I order you to do something, you bloody do it. If you do your job, it will be fine. But I'm sure you all know by now I was Royal Navy. I am used to having men flogged for disobeying me. It won't bother me to have the same done to you if necessary. Now get over there and fix the goddamn line."

The three men were silent for a moment before

nodding and the man Owen had punched went to do his bidding. Owen stalked back to the quarterdeck and resumed watching to ensure the now wide-eyed helmsman stayed on course. Owen sighed to himself, wondering if the man's failure to follow orders was a deliberate test of his resolve or whether he was merely one of those who needed to be prodded constantly. Applying punishment was not something Owen had ever wanted to do, but he understood the need for discipline on every ship afloat. Too many things could go wrong without it.

***

Owen found the November weather in Kingston far more bearable than during the first few sticky, hot summer months he had endured during the rainy season. The weeks turned into months so fast he couldn't believe it was now five full months since his life in the Navy came to such an abrupt end. The wound of parting from his former life still seemed raw when he thought about it, despite slowly growing less so. Of necessity he had learned much and being as busy as he was helped. But with most of the crops harvested and the product away to market, the demand to be constantly shuttling from Old Harbour to Kingston and back was considerably less.

Left with more time to himself, he worked to gain a better understanding of what was happening around him. He was fascinated to learn Old Harbour and, in particular, Kingston saw visiting merchant ships coming from a huge variety of ports. Sailors and ships arriving from the Guinea coast with new slaves came in to drop them off, before picking up sugar and molasses for transport to England. Once there they would offload the product and load provisions to take back to Guinea in an endless triangular route. Other ships from Newfoundland and Acadia, along with those from a host of American ports along the eastern seaboard brought provisions such as saltfish and corn along with lumber for casks and all manner of other products not available on the island.

Having personally seen the amount of trade goods moving back and forth he now had a better appreciation of how right Samuel was, for it was plain the owner of the plantation was undoubtedly far richer than he pretended to be. Both towns had active slave markets which came to life when one or more slavers appeared in harbour. The sums exchanging hands for their human cargo were staggering. A young male slave who appeared healthy and strong could command a fortune if a bidding war ensued.

For his part Owen was dismayed at the sight of the wretched people led forth in their manacles. Some seemed defiant and stoic, while others were shaking with fear. The majority simply seemed crushed and bewildered, still suffering from the effects of the horrific journey from Africa to here. On a few occasions Owen was forced to ferry some of the owner's purchased slaves from Kingston to Old Harbour. He did what he could to ease their situation by allowing them to remain on deck during the journey, ignoring the recommendation of the overseer John.

Owen also made a couple of trips to Black River

with cargo, which was a refreshing change for him as the trip to the distant port meant spending a full day at sea. The town was much the same as Old Harbour, with a host of warehouses and waterfront taverns and inns packed with sailors. The warehouses were also stuffed with the usual products to fill the holds of the ships, but this town did significant additional trade in cattle skins and logwood, which was used for the making of dyes.

But the problem Owen faced was even though a scant five months had passed since the beginning of his new life, it was already becoming a routine. Sailing back and forth to Kingston was not a challenge, while sitting in the taverns of Old Harbour where the majority of his days were spent was no relief. The one bright spot was Isabella.

***

"Hello Owen," she said, her face lighting up as he walked into The Spanish Rose.

With more time on his hands now, he was contriving to make opportunities to spend extra time with her every chance he could. The first few months he was so busy all he could do was send the occasional message to her, but gradually it had all changed. She dropped a mug of ale in front of him moments after he sat down before sliding into the seat opposite. She looked around to ensure they would be unheard before she spoke.

"Staying tonight, I hope?"

Owen smiled. "I thought it would be a good idea. Actually, I've made arrangements to stay two nights this time and, believe it or not, I'm taking the days off. I thought we could maybe do another trip to the beach?"

"Now you are talking. I'll have to make a few arrangements of my own, but this can be done."

"Excellent. Well, I need the break. I confess I am finding this work somewhat limiting. And some elements of it are, well—"

Isabella reached out and took his hand in hers.

"I am not surprised. I've seen the troubled look on your face a few times. Let me guess, you would like to be more than just a ferryman to a few places on the island and you don't like slavery any more than I do. Am I right?"

Owen nodded. "I'm a sailor, as I believe you pointed out to me months before. I like the broad, open ocean and seeing new places. And no, I don't like slavery. I know, it's how things work, but I don't have to like it. I don't want to be associated with it, in fact. Well, I've saved some money now and I'm in better shape, but I'm hardly rich. I'll start looking elsewhere for work, but I'll have to be careful. I don't want word to get back to Samuel about it."

"I think that's a good idea, Owen. But don't look too hard too fast, please. I'd like to enjoy having you around a while longer before you finally sail away and leave me once and for all."

Owen squeezed her hand. "We'll see, Isabella. Deciding I want to find other work is one thing, but finding it is another matter. And yes, in the meantime we'll just have to enjoy ourselves, won't we?"

Chapter Four
Jamaica
December 1772 to January 1773

The ale in the mug on the table in front of him was steadily disappearing as Owen sat in the shade on the waterfront tavern's verandah in Kingston. He had endured a long day of dealing with Samuel and a host of paperwork at the plantation warehouse. He had promised himself a drink as reward, but his thirst was too strong.

While tempted to wait until getting to The Spanish Rose for the drink, he knew Isabella would understand. The one flaw with the location of her Inn was it had no view whatsoever. Despite spending most of his days on board ships, Owen never tired of watching them come and go from the port. The endless tide of different people flowing past was also a source of fascination.

Finding himself drinking alone at the end of the day once again was a slowly growing source of unexpected discontent. Having a drink and spending time with Isabella was always good, but one of the things Owen hadn't realized he was missing badly was the simple camaraderie he had always found at the wardroom table when coming off watch on the various ships he had served on. After a hard day's work, having a drink with your mates was a simple reward Owen had not realized would be so valuable to him.

Drinking casually with the crew serving on *The Fair Mermaid* was impossible, for all Captains had to maintain a professional distance from their men and he would have been considered mad to ignore the rule with a crew of slaves anyway. While Owen had shared an occasional drink with the overseer Samuel, theirs was strictly a business relationship. Even having a drink with the overseer on his ship wasn't an option, for as time passed Owen realized he wanted to minimize the amount of time he spent with anyone associated with slavery.

As he stared at the almost empty mug before him it felt as if slavery was beginning to stain his very soul. He knew he needed out and this was the other reason for watching the ships come and go, for if an opportunity somehow appeared to meet his need, he wanted to seize it. Owen sighed and drained his mug, debating whether to order another. The serving girl was alert and came over asking if he wanted more, but even as she did Owen saw something from the corner of his eye which made him ignore her question. He stood to get a better look at a man standing on the dock in front of a nearby merchant ship.

"Sir?" said the serving girl, a puzzled look on her face as she asked the question a second time. "Did you want another?"

"Eh? Hmm, no," said Owen, distractedly pulling a few coins out to pay for his first drink. "I must go."

He wasn't certain the man who caught his attention was indeed who he thought he was, but he seemed familiar enough for it to be possible. Owen needed a better look, so he strode with purpose through the throngs of people on the waterfront finishing their duties for the day and heading for the taverns to quench their thirst. Owen still wasn't certain as he drew close, because the man had shifted position and now had his back to him. Owen's quarry finished talking to another man on the dock and turning, headed for the boarding plank of a nearby merchant ship tied up on the dock. Owen rushed forward to call after him.

"Sir?"

The man paused in mid step, about to board the ship, and he peered about with a quizzical look on his face. Owen had a bare moment to register the name of the ship was *The Sea Trader* before the man's eyes alighted on Owen coming toward him. An obvious sense of recognition slowly came over the man's face and his eyes widened as Owen spoke.

"Uncle Alan? Alan Giles? Is it really you?" said Owen.

This close to the man Owen was now almost certain his memory wasn't wrong, but his voice betrayed his uncertainty. The man before him was much older than Owen, with more grey hair than not. His face was weathered and lined, but he looked reasonably fit for what Owen judged to be a man in his mid-fifties. He was close to the same height as Owen, but what stood out was the similarity of their features.

"My God, I don't believe it. You are my nephew, Owen Spence, here after all these years. It is you, isn't it?"

"Sir, it is," said Owen, as he put out his hand for his uncle to shake.

Owen's uncle took his hand in a firm grasp and

pulled him closer for a brief hug.

"You are making me feel old, Owen. The last I saw you was well over ten years ago now. I think your mother, God rest her soul, had you dressed in a mock sailor's uniform, now I remember it. And the last word I had was you had indeed joined the Navy."

Owen stiffened. "I did, sir, but I am no longer in the Navy now."

The news brought another widening of his uncle's eyes. His uncle made to ask a question, but he stopped himself, obviously struggling to digest what he had heard. After a moment he shrugged and spoke.

"Well. There is clearly a story here and you must tell it to me. Hmm, I have business here in Kingston and my time is spoken for with some colleagues for dinner tonight. Would you be free to join me for dinner tomorrow night?"

"I would love to, Uncle Alan."

His uncle named an inn a short distance from the waterfront which Owen had never been to, but well knew was an expensive place to dine. After setting a time the two men parted. Owen was completely lost in thought still as he walked into The Spanish Rose and met Isabella. Despite his distraction a part of him sensed Isabella knew it and she proved him right by pulling him close and rubbing her breasts deliberately across his chest to get his full attention. Owen came to himself and held her close, explaining what had happened.

"And you think this man may be able to help you?" said Isabella.

"Maybe. I know he left for the Caribbean many years ago. My mother was his younger sister. The last I heard he had settled in Barbados and was running a trading business. God, I don't know, Isabella. Despite being apart, my mother and Uncle Alan were close."

Isabella clutched him even closer to her.

"I hope for your sake this is the opportunity you were looking for."

***

Owen dressed in his best clothes for the dinner, but they felt distinctly lacking in quality as he glanced about, looking at the other diners, while being shown to the table where his uncle was already waiting. His uncle greeted him warmly nonetheless and they were soon lost in conversation, catching up on family connections neither had seen for a long time. Owen's uncle had indeed settled on Barbados and married a local woman, but they had no children. She passed away a few years ago, but his uncle was still caring for a young niece of his deceased wife whose parents were also gone.

"Yes, I remarried again not too long ago, so the child has someone to care for her. I am at sea because of my business far more than I want to be now. You were fortunate to see me yesterday, for the business takes me everywhere throughout the Caribbean. Jamaica is always one of my first ports of call after hurricane season, but once I am done here I could be anywhere. But enough of me, what of you? I confess I am more than a little curious as to why you are no longer in the Navy."

Owen was ready for the inevitable question, but

he still stiffened, knowing he needed to be honest with his uncle about what had happened. He was spared from having to start right away as the first portion of their dinner arrived. An incredibly flavourful seafood broth soup with fresh bread served as the opening course and his uncle bid him to eat before it got cold.

Owen was amazed at how the soup complimented rather than overwhelmed the delicate flavours of the lobster and chunks of fish filling the bowl. As he slowly ate the soup he poured out his story, while his uncle topped up their wine glasses with a thoughtful look on his face. As Owen finished, his uncle rubbed his chin still in obvious thought.

"Owen? You mentioned there was some family history with your former Captain. What was his name?"

"Captain George Smithe, sir."

Owen's uncle groaned and scowled. "Oh God, that bastard again? Well, this all makes sense now."

"Sir?"

"Yes, I am aware of what he did to your father. I am also aware of his history out here. He is among the worst of the bloody worst of the plantation owners anywhere in the Caribbean. People like him make me ashamed to confess I share English heritage with him."

Owen was surprised at the vehemence and underlying anger in his uncle's voice, but he remained silent in response. After a pause to shake his head, Owen's uncle stared hard at him.

"So, you were suddenly set adrift and here you

still are. What have you been doing in Jamaica?"

Once again Owen was saved from answering immediately as their dinner arrived. The savoury chicken and local vegetables were done to perfection, but Owen wanted to finish his story, so he carried on with it between bites. His uncle remained silent, finishing his meal before Owen. He waited until Owen was done before topping his glass once more. With a bland look on his face, his uncle asked him what he thought of his new life and once again Owen felt the strain which came with knowing his answer somehow mattered.

"Sir, I have come to understand it is not for me. I took this work because I had to. It is not challenging and, if I may be honest, I don't like the people I must work with. Oh, I don't mean the slaves themselves. I have come to an understanding with them. They have learned I will be firm if I must, but I am also fair. No, the overseers I must deal with are—more than firm, they are harsh beyond belief. And they are most certainly not fair."

"In other words, you are a different kind of fish swimming in the wrong pond."

"Exactly, Uncle Alan. I have resolved to leave this behind, but making the resolution is easy. Finding a new life better suited to me is another matter."

"Indeed," said his uncle, as a tray of different English cheeses, a glazed cake with apple slices in it of a kind Owen had never seen before, and an array of different nuts appeared for dessert. The two men served themselves as his uncle continued.

"So, tell me, for I am curious. What do you think

of slavery, Owen?"

"What do I think?" said Owen, taking a bite of the cake to buy himself time to consider his response. He couldn't resist admiring the burst of flavour.

"I say, the cake is amazing, sir. Apples are a treat I haven't enjoyed in a long time. Well, you ask about slavery. I confess I have very mixed feelings, sir. I haven't spent much time on the plantation, but what I saw I know I wish I had not. Certainly, the way the overseers treat the slaves in their warehouses here in port and on my ship seems excessive. I suppose this doesn't speak well of them, coming from someone who has seen how punishment is delivered in the Royal Navy. The problem is money, though, isn't it?"

Owen paused to sample a few bites of the cheeses as he watched his uncle nod almost imperceptibly, before he continued.

"I find it incredible how much sugar is grown and sold on this island. As near as I can tell, better than three quarters of all the produce from Jamaica is sugar. I have much to learn about being a businessman, Uncle Alan, although I know what I am doing as a sailor. The thing is, even I can see the profits from all of this must be staggering to generate this kind of activity. And behind it all is slavery. I do not like it, but I do understand the importance of this to the economy. I just wish there was another way to get it done without using forced human labour. I know, you are a man of business and perhaps don't agree with me. If you don't, I hope you can forgive my humble opinion, but it just doesn't seem right."

"Indeed. And what do you think of the Royal Navy's use of the press?"

Owen was taken aback for a second at the sudden shift in topic, although he was well aware of what his uncle was referring to. The use of impressment, or the press as most people called it, involved the recruitment of men to serve in the Navy whether they wanted to or not. Officers in need of men would usually first try cajoling sailors with experience and in need of work in port towns to accept the joining bounty offered volunteers.

The problem was sometimes the need for men on the warship was bad. This need was especially so in times of war and the result was a press gang would be formed to search for men with experience of the sea. Those unlucky enough to be caught would find themselves whisked away to the ship without formality.

The forced recruitment was supposed to be limited to men with seafaring experience, but in practice more than a few landsmen found themselves snatched up and delivered to the harsh, unfamiliar world of a warship. Merchant sailors returning to England after months away sometimes found themselves pressed into service on a warship before they even set foot on land, dashing hopes of seeing family and home once again.

"I'll be honest, Uncle Alan. I never thought much about it, I expect because in time of war you do what you must in defence of your country. The press was in use by England long before I was born. Decades before? Maybe centuries even? It's just the way it works in the Navy and I never questioned it."

Owen sipped at the remaining wine in his glass before he continued.

"But I should expect the connection you are making is pressing people is perhaps another form of slavery, aren't you? Well, you may be right, uncle. Does the end justify the means? There are probably far more qualified people than me who can debate the point. If what you want to know is whether I like the idea of forcing people to be sailors, the answer is no. But then I love being a sailor, so I am perhaps biased. It's not an easy life, but I guess I don't understand why people need to be forced to do something so rewarding."

As Owen finally finished his uncle remained sitting in silence, swirling about the last mouthful of wine left in his glass. After a few more long moments he downed the remainder in one swift motion, setting the glass back on the table and leaning forward with elbows on the table to look at Owen again.

"Tell me, do you speak any other languages?"

Owen was taken aback by yet another sudden change in topic, but responded with ease.

"Well, yes. I can hold a slow conversation in both French and Spanish, although I cannot say I am fluent. My parents wanted me to learn them. If I were to practice, I'm sure I could improve."

"Well, this is better and better. Would you like to work with me, Owen?"

Owen's mouth fell open and his heart soared on hearing the words. He finished the wine in his own glass and leaned forward too.

"Very much so, uncle. Sir, I was not expecting this. I confess I was hoping you might be able to point me in the right direction to find something different. But I willingly accept whatever you have to offer. I no longer wish to do what I have been doing."

Owen's uncle smiled. "You haven't even asked me what I have in mind, let alone what I will pay you."

"Sir, I expect this will involve sailing, so I am content. As for pay, I am not concerned."

His uncle raised an eyebrow in question, so Owen named the sum he was currently being paid by the plantation owner.

"Uncle, I have no idea whether or not this sum would be fair pay for what you intend me to do. I am certain you will pay me what I deserve, though. As I said, I am content."

"Well, I may have to work on your negotiation skills a bit," said his uncle, a wry smile on his face. "But yes, I will pay you fairly. You will be on probation until I am satisfied, of course, and yes, you will be sailing to more places than just a few coastal ports on Jamaica. You should also bear in mind the men sailing with me are most certainly not slaves. Right, I must return to Barbados tomorrow and make some adjustments for this, but I will be back in early January. You can advise your current employer of your departure and settle your accounts with him. You will sail with me back to Barbados. Is this acceptable?"

"Uncle Alan, I will be forever in your debt."

Alan's uncle smiled and paid the bill, waving

away Owen's offer to pay something toward the cost of the meal.

"Nephew, with what they have been paying you, you can't afford to dine in places like this. I can."

Outside the two men made arrangements to meet at a specific time and date in January before Owen left, feeling as if he was walking on air.

***

Alan Giles wore a bemused look as he stood for a few moments watching his nephew walk away before turning to make his own way back to *The Sea Trader*. While he didn't feel as if he was walking on air, his step felt far lighter than he could remember it being in a long time. Having built his trading business to a point where he owned no less than three ships plying the waters of the Caribbean, he was finding the demands on his time onerous. He had two well paid Captains for his other ships, but finding a third with the right skills was proving difficult.

Being closer to age sixty than he cared to admit was also weighing on him, as was his health. He loved the island of Barbados and was now at a point where he simply wanted to end his days there enjoying life. Having no son to replace him running the business was his biggest problem. Finding his young nephew seemed a stroke of incredible fortune, even more so because both men had need of each other at the same time. He prayed this young man could be groomed to assume full control of it all.

The thought his young nephew might well be ideally suited to assume the other, far more important role he performed had also crossed his mind. While the other Captains he employed were capable enough, they were not suited to the task Alan Giles had in mind for Owen Spence. Well, time will tell, he mused to himself as he boarded *The Sea Trader*. He sensed his nephew might still feel a burning need to serve his country and this was good.

What his nephew didn't know was Alan himself had served as a spy for the Foreign Office for years now and it felt like the need for this service was growing ever greater than before.

***

Samuel finally appeared in Old Harbour one evening two weeks before Christmas, having finished the same journey from the plantation to the coast he and Owen had made months before. Owen sought him out as soon as he arrived at the dockside warehouse to tell him he was resigning effective Christmas day, for he had not had a break of any real duration for months. The overseer scowled and rolled his eyes on hearing the news.

"What bloody nonsense is this? You were going to be on probation with us for six months and then Mr. Westfall was going to give you a raise, remember?"

"I do remember, Samuel. The thing is I've received a better offer and I've accepted it."

"You haven't heard Mr. Westfall's offer, you fool. I just came from the plantation, where the two of us discussed this very question."

As Owen shrugged the overseer glared at him and named a monthly sum considerably higher than what he was paid in the first six months of his employment. Owen couldn't resist raising an eyebrow, but after a moment he shook his head. This time a look of total disbelief came over Samuel's face. The overseer finally recovered himself and carried on speaking.

"You're making me rethink what I'm about to say, but I'll try this anyway. Because I have assured him you know what you are doing, the other part of this offer is a chance at increased responsibility and opportunity to make more money than you know what to do with. Mr. Westfall is moving up the date when he wants to return to England. The offer is to put me in charge of the plantation and you in charge of all of our coastal operations. In addition to your guaranteed pay, there will be opportunity to share in the annual profits. It's five per cent for you and ten per cent for me, because I will still be the overall boss. In other words, if we run this properly, we could both make a fortune. Now, what do you say? Tell me you are giving up this ridiculous notion of leaving."

Owen shook his head once again. "I know you think I'm mad and I do appreciate your good opinion and generous offer, but I have an opportunity to do what I really want to. So no, I must decline. I am sure you will find someone to meet your needs."

"Do what you really want to? And what, dare I ask, is that?"

Owen turned and pointed out to sea, where the ships in the harbour stood out in relief against the backdrop of the rapidly setting sun on the horizon.

"Samuel, you may not understand this, but I am a sailor. I need to feel the truly deep water beneath the deck and to sail to different places. This sailing back and forth between Old Harbour, Kingston, and Black River is fine for a time, but it's not for me."

The overseer stared in silence at Owen for a few seconds before shaking his head as if to clear it of something distasteful clinging to it. Then he sighed.

"Right. Suit yourself, you lunatic. This just proves how wrong one can be about people. See me tomorrow and we'll sort out your pay."

With a final glance over his shoulder and a look of total disgust on his face, the overseer abruptly stalked away.

***

Owen spent Christmas with Isabella and her family in Spanish Town, meeting her mother and Isabella's young daughter for the first time. Isabella made it clear right away Owen was no more than a friend and would be leaving the island in a few short days, which he knew had to be done to put any notion of permanence out of her family's heads. Isabella herself had put on a brave face when he first told her what was happening, but Owen knew she too was disappointed.

After returning to Kingston Isabella suggested having one final day at the beach and Owen readily agreed. Her favourite beach was once again deserted, and they spread their belongings out on a blanket as before. Within moments Isabella stripped off her dress, making it clear what she wanted as she kissed him hard and moulded herself to him. Owen returned her passion and they lost themselves in each other's bodies once again.

They lay together afterwards, having exhausted their desire for a time. Owen felt torn as he stroked her side, listening to the waves coming ashore and enjoying the feel of the gentle breeze washing over them. He spoke when he could bear it no longer.

"You don't want me to go, do you?"

Isabella responded by pulling him closer and clutching him a little harder for a moment before answering.

"Of course not. But we both know you must and will go. I'm much older than you and you are a sailor. This was never going to last long."

Isabella rolled on top to straddle him, holding herself up with her hands on either side of his body. She laughed as Owen reached up with obvious pleasure to cup her breasts in his hands.

"You know I will be here for you if you are ever in port, Owen. But for now, I really do think some things at least must last a while and we should make the best of it while we can, don't you?"

***

Owen found on close inspection *The Sea Trader* was similar in many ways to *The Fair Mermaid*. His uncle's ship was slightly bigger and built to carry cargo like the other, but there were two major differences. This ship was a brig with two square rigged masts and a gaff sail carrying a complement of thirty men plus Owen. The other notable feature was how well maintained everything was. He was impressed, for the standards on display were high.

Owen approached his first real tour of the ship with what seemed the same level of curiosity the rest of the crew had for him. His uncle had still not made it clear what exactly he had in mind or whether *The Sea Trader* was ultimately to be Owen's, but it seemed possible. In a distinct sign this was likely, his uncle turned the ship over to Owen the second they were ready to depart.

"Take us to Barbados. I'll be in my cabin doing some paperwork."

Owen nodded, but his uncle was already disappearing in the entrance way to his cabin aft. Owen turned to the man standing beside him, who was watching him with a bland face, awaiting orders and appearing unsurprised at what was happening.

John Tate was a little shorter than Owen's six feet, but they shared the same sandy brown hair and slim, muscular builds. He also had the kind of weathered look which spoke of plenty of time at sea, unsurprising given he was First Mate of *The Sea Trader*. The one difference between them was age, for John also had the beginnings of fine lines around his eyes. Owen judged him to be in his late twenties in age. The two men had enjoyed little time to get to know each other to this point, but they both knew this would soon change.

"Let's get the men aloft, Mr. Tate. Once we get her underway and out of the harbour I'd like to have a look at some charts."

The First Mate nodded and turned away, issuing a stream of orders which turned *The Sea Trader* into a hive of activity. Owen rubbed his face and went to stand beside the wheel to watch the crew. Isabella had kept him up later than he planned to be the night before. He wanted to be fresh and ready for the first day of his new life, but they both had need to ensure their last night together for what would likely be a long time was memorable. Owen knew he would sleep well tonight.

They were two days at sea when the test came, as he expected sooner or later it would. Owen was slowly coming to know the various men and, so far, had found little to complain of any of them until now. Owen caught the unmistakable scent of rum about one of the common seamen and confronted the man about it. Finding the man was drinking wasn't unusual, for sailors on board merchant ships were entitled to their rum ration just as they were aboard a Royal Navy ship. Unfortunately for him, he was already drinking long before anyone was supposed to be, using a personal supply he had somehow spirited on board.

The sailor gave him a surly look in response to Owen's query and made the mistake of denying he was drinking. Owen shook his head in disbelief, before pointing to the small bulge in the pocket of the man's slops and ordering him to hand over the contents. The man scowled and pulled out a small flask, which Owen grabbed and flung overboard. The sailor was shocked.

"That was mine! You can't do that!"

"Yes, I bloody can. On this ship you follow orders in future. You will not be drinking before time."

"Who the hell are you to order me about? You're not the Captain—"

"Ah, but right now I am. So, when I give you an

order, you do it."

"What do you think you're going to do about it? This isn't the bloody Royal Navy where you can flog me for no reason. I—"

"And now I've had enough," said Owen, grabbing his shirt at the collar and pulling him nose to nose. "You are correct, this isn't the Navy, so I won't have you flogged. But if you continue this you are going to find yourself locked in the hold the rest of the way to Barbados with minimal rations. With any luck you can catch a rat or two you can eat. And if you don't like this and you think you are tough enough to take me, go ahead and try. See what happens."

The sailor scowled, breathing hard as if tempted, but after several long moments he sighed.

"Sir. I understand. I will not disobey you again."

Owen loosened his grip and smiled pleasantly as he pushed the man away.

"Excellent. I'm glad we understand each other. Now get back to your duty."

Owen saw two other seamen standing nearby who had obviously watched the whole encounter as he turned to make his way back to the quarterdeck. He stared back at them, arms folded in silence, until the two men understood his meaning and went back to their own duties. The other man Owen knew was watching the scene was the First Mate manning the helm, but he said nothing as Owen passed by and went below to his quarters.

***

Captain Giles heard the knock on his cabin door and called out a command to enter, for he knew it would be the First Mate coming in response to his summons. He waved the man into one of the chairs in front of his desk. After pouring the two of them shots of rum to sip the Captain sat back in his chair, shifting to make himself comfortable again.

"Well, John? It's been almost a week and we have made good time. What do you think?"

The First Mate gave an almost imperceptible nod. "He'll do."

"How is he with the men?" said the Captain, rubbing his chin.

"I confess I had my doubts, but he seems to have gained their respect. He picked up on the fact that arse Cranston had smuggled rum on board again before I did, and he seems to have put some fear into him. We may have to do something about Cranston one of these days. In any case, he certainly knows what he is doing with the ship and the men have noticed it too. Took him a while to get used to how she sails, but I've had no qualms leaving him to stand watch. He knows his business with navigation. I can work with him."

The Captain downed his drink and smiled. "Excellent."

"Captain? Have you talked to him about the idea of giving him the other duties yet?"

"No. It might come later, once I am certain he is the man for this. He seems promising enough I plan to mention him to Sir James Standish in Barbados, though. All in good time."

***

Owen was surprised to get an invitation from his uncle to dine with him, but he accepted readily. His uncle offered a toast with his wine glass to Owen as the Captain's servant placed their first course of soup on the table before them.

"Well, congratulations, nephew. We will be in Barbados tomorrow. I've been assured you know what you are doing with the ship."

"Thank you, uncle," said Owen, raising his own glass in return. The two men began eating their soup as Uncle Alan spoke once again.

"In case you are wondering, the plan is to assign you this ship in due course. I am not done with it or you just yet, however. You and I will need to take a little trip with her, perhaps next month. For now, though, I would like to know what you think of the crew?"

Owen shrugged after considering his response.

"They know what they are doing. They aren't very different from sailors in the Navy. If an opportunity for the usual kinds of mischief arises I expect they will take advantage of it, but I am not concerned. There is only one of the common seamen who might bear closer scrutiny. On the other hand, this John Tate is very good as the First Mate. I expect he was the one giving you assurances about me. I confess I am a bit curious about him, uncle."

"Oh?"

"I appreciate you are considering me for command of this ship, but this man seems fully competent. Have you given thought to him for a similar role?"

Owen's uncle gave him an appraising look as he finished eating the soup. The bowls were whisked away within moments and their main meal of roast chicken appeared before them. Owen's uncle waited until the server disappeared before continuing.

"An astute question, Owen. The answer is yes, I offered him a command long ago, but he is not interested. I've come to understand he is also not suited to it either."

"Really?" said Owen, with a puzzled look on his face. "Can I ask why?"

"A couple of reasons. He was born in England, but his family moved to Norfolk in the Virginia colony when he was younger to start a business. The problem is matters have been getting rather tense between the so-called patriots and the loyalists there for a long time now. His family are loyalists and were very early victims of the tensions. I don't know all the details, but the result was they were forced out of business. To escape it all they ended up moving to Barbados where they have other relatives who helped them. As a result, he hates these American patriots with a passion which wouldn't serve him or me well, for if you are in business sometimes you have to do business with people you don't like."

"I see."

"The other reason which I expect may sound strange is I think he understood better than I the fact he is not a leader of men. It isn't a criticism, of course. I think if he pushed himself he certainly could serve as a Captain, but he wouldn't be happy about it. It's dealing with the people, you see. He doesn't like having to discipline or bring others into line. He could do it, but he would be frustrated constantly. He is a very straightforward person who believes in doing a job to your absolute best without let up, and he has no time for anyone who doesn't meet the same standard. In other words, in all other respects I trust him with anything. This may not make sense, but I now know he would make a very imperfect Captain. On the other hand, he really is the perfect First Mate."

Owen nodded between bites of his dinner. "I see. I agree, some people are not suited to be leaders."

"Indeed. And yet some people seem fated to be leaders on a very large stage. Fascinating, isn't it? I think there are some most interesting people coming to the fore in these difficult times we are in and they may take the world in a whole new direction."

"Let me guess, you are thinking about the Americans, aren't you?"

"I certainly am. They are in a difficult place right now. Many want change and many want to keep the status quo. I confess I personally am rather torn about it all. By and large, I like the Americans. They are proving very resourceful, but they are also not happy about how they are being treated. I would like to see positive changes which work for everyone, because I love England and don't want to see her at risk. But I fear they are at a tipping point with their frustration. We have a challenging future ahead of us."

The two men ate the rest of their meals in silence and were left with the remnants of their wine to finish. Owen's uncle toyed with his wine glass as he finally spoke once again.

"We were speaking of slavery the last time we

had dinner, weren't we? Tell me, have you ever heard of Granville Sharp?"

Owen rubbed his forehead in thought. "Um—yes, I believe I have, uncle. He is a distant relative of ours, is he not? I don't recall ever meeting him, though."

"He is indeed a relative. He is a cousin on my mother's side. You don't remember reading about him in the newspapers?"

"No. I confess I haven't had much time for it, either in the Navy or in the last several months. I do like reading them, though. Have I missed something?"

"Hmm—well, yes. Granville is another man who is evolving into a leader on the world stage, and he is doing a fine job. I will fill you in about him at our next dinner together. But for now, it is early to bed. We will have a busy day in Barbados tomorrow."

Chapter Five
The Caribbean
February 1773

Carlisle Bay was as crowded with Royal Navy and merchant ships as the last time Owen was there, but *The Sea Trader* worked her way inshore to the dock his uncle used for his trading operation without much difficulty. In the three weeks since their arrival this was where they remained, for his uncle was extremely busy from the moment he stepped ashore. Owen and the crew of *The Sea Trader* busied themselves with offloading their cargo and slowly loading new shipments of goods as they arrived, along with fixing a variety of small problems with the ship. She would be ready to go when the time came.

Owen kept to himself on the ship, but was forced to dine ashore on nights when the cook was given shore leave away. While there were numerous taverns and inns in Bridgetown, not all of them served the quality of food Owen expected and he had his favourites. He was aware the Royal Navy officers on the various ships in harbour felt the same way, so it was inevitable Owen would encounter someone he knew sooner or later.

A party of four Lieutenants came into the tavern Owen was in while having dinner with John Tate and one of them was an officer he had served with on his first ship. The man recognized Owen and came over, but the conversation was awkward and mercifully brief. The officer didn't ask why Owen was in civilian clothes, making it obvious the man knew what had happened.

John watched the whole encounter in silence, but as the officer walked back to his own table Owen knew his First Mate was curious. Owen sighed and told him his story. As he finished, he reached for his mug of ale to down a portion and gauge John's reaction. The man kept a bland face as he finally nodded and took his own drink.

"So, you and your family were wronged by a bunch of bastards. I expect the Captain told you my story, of course. I know what it feels like, so I guess it makes us a good fit. You uncomfortable here with them? We can go elsewhere."

Owen took a moment to think about the notion and glanced one last time in the direction of the Navy officers before he spoke.

"Yes, I'd say we are a good fit, John. He did tell me a little about you, but not much. You know, I was expecting this would happen sooner or later and now it has, I somehow find I don't really care what they think. It's the past, so let's have another. I'm buying."

"Sure," said John, toying with his mug and looking thoughtful before finally carrying on as Owen signalled for another round of drinks.

"He would have told you I'm from Norfolk and my family was forced out, right?"

"Yes, this would be all I know."

John nodded. "What you really need to know is I hate liars. People who say one thing and then do something completely different. Stab other people in the back. Those rebel bastards in Norfolk drove us out, Owen. Some of them were people who claimed to be our friends, but weren't. My father was a trader and he had a general store, selling goods from everywhere. He was loyal and wanted to stay loyal, so a few of the rebel leaders decided to make an example of him. Bastards started threatening people who wanted to do business with him. I don't know why it's a crime to have an opinion, but these buggers made it that way. And when he stood up to them, they decided to make him pay. Despite the fact they were allegedly friends."

As John paused to sip his drink Owen frowned. "Make him pay? How so?"

"He was waylaid on his way home with my older brother one night. Both were dragged into an alley and beaten real bad. I still can't believe they survived, given their injuries. Neither of them has been the same ever since. I was away at sea and knew nothing of it, but by God I was angry when I returned. I was ready to make some people pay, but they forbid me to do it. My father said it was only going to get worse in Virginia, and I'd say he's right about it. Anyway, the wheels were already in motion to move to Barbados. My father has a brother here and he helped a lot to get the family settled. I was fortunate to find a position with your uncle and here I am. And I expect you have a problem with liars too, after your experiences."

"I certainly do and yes, it seems we have much in common," said Owen, pausing as fresh drinks appeared in front of them. He raised his mug in toast.

"I'm also thinking it would be fair to say I've

found a new friend, John."

John raised his in return. "I would say so, friend."

***

Owen's uncle was staying at his small estate south of Bridgetown near Saint Lawrence Gap, an area Owen knew was filled with similar such homes fronting several wonderful sandy beaches. They hadn't seen much of him, but he finally sent a message he wanted to take Owen with him around the island the next day, although no explanation as to why was given. Owen was curious, but told John the ship would be in his hands the next day.

Right on time his uncle drove up on the road beside the dock in a small carriage drawn by one horse with room for up to four people. A young girl was with him in the carriage and she climbed down to greet Owen, while his uncle remained where he was in the driver's seat. As she reached the ground she paused for a long moment, staring up at Owen with wide eyes and obvious interest.

"Hello Owen," said Uncle Alan. "Sorry I haven't had much time for you lately, but today we make amends. I believe I mentioned to you I have a niece under my wing. This is Elizabeth Giles. She is twelve years old, but I sometimes think she is double her age, given how smart she is and how easily she wraps me around her little finger. Beware, she might do the same to you."

"Really, uncle?" said Elizabeth, giving him a mock frown with one hand on her hip before turning to Owen and offering her hand.

"Uncle has told me about you, sir. I am pleased

to meet you."

Owen smiled and took her hand, impressed at the poise she was displaying. He gave her a brief bow and brushed her hand with a quick kiss as the girl was obviously hoping for him to do.

"I am enchanted already, Elizabeth. It is always an honour to meet a pretty lady."

Elizabeth beamed with delight and Owen was almost certain her eyes twinkled as she gave him an appraising look, letting her hand linger in his for a couple of seconds longer than what would be normal. While the girl was only twelve years old, Owen judged it possible she might blossom when she was older. Her straight, sandy blonde hair framed a pleasing, strong face, but what stood out was her piercing, dark blue eyes. She was six inches shorter than Owen and seemed too gangly and thin to properly fill out the dress she was wearing, but he suspected this would change soon enough.

"I'll be thirteen in November," said Elizabeth, with a wistful hint to her voice, as if she were hoping it would come sooner. She blushed as Owen gave her an even wider smile and, recovering herself, she pointed to the rear seat of the carriage.

"I am to sit in back, while you join Uncle in the front so the two of you can talk."

As she made to climb aboard on her own Owen offered her his hand.

"May I help you up?"

She stopped, one hand already on the carriage side to pull herself up. She bit her lip briefly before smiling as she nodded, taking his hand once again. Once she was settled in the carriage Owen climbed up himself to find his Uncle grinning at him.

"You won't be able to say I didn't warn you, Owen."

"Uncle!" said the girl, sounding mortified as she gave him a light slap on the arm.

Her uncle laughed and gave the reins a shake to start the horse moving.

"I think I told you Elizabeth is my niece from my deceased wife's side of the family, did I not? Her own family is gone too. She took my surname when she came to live with us. I confess I've come to love this little imp as if she were my own daughter."

"Uncle Alan is the only family I have here now, and I do love him too, even if he does tease me unmercifully," said Elizabeth.

Owen's uncle steered the carriage with practiced ease through the crowded streets of Bridgetown, but the crowds thinned soon enough. They continued past the outskirts of town and on to a pleasant country carriage path winding through patches of foliage sprinkled with brightly coloured flowers. Fields with young, green sugarcane plants waving in the light breeze appeared, stretching onward to the far distant horizon. Owen's uncle talked of his business as they went.

"So, I thought you and my niece here would like a day in the country for a change of pace. I'm combining this with a little business while we are at it. If one is in the business of providing trade goods it pays to know what kind of situation the people you deal with are in and, more importantly, what they want to buy. The fellow we are going to see today has a large plantation. He is one of the more civilized ones as far as plantation owners go, for he at least acknowledges owning slaves is problematic if you justifiably want to call yourself a civilized person. He has a dilemma, however, for he still owns them and looks the other way when his overseers get too zealous in their duty."

"It makes sense to find out what he needs, uncle."

"It is also even better to find out what he thinks the future holds. I may not agree with him on some things, but knowing his thoughts has proven useful to me in past."

They eventually turned onto a side lane following yet another cane field before it gave way to a broad, well-manicured lawn dotted with flowers and trees fronting a large manor house gleaming white in the now late morning sun. Beyond the manor house numerous buildings of various sizes could be seen, with several black workers moving about their tasks. Owen judged this plantation was roughly the size of the one he had served in Jamaica. After leaving the horse and carriage with a servant they were ushered to chairs set on a wide, shady verandah.

The owner and his wife joined them as they were all served cool fruit drinks to sip. His wife was soon in animated conversation with Elizabeth, while Owen's uncle and the owner began talking about business and politics. After being introduced Owen stayed silent to observe what the two men were talking about.

He quickly realized the man was not at all optimistic about the future. The duties he was being forced to pay combined with rising prices and occasional shortages of food and supplies were combining to squeeze his profits far more than he liked. Owen felt little sympathy, for from what he could see this man was as wealthy as his colleague in Jamaica.

They took their leave after an hour of conversation. As they returned the way they came back down the long laneway they were forced to a halt when a mixed working party of male and female slaves with two overseers crossed their path. One of the women glanced aside at the carriage and stumbled on an unseen rock in her path, causing a chain reaction of slaves tumbling into each other and falling to the ground.

An overseer immediately began striking those on the ground with his short whip, but one of the male slaves pushed him away from the women, trying to help them get up. The other overseer had a short club which he drove into the slave's stomach, causing him to double over and cry out in pain. From behind him Owen heard Elizabeth cry out in horror at the brutality on display. To his amazement, she stood up in her seat and stamped her foot as she screamed at the two overseers.

"Stop that! Give them time to get up!"

The horse gave a start and shuffled about, surprised by everything going on, but Owen's uncle reined him back in. As he did one of the overseers glared over at the occupants of the carriage for a long moment. The man said nothing and turned back to the slaves who were struggling to get fully on their feet. He kicked hard at the one remaining woman on the ground and she cried out in pain from the blow, but she found her footing and joined the others.

Within moments the little group was once again on its way and the laneway was clear. Owen and his uncle both looked back at Elizabeth to ensure she was all right. The girl was still wearing an angry look as she stared after them, but was settling back on the seat once again. She finally turned to her uncle, her face set hard.

"I'm sorry, uncle. That made me mad."

"I know, sweetheart. I don't like it either. Let's go for lunch. We can talk about it then."

They spent the next hour travelling a winding route, eventually linking with a well-travelled coastal road. Owen judged they were somewhere south of Bridgetown by the time they finally pulled up at a large oceanside inn. From the roadside where they stabled the horse and carriage there wasn't much to see, but inside was another matter. The inn had an enormous open terrace supported by a large rock wall built up along the beach to keep back the waves. A high, thick thatch roof offered shade and opportunity for the light ocean breeze to keep them cool. A server recognized Owen's uncle and simply waved them through.

"She is already here Mr. Giles," said the woman with a smile.

Owen's uncle led them to a table right on the water's edge, where Owen could see they would be able to watch the waves wash up against the wall beside them. A woman of roughly the same age as his uncle with light, coffee coloured skin rose from the table to hug Owen's uncle. He gave her a loving smile before introducing her to Owen as his second wife Mary.

"This is our favourite place to eat in all of Barbados, Owen. Coincidentally, we live not far from here, so you can imagine they know us well here. We also know the menu, so may I order for all of us?"

"Of course, uncle. I am in your hands."

The starting course consisted of sticks of breaded and fried flying fish for dipping in a spicy, hot yellow pepper sauce which Owen couldn't get enough of as he washed it down with a mug of fresh ale. The simple main course of steamed lobsters cooked with butter, salt and pepper, and grated cheese along with local vegetables came soon afterwards. As they worked their way through the meal Owen's uncle brought the conversation around to what they saw earlier in the day.

"So, as you saw this morning Elizabeth here doesn't much like slavery, Owen. And as I mentioned, neither do I. You remember a while back I told you about Granville Sharp, right? Well, our relative is a good man, Owen. While many people are coming to deplore slavery, he is actually doing something about it. He won a major victory in the English courts last year."

"Indeed? What was it about?"

"A slave named James Somerset was taken from America to England, where he was able to escape in 1771. He was recaptured and was going to be sent back to America, but Granville learned of what had happened. Somerset's plight was covered in the newspapers and the public funded a legal team to take the man's owner to court. Granville was already studying law surrounding slavery in depth and he helped them with their arguments. The judge took his time prevaricating as long as he could, but in the end he came out with a rather narrow ruling last summer to the effect English law did not allow forcibly taking someone from English soil into bondage. In other words, everyone in England is free and slavery is not permitted there."

"This is incredible, Uncle Alan. What does it mean for slavery here?"

"Good question. Unfortunately, right now, it apparently means nothing. This ruling seems to apply only to English soil and not to English territories or colonies like Barbados. There are still disputes ongoing over the true meaning and impact of this, but regardless, it is a major achievement. Sadly, I think the road ahead is still long, but I also believe a day will come when everyone in England will come to understand the horror of slavery and forsake it once and for all."

"I hope the day comes soon, uncle," said Elizabeth, as the heat in her voice betrayed how strongly she felt about it. "I may be just a girl, but I know the difference between right and wrong, and this is terribly wrong. If some means to help end slavery ever comes my way, you can be assured I will take it."

"I know you will, sweetheart," said Uncle Alan, giving her a loving pat on the shoulder. "Someone has to. Anyway, the reason I mention this is to ensure you understand where we stand. I was one of the people who contributed to the fund for Somerset's defence and I will continue to support them with what I can. My problem is I live with a contradiction every day. I know sooner or later it will occur to you that much of the business I do is with people involved with slavery and this will inevitably make you wonder if I am saying one thing while doing the complete opposite."

"I hadn't thought this yet, Uncle Alan, but I expect you are right. Sooner or later it would cross my mind."

"Indeed. It certainly feels like I am having it both ways. The trouble is the economies here in the Caribbean all to one extent or another depend on the sugar trade. Not completely of course, but there is no question sugar is dominant. In turn, the sugar trade depends on using slavery. And the British economy is addicted to the money the sugar trade brings. So, I console myself with the thought I am doing what little I can to try and change all of this. I know it won't happen overnight. Because the profits I make from dealing with the slave owning plantations may someday help end this madness is a small irony I like. But it still troubles me I have to make a living and inevitably my doing so goes some way to supporting this madness."

"This isn't all your Uncle has done, Owen," said Mary, stepping into the conversation for the first time. "My daughter and I were house slaves he and his first wife purchased and set free years ago. They began paying us a wage as employees and we couldn't believe it at the time. Your Uncle won my heart with his kindness. There aren't many men like him."

Mary reached across the table and took his hand in hers as she finished, as her husband smiled.

"Uncle Alan?" said Elizabeth, wearing a tentative, questioning look as she finished the dessert the servers had placed before all of them. "Have you told him about the other work you do?"

"Well, not in detail, but now is perhaps as good a time as any. Owen, I have no secrets from these two, in case you are wondering. I do indeed have another role, which is not for everyone's ears, so you must keep this to yourself. I actively gather information and I talk to diplomats everywhere I go. I prepare reports on what I have heard. I do this on behalf of the government, Owen. They need information, you see. Everything is important, even small pieces of information which may not seem like much. The situation here in the Caribbean is—fluid, especially with what is going on in America. And with the direction it all seems to be going, I fear yet another war may come to plague all of us. I am not alone with this fear. So, I do what I can for my country. It may break my heart my country is so addicted to money it must rely on slavery, but I love my country and will do what I must to help."

Owen frowned. "I confess I have not paid much attention to what has been going on in America, Uncle. What is the problem?"

"Answering that question would make for a much longer conversation, Owen. Personally, I think the real issue is actually what is being done to the Americans. I confess I rather like these Americans, as I think I mentioned to you. They are proving very strong and resilient despite being forced into a difficult situation. I just wish they weren't relying so heavily on slave labour too. In any case, there is someone I want you to meet, Owen. He is away right now, but when he returns we will have a conversation with him. In the meantime, though, you and I will be making another trip. I will be honest, Owen. I need to see you in action as a negotiator. If you can satisfy me as to your skills in this regard on this trip, the ship will be yours to command."

"All right, Uncle. Where are we off to?"

"The Spanish Main, nephew. Have you ever been to any of the ports on the Main?"

Owen's eyes widened in response. "No, but you certainly have my interest. I thought trade with the Spanish had waned."

"Hmm, well, it has. Those greedy fools in the South Seas Company ruined it all. The contraband trade in slaves and other wares with the local officials grew so blatant and outrageous the authorities in Spain couldn't ignore it anymore. More to the point, the tax revenues they were missing out on were enormous, so they cancelled the exclusive authorization for the Company to trade with the Main and it all fell apart. It's why the government finally authorized a number of free ports on Jamaica and Dominica to compensate for the loss of trade. But even though the Spanish are fully managing their own trade in slaves now, their need for other goods hasn't disappeared and this is what we will be dealing with. After we pay their duties, of course."

"I expect I have much to learn, Uncle."

"You do and you will. Look, for now all I need you to do is to watch and learn. If you meet my expectations, and I think you will, I really just need you to be a sponge. Listen to those around you, watch who is doing what. Keep your eyes and ears open."

"I can do that, Uncle."

"Excellent. Well, I will take you back to the ship. Mary and Elizabeth will make their own way home. I want to be on my way to the Main two days from now, Owen."

As Uncle Alan paid the bill Owen made to take leave of the two women. On a whim he once again bent to kiss Elizabeth's hand and she gave him a glowing smile before the women walked away. Owen thanked his Uncle for the meal as they climbed back into the carriage. Owen's uncle explained what he wanted done in preparation on the ride back. Owen felt he needed time to digest everything he had learned, but he had much to do and little spare time to do it with. He had confidence he could succeed, though. And best of all, his future now seemed much brighter than before.

***

The fierce sun of late afternoon combined with the minimal breeze helping them limp slowly into harbour would normally have left Owen feeling as energetic as a lizard digesting a large meal, but he was fully alert, for the first stop they were sailing into was yet another historic Caribbean port he was curious to see. The deep-water harbour of Porto

Bello, located on the Caribbean side of the northern tip of the isthmus of Panama, was surrounded on either side by low hills covered with thick, heavy tropical jungle. A small, nearby river flowed through a wide delta into the ocean. To someone unaware of the history there would seem little reason to establish a significant outpost in this spot, but this was once one of two major ports the Spanish used as a transit hub from which the riches of the mines of Peru could flow through on their way to Spain.

Because of those riches the British had attacked and plundered Porto Bello several times. The settlement was established in 1597 and not long after in 1601 the English privateer William Parker captured it. Captain Henry Morgan, another privateer who later went on to become Lieutenant Governor of Jamaica, did the same in 1668. The latest such effort was during The War of Jenkin's Ear in 1739, but the Spanish had reclaimed it two years later. The wealth plundered each time from Porto Bello ensured the raids and the port now enjoyed a legendary status in the minds of the English public.

Owen's uncle was standing beside him as they drew closer, aiming for an open spot along the waterfront docks. Two other merchant ships of roughly the same size as *The Sea Trader* were already tied up. Owen's attention was focused on the San Geronimo Fort, which still defended the town even after being attacked so many times, when he heard his uncle curse aloud in surprise. Owen turned and saw his uncle standing tense like a hunting dog, staring intently at the nearest of the merchant ships.

"Uncle Alan?" said Owen.

His uncle pointed to the ship's flag stirring limply in the breeze which Owen had not seen.

"I am curious as to what a Frenchman is doing here. The French have not done much trading along the Main. This is exactly the kind of thing you will need to have an eye out for, Owen. Anywhere the French are trading and travelling to, we want to know why. More importantly, we want to know what they are doing. In fact, I think I have seen this ship before. If it is the one I am thinking of, we need to find out who her Captain is."

"Uncle? What about the other ship? It looks to have a Dutch flag."

"I am less concerned about him, but we will need to dig for information on it, too. The Dutch ship I am not surprised to see. This French ship is another matter."

Owen grunted acknowledgement and would have quizzed his uncle more, but the task of safely docking the ship was commanding his attention. He was curious as to what reception an English trading ship would get, given the history of the place, but the Customs officers who boarded the ship as they finally docked seemed cordial enough. When he made an effort to speak to them in their language it also helped, along with the smell of stale wine surrounding them. He gave them a quick tour to show them the merchandise they had in the hold matched the manifest listing it all and as he did Owen marvelled once again at the amazing variety of goods they had to offer.

The surprising part was how mundane some of it seemed, yet how far it had all come to be sold in a Spanish market on a different continent. English textile goods such as clothes along with hats, gloves, shoes, and even furs would soon be for sale. Owen was amazed to learn one crate even held pots of English mustard. English manufactured goods ranging from simple items such as pots, pans, and small hardware items to more complex items such as watches, clocks, and jewellery formed another cluster of wares. Even a few large items such as furniture were included.

While all of this had certainly come a long way from England, the bewildering array of wares from Asia outmatched this. Owen's uncle assured him the host of exotic spices such as peppercorns, nutmeg, cinnamon, and cloves they carried would fetch high prices and be snapped up willingly by the locals, despite the high duties the Spanish government would charge. The Chinese porcelain, rugs, and draperies they carried would do the same, for all of this was impossible for the locals to get from anywhere else.

The inspection was as cursory as Owen's uncle predicted it would be. The customs men opened a couple of crates for appearances and compared what they saw against the manifest. Ten minutes after boarding they were back on deck and after applying an official stamp to the manifest Owen's uncle offered the senior of the two men a small, heavy purse. The man nodded his appreciation and left the ship with the other in tow.

"Well, that's the first bribe behind us. Those two couldn't wait to get back to the tavern. I expect they'll be drinking from the more expensive bottles for the rest of the day."

"The first bribe, uncle?" said Owen. "There are more to come?"

"Oh, yes. In a larger port like this you have to deal with the local Governor in addition to the minor officials who board us. The Governor and his duties will cost us rather more than what those two did. In the smaller villages we will stop in it will just be the local customs men."

"Isn't all this eating into profits too much?"

Uncle Alan shrugged. "Yes, but it is a cost of doing business in places like this. As I told you, the specific wares we have brought aren't made here. We can therefore charge what we want as long as no one else is here selling the same goods. Well, we may have to negotiate a bit, but we aren't going to lose out. The duties they add on are in reality paid by the locals and not us, because we factor these into our prices. There is risk, of course. Our manifest lists everything we have, but not the proper quantities of it all, you see. In other words, we can work some side deals with the local merchants to give them a chance to make money too, without the bother of duties."

"So, we really are smuggling to the Spanish Main as in past?"

"We are, just not to the same degree and, no, we certainly aren't making the kind of outrageous profits The South Sea Company made. Of course, we risk some overzealous Governor or even the

Spanish Navy boarding us to do a detailed inspection. We would have some explaining to do if they were to find the discrepancy between our manifest and the reality of what we have. But we have unique goods to sell, and the lesson here is those who risk the most will realize the greatest rewards, Owen."

"I see, Uncle. It makes sense."

"The key in any transaction is to ensure everyone involved comes away feeling their interests have been taken care of. I was not surprised when the Spanish cancelled the arrangement with The South Sea Company. Those greedy idiots didn't allow for the Spanish government to receive a reasonable share of the action, which makes it a perfect example of what I am talking about. And now, before we do anything else, we need to go see the Governor."

"Don't we need to send word and ask for an appointment?"

Uncle Alan grinned. "Even if he's in bed with his favourite mistress he'll stop what he is doing and come to greet us. We're bringing him the means to spend even more time with her in future. Let's go."

***

The Governor's mansion wasn't far from the waterfront, perched on a small rise of land to capture whatever breeze could be found at any time. As the two men made their way to the entrance the Spanish soldier standing guard stepped forward to greet them. They had just finished explaining who they were when the door opened, and a servant showed two other men out. Owen was surprised to see his uncle stiffen and give a start of recognition at the same time as one of the newcomers. Owen's uncle was the first to recover, bringing a smile with no warmth in it to his face.

"Well, it is Paul Allarde, is it not? It has been some time since we met. Boston, wasn't it?"

"It was. And you are Captain Alan Giles, aren't you?"

"Indeed. This is my nephew, Owen Spence."

"And this is my First Officer William Bains, sir. What brings you to Porto Bello?"

Owen's uncle eyed the First Officer briefly, before turning back to the Frenchman and shrugging.

"Trade, of course. Which I suspect is why you are here? That must be your ship in the harbour."

"It is, sir."

"I must say, you are a bit far away from your usual routes, aren't you?"

This time the Frenchman shrugged. "My home of Martinique is no more or less distant than Barbados, which if memory serves is your home base. We all have wares to sell, don't we?"

"Indeed. Perhaps we can share a bottle one night over dinner?"

"No, we are departing no later than dawn tomorrow morning. We may even leave later tonight if we can, as my crew were almost done making ready when we left to come here. I have a couple of merchants to finish some matters with hopefully tonight. We have already been here a day too long and I am behind schedule. We were just giving our parting regards to the Governor. Perhaps another time."

"I see. Another time then. Good day, sirs."

Owen's uncle stood staring after the two men as they walked away, chewing his lip in thought. Owen finally could resist no longer and spoke up.

"I'm surprised you know him, uncle. Is there more to this story?"

"Oh yes, most certainly. We will discuss it later. Let's go see the Governor."

As Owen's uncle predicted the Governor made them wait less than ten minutes before they were ushered in to see him. Governor Sanchez scrutinized the stamped manifest briefly before engaging in a negotiation with Owen's uncle regarding the official duties and his fee. The discussion didn't take long, for both of them knew the rules of the game and they had played it many times before.

After another pouch of coins was passed across the desk, heavier and larger than the one given to the customs men, the Governor became positively cordial. Glasses of a smooth Spanish wine were shared out from a nearby decanter and the three men toasted to future profitable relationships as the Governor applied his personal stamp to the manifest confirming duties were paid. After a few minutes of general conversation Owen's uncle steered the conversation around to the presence of the French ship, casually expressing wonder at what they were doing here.

The Governor laughed. "Come, Captain Giles. You need not be so circumspect with me. I have no more love for the French than you do. Perhaps even less, come to think of it. They are indeed here trying to sell their goods and they also want information, both of which is what you are doing here too. Any hint Spanish authorities along the Main want to have a friendlier relationship with the French would be welcome news to them, and bad news to you."

Hugh's uncle gave a wry smile in return. "All very true, Governor. And what do you want? We have talked before of putting the excesses of the past behind us."

The Governor shrugged. "None of this is up to me, as you well know. Spain will set her own course through this. We are steering for the middle ground just now. If the local French traders want to be here, we have no objection, the same as we have no objection to you. As long as you pay your duties and my fees, of course."

The Governor was unable to resist laughing before he continued.

"The problem we have with France is Spain shares a land border with her, while you do not have this perhaps questionable honour. But the one problem I suspect we do share is I think the French are beginning to take active interest in what is going on in your American colonies."

"Indeed," said Owen's uncle with a frown. "And what makes you say this, sir?"

"Well, for one thing, his First Officer is from Norfolk, Virginia, and for another they both hinted changes are coming. I am not normally blunt, you understand, but they both certainly were. Theirs was a thinly veiled message to the effect they will remember who their friends are when the time comes. Whenever this may be. And I tell you this also because we all know you serve in the same capacity as the two of them for your own side."

"Well, this is the first I have heard of the Americans engaging in this sort of business. Thank you for the information, Governor."

The Governor shrugged. "I have no loyalty to them, any more than to you. I do like the civilized behaviour you at least display, and I mistrust their motives more than yours. It concerns me because when France decides to be more aggressive about anything it usually ends up involving us whether we like it or not. French aggression on the other side of the Atlantic is one thing, but I start to take notice when the same behaviour begins appearing in my part of the world."

"As would I if I were in your shoes, sir. And the Dutch ship? He is one of your usual visitors, is he?"

The Governor nodded. "Yes, this fellow does a routine and regular trade between Aruba and the other Dutch islands and along our coastline. I expect you will find Captain De Ruyter dining at The San Geronimo Inn if you want to talk to him. I was there with him last night, but he loves the food so much I'd be shocked if he was anywhere else tonight. "

As he finished speaking the Governor downed the remainder of his wine. Owen and his uncle took it as a signal to do the same, rising from their seat as they did.

"Thank you once again, Governor. I may take you up on your suggestion to find Captain De Ruyter," said Owen's uncle. "By the way, we will be following our usual trade route stops along the coast north as far as Limon."

The Governor waved a languid hand to signal he agreed and yawned.

"I will have my clerk send you the usual note with my approval for your trading voyage."

Once they were outside Owen looked around to ensure they would be unheard before he spoke.

"I must say, this was most interesting, Uncle Alan. So, what is there I need to know about all of this?"

"Governor Sanchez has been around a long time and in many ways is his own man. For whatever reason he has always been helpful. Because we pay him a little more than would perhaps be normal likely helps. As for this Frenchman Paul Allarde, you must be extremely wary of him if you encounter him in future. I've had word he is—dangerous. If it was in his interests to knife you in the back he would not hesitate. And given he is now sailing with an American who is apparently in the same line of business makes him doubly interesting."

"And it seems we are indeed more than just businessmen, aren't we? Who are we really working for, Uncle?"

Owen's uncle looked aside at him as they continued walking back to the harbour.

"Well, I did mention I prepare reports for the government, right? I'm sure it is obvious by now we are spies, nephew. We gather information. I will explain all back in Barbados. There is someone you really must meet. But for now, the dinner hour is upon us. Let's go see if we can find this man De Ruyter. "

***

Owen and his uncle found the Dutch Captain exactly where the Governor predicted and as he was alone, they all sat together to enjoy a meal. Owen's uncle had not met him before, but the two Captains soon realized they had acquaintances in common. The conversation predictably shifted to business and politics as they dug into their meals.

"You realize, sir, there is a war coming, do you not?" said Captain De Ruyter.

"Perhaps. I would hope not, but I believe I understand why you think so. Or perhaps I don't. Do you know something I am unaware of?"

The Dutchman shrugged. "Oh, I do not hope for war, sir. And no, I expect I know no more than you. But I am a realist when it comes to business and to survive, I must read the signs correctly. Because my country is a small fish surrounded by much larger fish, there is no room for error. My colleagues and I are all paying close attention, sir. War is bad, but it also means profit. We will be ready to seize the opportunity."

"It's looking so very grim, is it?" said Owen's uncle, in between bites of his savoury spiced and grilled fish. "What signs are pointing this way?"

"What the French are doing, of course. This Frenchman is not the only one of his kind plying the seas, but there are more of them than ever now. They are all becoming much more—aggressive would be the best word to describe it. I had a drink with this fellow in port the other night. He is the worst of the lot so far. He was rather pointed with me about who we should be friends with. And then there are these patriots in America. Unless you people do something about them soon, you will be at war before you know it."

"And who are you friends with, sir?"

Captain De Ruyter smiled and raised his glass of wine in toast.

"We are friends with everyone these days, Captain Giles. Especially anyone who can make us money. As I said, we are a small fish, but money buys lots of things. Sometimes this includes friendship."

As they finished their meal all three men rose and shook hands before paying the bill and making their way back to their respective ships. On reaching the waterfront Owen saw the French ship had already freed the lines tethering her to the shore and was getting underway to depart. Stepping aboard their own ship they found John Tate standing at the railing watching the Frenchman leave with a dark scowl on his face. Owen had never seen him look so angry.

Two members of the crew were standing nearby doing the same as the First Mate. With a start Owen realized both men had clearly been in a fight. One was sporting a black eye while the other had bled profusely down the front of his shirt and was holding his nose. Owen and his uncle looked at each other in shock.

"John? What is it? What the hell happened?" said Owen's uncle.

The First Mate remained scowling for a long

moment before finally turning away.

"Sir, you see the ugly bugger standing beside the wheel of their ship? The one who is even now staring at the three of us. He is William Bains. It was his father who drove my family out of Virginia. And yes, this bastard is as evil as the rest of his family. I swear to God if he and I ever end up alone in a dark alley together only one of us is going to walk out alive."

"Good Lord, I had no idea of the connection, John. I was already very concerned he was in company with this particular Frenchman and now I am doubly so."

"And well you should be, sir. The Bains family is well known in Norfolk for being among the most radical of the lot agitating for change, which says plenty, because Norfolk is filled with those bastards. They have extensive ties beyond Virginia too. I wouldn't be surprised if they are stirring people up behind the scenes at every chance they get."

"I see. But what happened to these two men?"

"Captain," said the sailor with the black eye. "Mr. Tate here gave us shore leave, so we went for a drink. What we didn't know is there were three of those frog bastards in the same tavern we went to. They apparently were given one last bit of leave too before they left. When they realized who we were they started insulting us. We gave them less than we got because there were three of them against the two of us."

"And I didn't know what was happening until they finally returned to the ship, Captain," said John

Tate. "I saw some men return to the French ship in a hurry and they made ready to depart almost as soon as they were aboard. It wasn't until then I realized William Bains was part of the crew."

The men all stood in silence as they watched the ship gather speed to tack out of the harbour. Uncle Alan finally turned back to speak. His face appeared cast in stone.

"Well, gentlemen. You will all need to have an eye out for this ship and be wary if you encounter it again. Who knows, opportunity for a little pay back may come your way. But before you engage in any of that, remember I want to know what they are up to. I think this ship is aptly named."

Owen nodded his agreement, for the French ship was named Le Mystere.

***

"This is impossible!" said the Spanish merchant with a scowl on his face as he waved his arms in obvious disgust. "I cannot believe you English charge these outrageous amounts. I offer you something reasonable and you drop your price by almost nothing. How do you expect to do business with us? Everyone along this coast is poor. I must make some kind of profit."

Owen tried to put what he hoped was an understanding, but apologetic look on his face as he gave a small shrug in return.

"We must make a profit too, sir. If your government weren't charging us such ridiculous duties it would be better. You can't expect us to pay them, can you? They are a cost of doing business."

After yet more arm waving and threats to walk

away, they finally finished the negotiation ten minutes later, and Owen made his way back to the ship with his uncle beside him. The trip had worked out well, for they had finally sold the remainder of their wares. They had stopped at several small communities along the coast, culminating in their last stop of Limon. Owen had conducted the negotiations with the locals each time.

"Well, congratulations, nephew. You are learning fast. I think you actually pulled off a better deal than I could have with this last one. It will make up for some of your earlier mistakes. And by the way, don't pay much attention to his protests. He will make profits from trading with us too, although perhaps not as much as he thought he would."

Owen laughed. "I'm glad, uncle. And my Spanish is getting a little better every day. There is still much to learn, though."

"Lots of time to keep learning in future, but now it is time to sail for home. I confess I am looking forward to turning this ship over to you. I miss being away from Barbados. It is time for a new chapter in my life."

"I am so very grateful for this opportunity, uncle. And I'll be even more grateful to get away from this coastline. I hadn't thought it possible for the mosquitoes to be as bad as this. I really don't know how the locals survive."

"They use mosquito nets just like us, nephew. But I confess I've wondered about these people myself. This coast with its endless jungle has a beauty all its own, but I'll take Barbados any day. And Barbados has far less mosquitos. Let's go home."

***

The shade of a stand of palm trees further up from the beach served as a perfect location for their lunch, with enough of a light breeze to make the warmth of a late February day in Barbados bearable. The home Owen's uncle owned was perched on a slight rise well back from the beach, with a wonderful view of the shoreline and ocean beyond. A table was brought out and set for the four of them to eat a lunch of cold chicken, fresh salad, and a dessert dish which looked temptingly sweet. Once again, Elizabeth, Mary, and Uncle Alan were present.

"The trip was a success, Mary," said Owen's uncle as he finally joined them at the table. "You will be pleased to know Owen here will be taking command of the ship from this point on. I will dedicate my time to organizing matters here in Barbados henceforth and you will be stuck with having me around far more now."

Mary reached out and grasped her husband's hand in hers as she smiled.

"It's a problem I am happy to grow accustomed to, Alan. Leave me my own time to spend tending my garden and we will do just fine."

As Owen's uncle laughed Elizabeth spoke up. "And this means Owen will be back to visit us regularly, doesn't it?"

Her uncle eyed Elizabeth with a tiny smile at the corner of his mouth before he responded.

"You sound rather happy to hear it, my love. Are you already making plans for him?"

Elizabeth blushed and glanced quickly at Owen before giving her uncle a mixed look with equal parts of obvious exasperation and embarrassment.

"And what if I am?" she replied, a defensive tone to her voice. "I expect Owen might like to see more of Barbados with me. There is plenty to see and do. He isn't going to be working all the time, is he?"

Owen saved his uncle from having to reply. "Elizabeth, I will be happy to join you some day for a little tour of the island, if Uncle Alan approves. It really is beautiful, isn't it? Perhaps we can all do what the French call a picnic or something similar?"

"Hmm, well I rather suspect Elizabeth was hoping to have you all to herself," said Owen's uncle with a grin. "But we shall see. He is going to be busy at least for now, for there is always yet another task for a ship Captain. But Owen, the fellow I told you about has returned to Barbados and I have arranged for us to meet him in a few days. Once we introduce you and have a conversation, we will sort out where you are off to next."

"I look forward to it, Uncle Alan."

As the conversation turned to other topics Owen's mind drifted and he stared out to the far horizon. He had no idea where he would be sailing next or exactly when it would be, but he knew it would be soon and he was content.

Chapter Six
Barbados
March 1773

Uncle Alan appeared on the wharf at the appointed time and walked up the boarding plank to the deck of *The Sea Trader*. Owen was ready to go to the meeting, but his uncle surprised him by inviting John Tate to join them without providing an explanation. John seemed as surprised as Owen, but at Uncle Alan's suggestion went to change out of his stained and weathered everyday slops he wore about the ship to something more presentable. They made their way off the ship when he was ready and walked toward the main business district of Bridgetown on Broad Street. Uncle Alan gave John a sidelong grin as they went.

"I normally wouldn't have suggested you change clothes, John, but I believe the fellow we are going to meet today has the notion we are going to have lunch together. If I know him, it will be at The Boatyard Inn. They have been known to refuse entry if you are dressed like you have spent the day mucking about in the hold of a ship."

A few minutes later Uncle Alan stopped in front of a nondescript looking two storey building filled with lawyers, accountants, and insurance firms as tenants. He led them upstairs and entered one with a sign on the door announcing the law firm of Smith, Wesley, and Fowler was inside. A bespeckled clerk looked up and gave Uncle Alan a brief nod of recognition before going back to his work.

Four other inner doors led to offices which

presumably belonged to the various lawyers. Owen followed his uncle as they all made their way to one of the doors, which he stopped at and knocked on. The three men all entered on hearing acknowledgement from within and they crowded inside, for the inner office was tiny. The man who was working at a desk with a stack of paperwork on it rose to his feet on seeing his visitors.

"Alan, thank you for coming. You are saving me from this pile of correspondence I have to deal with. I can wish for far better things to do with my time, but the paperwork never goes away."

"Sir James, it is good to see you again," said Owen's uncle, waving a hand in Owen's direction. "I'd like to present my nephew, Owen Spence. This fellow beside him is the First Mate *of The Sea Trader,* John Tate, whom you have heard of from me before. Owen, John, this is Captain Sir James Standish. He is British Royal Navy."

"That is retired Royal Navy, gentlemen. Alan, I have made arrangements for all of us to dine at our usual haunt. While this office is a better place to discuss confidential matters, it is far too small for the four of us. As you can see, I don't even have enough chairs. At some point I'm going to find better quarters of my own for myself and get a clerk to deal with my paperwork, but for now it serves my purpose. Give me a moment to lock things up and we shall be off."

Owen looked around the room and saw he was right, for even if he had enough chairs for the four of them there would barely be enough space to seat them comfortably. As the Captain took a few moments to put everything away Owen studied him with interest. Owen judged him to be in his early forties in age given his greying hair around the temples and his weathered, tanned face which spoke of many past days at sea. Owen knew the women would find his handsome patrician looks and his well-dressed appearance attractive. The strange part was it all seemed incongruous given the Captain had made it clear he was retired. Most Royal Navy Captains of his age wouldn't even be entertaining thought of retirement for at least another twenty years or more.

The notion perhaps there were medical reasons for the retirement crossed his mind, but he dismissed the idea almost as soon as it came. The man before him was roughly the same height as Owen but quite lean, with no hint of fat apparent on him. He moved about with a subtle hint of power and strength which made Owen certain this man was extremely fit for his age.

Another factor making him attractive to women was the unmistakable aura of command about Sir James which Owen had immediately sensed. In his time in the Navy Owen had met others who exuded the subtle confidence people around them would assuredly follow their lead without question. Owen held no doubt this man had achieved a level of leadership skills which justified his confidence. But the more Owen considered it, the more it seemed so very strange an officer in the obvious prime of his life and career would be retired.

Sir James finished what he was doing and led the way out, locking his office door as they left. After walking a few blocks down Broad Street they found themselves in The Careenage area, a small inlet in the heart of Bridgetown lined with ships, wharves, and a host of small businesses catering to the needs of the ships. Shops with butchers, fishmongers, bakers, and even small blacksmiths all clustered together along the street doing a steady trade. The men had to weave their way through the narrow streets filled with a mix of black and white people all bustling about their business.

As Uncle Alan predicted they went straight to The Boatyard Inn, which proved to be a large nondescript looking building along the waterside. When it came in sight Sir James pointed it out and told them it had a large dining area perched on the second floor. Sir James was warmly greeted at the entrance by a server, who motioned for them to follow him. Owen had heard this place had an exclusive and expensive reputation, but never been here himself.

After climbing the stairs up to the second floor they went through the interior of the seating area for meal service to an open-air terrace beyond and Owen realized as they did the reputation was deserved. The high ceilings with crown mouldings, hardwood floors, expensive furniture, quality cotton tablecloths, and what he soon saw was real silverware on the tables all meant the bill for this meal would be far beyond what Owen would normally spend. Fortunately, he was certain it wouldn't be his problem.

The server took them to a table for four set off to the side of the covered terrace overlooking the host of ships moored in The Careenage. Both Sir James and Owen's uncle looked around to ensure no one was seated close enough to them to overhear anything they said. Sir James pointed to the closest table and the server nodded acknowledgement, with neither man saying a word. After ordering drinks for them all Sir James smiled as he spoke.

"The benefit of being a regular customer here is they know my preferences. They won't be seating anyone nearby unless they absolutely have to, so we can speak without fear of being overheard."

"How was your trip, Sir James?" said Owen's uncle. "You were away for quite some time. Boston, wasn't it?"

Sir James sighed. "I was gone too long, and my woman has been complaining about it ever since I got back. And yes, it was Boston. I had to make a side trip to Bermuda to make some connections with people there, too. I mislike what is going on out there, Alan. Bermuda is a key port for us, but I swear sometimes they think they are simply another one of the mainland colonies. God knows they feel they have much in common with them."

"It's getting that bad, Sir James?"

"Let's just say I don't like the direction matters seem to be taking. I did a little more digging in some places which are—hmm, rather less pleasant than this establishment in both ports. And this is why I am very much hoping these two fellows will be able to help. We need it."

"I am confident they can, Sir James."

The server appeared with their drinks and Sir James ordered some small appetizers for the table, assuring them they would enjoy everything on offer.

"So, Owen," said Sir James, turning to him as the server left. "You were once Royal Navy."

Sir James had stated this as fact and not as a question. Owen was waiting for this, knowing it likely Sir James would be aware of what had happened.

"I was, sir. I assume my uncle has told you the story. I assure you I was not guilty of what they charged me with."

Sir James nodded. "I do not doubt you, sir. It pains me to say this, but there are some people in the Navy who should understand the meaning of honour and fail miserably at doing so. Your former Captain is at the first person who comes to mind when I think about this. I have some prior experience with him, but fortunately I am more senior on the Captain's list than he is despite being a bit younger than him. I also have plenty of influential friends."

Sir James smiled to emphasize his last point, before pausing as he turned to Owen's uncle.

"Have you told these fellows anything about me and what I do?"

"Not much, Sir James. George has some understanding, but only what he needed to know in limited situations. Owen knows you work for the government."

"Very good. Gentlemen, it is true I am indeed retired from the Navy, but I am still employed by our government. And as of this moment, I expect you to maintain secrecy about anything I tell you from here on. Do you understand and agree?"

Owen and George looked briefly at each other before nodding agreement.

"Excellent. Gentlemen, I am employed by the Foreign Office. In public I pretend I have strictly diplomatic duties these days, but in reality, I am a spy. As much as I enjoyed my career in the Navy, I was convinced by friends in the Foreign Office I could better serve my country by doing this. My domain is the Caribbean and, to be blunt, there is not enough of me to cover it all. This is where you two come in. Alan here thinks you two could make an effective team, using your role as traders to cover for anything sub rosa you become involved with. Owen, as a former Navy officer you once had a role giving you a chance to serve your country. You would justifiably have cause to turn this opportunity down, because in a way your country has already rejected you. But I think you should disregard this. This is about service to the people and your country, which is far more important than the greedy, ignorant fools who look only to serve themselves. I am offering you another opportunity to serve, albeit in a different way. What do you say?"

To this point Owen had sat in silence, listening to Sir James's words, but inside his heart was slowly pounding harder and he felt as if it would soar enough to lift him skyward. He paused a moment to compose himself before responding.

"Captain, I wasn't given much choice about my path in life when I was younger, but I came to love being a sailor and serving my country in the Navy. It felt as if I had lost my reason to exist when I was dismissed from the service. And now thanks to you and my uncle I have a second chance. I don't know how to thank both of you. Command me, sir. I will do whatever you ask."

"Very good," said Sir James, smiling as he turned to John Tate. "And you, Mr. Tate? You have already served Alan here on occasion with a few small tasks. Are you willing to take on more and work with Mr. Spence here?"

"I am, Sir James. Mr. Spence and I are coming to know each other better. I can work with him. I will also be honest with you. If doing this means I can help deal with the rebellious scum out there, I am all for it."

"Indeed. Dealing within reason, of course. Well, I think you have both made a decision you will be glad of in future. I confess I wasn't certain about it when I did the same, but I have come to rather enjoy what I do. There may not be much glamour in it, but the life itself is its own reward. Anyway, I'd like both of you to understand Alan and I are of one mind about what is going on in the Caribbean and America. We are trying to quietly make it all better by changing people's minds and there are many others out there who are just as appalled by the situation as we are. We view the people in America as family, even if some of them are rather wayward."

"Sir James is correct, gentlemen," said Owen's uncle. "Both of us would like to see a future where all of our colonies prosper and do it without the appalling use of slavery to achieve it."

"Yes, but it won't happen overnight. Well, if you are going to help us, I suspect you need a more in depth understanding of what is going on in the world. You also need to know what is expected of you. I believe Alan here has had you both more or less passively keeping your eyes and ears open until now, correct? His role has always been to simply gather information passively. I am proposing a rather active role, more in line with what I do on a regular basis. This means seeking out people who may have information we want without alerting them to why we want it. It means frequenting taverns occupied by unsavoury and perhaps dangerous people. It also means going to brothels and paying the whores for what they know. Men talk to them about things they shouldn't, of course."

Sir James paused a moment to eye John Tate.

"It may also mean spending time drinking with and being pleasant to someone you would rather throttle, Mr. Tate. But it won't all be unpleasant situations to endure. You will still need to talk to local British diplomats, who will be sent messages to let them know they can speak freely to you. Merchants from other nations will also be a source. In reality any information is good. You may pick up on something which seems unimportant to you, but may be vital for me to know. And if you find someone with critical information we need, you may be asked to do whatever it takes to get it from them. Of course, this is the kind of thing I already do, but as I said, there is not enough of me to go around."

Sir James sat back in his chair and took a long pull of his ale before looking from Owen to John.

"I am hoping it is also now clear you may find

yourselves in difficult situations where you may have to resort to using weapons to get yourself out of trouble. And no, I am not joking. Positions are hardening everywhere and when this happens, it doesn't take much for a situation to escalate to where weapons are involved. Are you both all right with this?"

"No problem," said John Tate. "And don't concern yourself about my ability to do this. I may not like it, but if I have to be nice to some arsehole to get the job done, I will."

Owen smiled at his First Mate's response and nodded his agreement too.

"Excellent, we can brief you on some relevant background while we eat," said Sir James, as the server came over to the table to deliver several skewers of grilled, savoury fish and meat. Before the man could leave Sir James stopped him so they could order their main dishes. After the four of them had ordered and the server departed Sir James took another sip of his drink, looking at Owen's uncle while everyone began working on the appetizers.

"I confess I was rather taken aback when I read your report about this Frenchman out of Martinique appearing in Porto Bello, Alan. I am particularly concerned he seems to be in league with an American. I have only heard rumours of him before, but I have sent some questions out to a few friends to see what they know. I have my suspicions about what is going on and if I am right, it is not a good sign. And yes, John, I am aware you have some past history with him. What I am interested in is what he is doing now."

"Sir James?" said Owen. "What is your specific concern about these men?"

"This bloody Frenchman Paul Allarde is a spy, Owen. He is effectively my counterpart here in the Caribbean. I believe he reports directly to the Governor of Martinique. Naturally, anything he does is therefore of interest and if he is casting his net wider for information and trying to perhaps coerce the local Spanish authorities on behalf of his masters, then we need to know this. To my knowledge this is the first time he has had an American sailing with him, and it would be nonsense to think it coincidence. I am concerned the rebellious factions in America are doing more than talking now."

"These bloody Committees of Correspondence again, Sir James?" said Owen's uncle.

"Yes. It has gone beyond mere idea to reality. Of course, Owen and George know nothing of this. Gentlemen, you know the various American colonies are separate entities. It was almost a year ago we got word talks between the various colonies about their shared concerns and interests started. The name stems from the suggestion to form committees to correspond with each other and discuss what to do about the situation. More recently in November of last year we learned they went beyond talk and actually formed some."

"Why is it a problem if they are just talking, Sir James?" asked Owen.

"Hmm, if it all was just talk I expect we could live with it, except one of the committees seems to have a rather shadowy mandate. Gentlemen, we have learned this specific committee is tasked with actively soliciting and handling all manner of secret intelligence. And I fear this fellow Bains is either a representative on the committee or is employed directly by it."

"I see your concern, Sir James. If this is the case, they are doing far more than talking. I guess the question is exactly how active do they plan to be."

"Precisely, Owen. And sadly, most everyone I know in the Foreign Office thinks they are rapidly giving up on being passive. It didn't have to be this way, but it is. We have been stumbling our way toward this point for a long time now."

"Forgive me, sir, but I find myself woefully behind on world events driving this," said Owen. "What is at the back of all this?"

Sir James shrugged. "Struggle between nations has been a fact of life for centuries and we should not be surprised we are enjoying our share in our lifetimes, but if you want something recent to consider then look to the French and Indian War of the last decade for starters. We incurred enormous debt to defeat the French in America. The government brought in the Stamp Tax and other tariffs to pay for it all. It all seemed reasonable enough on the surface to increase taxes because of all the money spent to ensure the security of the colonies, I suppose. The problem is it isn't universally applicable to all of our colonies around the world. Not surprisingly, the first signs of trouble over it happened in Boston."

"I did hear about this. It was a couple of years ago, was it not? They call it the Boston Massacre."

"Yes, it was 1770. It started with a minor incident involving a soldier and escalated into protestors being shot. The patriot agitators have used it ever since to stir up passions and justify increasing push back. It got even worse last year when they burnt a customs schooner off the coast of Rhode Island. No one should have been surprised smuggling activity increased massively as a result of all the taxes."

"Are they really so bad, sir?"

"Oh yes," said Owen's uncle. "Let me give you an example. The women all need pins and needles to do their sewing, right? The price of a simple pin or needle in America went up well over 100% last year because of the taxes. Of course, they weren't terribly expensive to begin with, but when times are hard every bit counts. And these are essential items as far as the wives and daughters are concerned. And believe it or not, our government in their wisdom has prohibited local production of pins and needles. They all have to come from England. The women now refer to the need to save 'pin money' to buy more. The result is it has become yet another rallying point of contention. Obviously, we have not endeared ourselves to them."

"When it really went from merely bad to terrible was last year, though," said Sir James. "All the speculation in East India Company stock created a bubble which burst, and our banks have suffered enormously as a result, especially those in Scotland. It all spread around the world, of course. Obtaining credit is now extremely difficult in America. This adds fuel to the flames, because The East India

Company is on shaky financial ground as a result. As your uncle here can attest, this is almost unbelievable. It is the Company who collects all revenues from India, not the government. The system of corruption, kickbacks, and bribes in place there is almost beyond belief. And the wealth they continue to gain from it is staggering is scale."

"Good God, I had no idea. Why does the government allow this?"

"Because there are far too many greedy fools out there interested in only their own welfare, nephew," said Owen's uncle. "What is going on in India is going to lead to major trouble there, too. In any case, I trust you now understand the problem here. The American colonies look at this situation and demand the costs of the French War be shared by all fairly. It seems rather outrageous the only people benefiting from the enormous wealth being generated by India are The East India Company shareholders. Bear in mind by defeating the French here we were able to reduce the French threat to the Company operations."

"I hope you both have a better understanding now," said Uncle Alan. "Sir James is not exaggerating any of this. I do what I can for him, but the need is only growing. The men sailing on the other two ships I own are aware I always want to know details of what they saw and heard, but they do not know why. Sir James and I deem them capable as far as doing their job goes, but beyond this we are not clear they would serve the kind of purpose we would like you to have."

"Indeed. I fear we are headed for troubled

waters, gentlemen. Alan and I will do what we can to turn the tide and influence a more positive outcome, but we can only do so much. And if it comes to war, we want to do what we can to make it as short as possible."

"Sir James?" said John. "You mentioned dealing with diplomats a while back. I know a lot more about being a sailor than dealing with proper gentlemen. Are you expecting me to be involved with them? I confess I will probably need a lot of help if so."

"Actually, I think what Alan here and I have in mind is a partnership between you two, where you support each other with different roles. Owen was an officer, and he would have at least some experiences dealing with them. You have experience dealing with some of the rougher sorts of people you will encounter. But give yourself some credit, Mr. Tate. You work with your Captain all the time and he is certainly a gentleman. I think there is a middle ground where the two of you will be able to support each other perfectly. Owen here is also used to dealing with ordinary seamen. I'd say you are both more capable than you think."

Uncle Alan peered at both Owen and John in silence, obviously assessing them both, before finally speaking.

"Well? Do either of you have any more questions?"

"Only one, sir," said Owen. "What are the next steps?"

"Your uncle and I will collaborate on trading routes for you. We will attempt to dovetail his trading activities with my needs. He needs to make a profit, of course, but if I need more information from somewhere a way will be found to have you appear there. And if you can't be where I need you, I will go there myself. At the moment, I think you will be making regular visits to both Boston and maybe to Bermuda. I have serious concerns about what is going on in both of those places, and Boston in particular."

"Sir James? Suppose I learn something of importance, but need to carry on with what I am doing. Can I write you?"

"Thank you for reminding me. I most certainly want you to write to me immediately if time is critical. Before you leave on your first journey, I will provide you with a cipher to use. We must be very careful with what we say in any correspondence, for we don't want others reading it, even if they are friends."

"Sir?"

"Gentlemen, any mail coming through our postal services which appears of interest to the crown is set aside and opened very carefully. This is a little secret not many people know, so please keep it to yourselves. Of course, we obviously would not want our enemies reading our letters, either."

"I see. Very good, sir. I have no more questions."

Sir James looked at John, who simply shook his head.

"Excellent. There is one last thing. You will be provided with some extra funds to be used with discretion. Gold has a way of loosening tongues. We always have to be careful with the information it buys us, because there are more liars born every minute, but it serves its purpose. Naturally, I am accountable to others, you too will have to account for your expenditures in turn."

"Sir James, please be assured we will be extremely diligent with it. John and I have discovered we have a mutual dislike of liars. We will be on guard."

Chapter Seven
The Caribbean and America
April 1773 to July 1773

The jarring, metallic sound of cutlass blades smashing into each other filled the air around a few small knots of bare chested, struggling men on the deck of *The Sea Trader*. Despite the light breeze carrying them north from Barbados, Owen's body was covered in a sheen of sweat as he parried the blade of a black sailor named Wilson Jones yet again. He was almost at a point where he feared he could no longer swing the blade when John called time for the men, as the sand in the glass timing an hour of exercise had finally run out. Owen stepped back and raised his cutlass to the vertical to signal he was done, as did his opponent.

Jones was one of two black sailors serving on the ship. Owen found he needed more time to get to know the normally taciturn man, who made a point of doing his job while keeping well to himself and avoiding interaction with others. Although he did his job well and without complaint, the deliberate distance the man kept gave some a first impression he was almost simple minded. Owen slowly came to understand this was far from the truth and to learn more he asked John about the sailor's history. As someone cut from practically the same mould, John's response was short and to the point.

"Jones? He knows what he is doing, and he is far from stupid. He was a slave your uncle freed."

Owen simply grunted his thanks, knowing it was all he was going to get out of John, so he decided to watch and learn more. The choice to do so was more than simple curiosity, for with the growing likelihood of conflict on the horizon Owen knew he and his men could be fighting for their lives together. Knowing your men and who you could count on in a tough spot was essential.

After having thought long and hard about their new role and what might lie in their future, Owen had approached his uncle with a request to significantly increase their stockpile of weapons on *The Sea Trader*. His uncle saw the sense in the request and readily agreed. They soon procured a range of privately made boarding axes, pikes, cutlasses, and sea pistols, all of which were similar in design to those used by the Royal Navy.

Fitting out *The Sea Trader* with more than the few swivel guns she already carried would be a longer process, but his uncle promised to give thought to what the ship should carry for defence and where to procure them from to fit her out on her return. As soon as they left port on their way north Owen instituted a regular program of practice with the weapons, patterned on his experiences in the Navy. He knew a couple of the men were questioning the need privately, but after a few sessions he also knew every one of the men were looking forward to them as welcome deviations from the daily routine. Those who had never used such weapons before were first started with makeshift wooden facsimiles.

Wilson Jones disdained any notion of using anything other than the real thing and he learned fast. A naval cutlass in his hand almost seemed a child's toy, for Jones was huge. Wielding the heavy blade seemed to require little effort on his part. Owen judged the sailor to be four or five inches shorter than him, but the man was almost half again his width with broad, heavily muscled shoulders and thick legs carrying his frame. Owen was certain he would simply bounce off the man even if he ran into him at full speed to knock him over. And at the end of the session with him Owen had a large bead of sweat about to drip off the end of his nose, while Jones was only now beginning to breathe heavier.

The men all walked over to a small tub filled with clean water which had a stack of rags beside it to sponge themselves clean of the sweat. As Owen stood beside Wilson he peered aside at the sailor trying to gauge how old he was. A few tell-tale, fine lines around his eyes and the barest hint of grey in what was left of the man's short hair told him Wilson was likely no younger than thirty years old and it wouldn't be long before the man would be completely bald. The sailor sensed Owen's gaze and looked back at him, a question in his eyes.

"You are very fit, Wilson. I am impressed."

The sailor grinned, displaying a row of brilliant white teeth before he responded.

"Thank you, sir."

"And you have done well with the cutlass. I don't think I've seen anyone learn the standard cutlass drill so fast. And you were using the pikes and boarding axes like you were born with them in your hand. Have you ever used a swivel gun or served a cannon?"

The man's face crinkled in surprise for a brief

second.

"No, sir. My previous master would never have wanted me to learn anything like that."

"Hmm, well, I'm certainly not your master, but I am the Captain and I very much want you and the rest of the men to learn. I think you are more than capable and we all may need to defend ourselves one day."

Wilson was silent for only a moment. "I am interested in learning, sir."

"What's your story, Wilson? I would like to know."

This time the silence was longer, as the sailor took his time pulling his shirt back on to think about his response.

"I was born a slave, sir. I worked on a plantation in Barbados. My master chose me to work on his trading ship and this is how I learned to sail. When he sold his plantation and returned to England, he sold me and the ship to Mr. Giles. I confess I was amazed when Mr. Giles freed me and gave me work. And here I am."

"Indeed. We must have a drink some day and talk more. Please go relieve Mr. Tate at the helm when you are ready."

As Owen walked away and headed for his cabin, preoccupied with thoughts of their next destination, he missed the brief look of surprise flashing across Wilson's face. The look changed to one of a man in deep thought, before he turned away to follow his orders.

The Sea Trader had made slow progress north from Barbados through the month of April and now into May, stopping in every British port in the Leeward Islands along the way. Owen had arranged to meet the local Governor in each port to pass on letters from Sir James Standish and to establish his secret credentials with each of them. To a man they were universally pessimistic about the future and all of them felt a growing sense of unease about the supply of provisions and food for their respective islands. While none were dire, disruptions in the availability of regular supplies were no longer unusual.

Owen knew he would gain a far better sense of what was happening in America once they made it to their next destination of Charleston, South Carolina. Uncle Alan had given him contacts to use for the sale of a good portion of his cargo of sugar, molasses, and rum. Owen had never been there before and was curious to see it.

The Sea Trader sailed into Charleston harbour with the dawn, making straight for an open spot along the large waterfront docks of the peninsula the town was situated on. Owen was busy from the moment they tied up, dealing with customs officials and making arrangements to briefly meet the local Governor. The rest of his days were a blur as the contacts his uncle had provided were only too happy to barter for the goods he had brought, but the bargaining was hard. When Owen protested, they all complained of growing disruptions and unrest affecting the supplies they could offer in return.

After finalizing the last of his sales Owen found Wilson back at the ship on his return, waiting with the rest of the men for word they could offload the remaining cargo Owen had arranged to sell. Owen was unhappy what he got in return was a much smaller portion of salt fish and lumber than he expected, but it was the best he could do. John was delegated to trawl the local taverns for information from the moment they arrived, but had yet to return.

Owen hoped to be away with the dawn tide, for even though it was only late May the humidity in the town was severe. As Owen finished explaining what he needed done with this last load both Owen and Wilson had a sheen of sweat all over them, despite the fact neither were exerting themselves. A series of sudden passing rain showers throughout the afternoon did nothing to alleviate the situation.

"My God, this heat is brutal," said Owen, wiping the sweat off his brow yet again.

"It certainly is, sir. At least we will have this done before the day is over," said Wilson, pausing to down a ladle of fresh water from a nearby tub. He stopped a moment before leaving to join the other men, staring past Owen to a nearby spot on the waterfront.

"Mr. Spence? Are we leaving soon, I hope?"

Owen knew where he was looking and why he wanted to leave sooner than later. *The Sea Trader* had tied up at a dock right beside the landing area used by the slave traders. The consequence was a distinct stench from the seemingly endless tide of slaves being transported each day to the main slave market in town, which was being carried their direction by the wind.

Although new arrivals were briefly quarantined

on nearby Sullivan's Island and at least some effort was made to make them presentable for sale, the smell was still overpowering. With hundreds of them being led in chains to the market the smell would not disappear anytime soon. Overseers with short whips struck any of them they deemed to be lagging in the long lines being led away.

Owen did a rough calculation based on what he was seeing and estimated it would be close to two thousand slaves being sold before the day was done. Owen shook his head in dismay as he looked at the scene once again, before turning to find Wilson watching him in silence. The two men shared a look with each other without speaking, as John appeared and came on deck. Wilson went to attend to the cargo as Owen greeted John.

"Captain? I've been in three different taverns and the talk is all the same. There are rumours this Tea Act is going to be passed in Parliament and everybody is unhappy about it. Actually, unhappy doesn't describe it well. Livid with anger would be a better description, which explains why there are more soldiers patrolling this place than I remember."

"Yes, I heard the same from the various merchants I talked to and I agree."

Owen sighed inwardly, for this was news everything Sir James and Uncle Alan feared was coming to pass. The Tea Act would confer a monopoly on the importation and sale of tea to The East India Company. The problem was Dutch traders could smuggle tea to America and charge far less than the Company, making the Americans feel they were being gouged to help prop up what they saw as greedy owners of a private company.

"The only other point of interest is there are at least three French ships in the harbour," said John, intruding on Owen's thoughts. "I think they are all from Martinique and Guadeloupe and they are selling the same products we are. At least, on the surface they are. I recognize none of them."

Owen sighed. "It would explain why the price I am getting for our goods is less than I wanted."

"Sir?" said John. "Do we have to stay here tonight? We've been here a week."

"Hmm. Tide isn't with us, John."

John grunted acknowledgement and looked around them. The tidy streets and buildings of Charleston perched on the tip of the peninsula made a pleasant, picturesque scene, but the image of a barge from Sullivan's Island filled with yet more slaves heading to their destiny being tied up at the dock made John the one to shake his head this time.

"Sorry, Captain. I asked a question I already knew the answer to. Wishful thinking."

***

The weather in Boston in the middle of June was much easier to bear. With a steady, but gentle offshore breeze the late spring heat was pleasantly moderate. In contrast the inner temperature of the residents of Boston was a raging inferno. Owen sensed it from the moment they tied up at the waterfront docks, as they received several dark stares from passing workers and tradesmen along with a few choice curses sent their direction. The glares eased a little when the dock workers realized

The Sea Trader was sailing out of Barbados and not delivering tea, but the flag at her masthead was like a magnet for the anger simmering below the surface.

Owen's days became a blur of activity much like their stop in Charleston, as he made contacts to sell most of the remaining bulk of his wares. Once again, hard bargaining was needed, and he was meeting with even less success than he had in Charleston. Despite the fact he had nothing to do with The East India Company, by sailing under a British flag he was already guilty by association.

The Foreign Office diplomat Sir James asked him to visit confirmed what Owen was experiencing was related to the Tea Act. Sir Ross Stanhope had a nondescript office near the waterfront in Boston, which bore an eerie similarity to the one Sir James had in Bridgetown. The parallel ended there, however, for Sir Ross was at least twenty years older than Sir James. The diplomat looked up with interest from the letter of introduction Owen provided, studied Owen for a moment, and reached for a decanter on a nearby side table.

"Brandy? It's rather good. The black market here is so robust we even get the best product every now and then."

Owen gave a rueful smile and gratefully accepted a glass, acknowledging after his first sip the man was right.

"This is indeed very good, Sir Ross. The smuggling is that bad, is it?"

"Oh yes, it is becoming an art form here and, yes, I expect your reception was less than pleasant.

No one sailing into this port with a British flag is getting a friendly reception and especially not ships filled with East India Company tea. My friend Sir James and I told our masters not to pass this legislation, but they aren't listening. Mark my words, there will be consequences. So, what did Sir James tell you about me?"

"Hmm, very little, Sir Ross. I gather you serve in a similar role as he does?"

"I do, but I don't rove about much anymore, unlike Sir James. I prefer to stay put and keep my ear to the ground. And there is plenty to listen to here. I have a small network of—friends, some of whom aren't really friends unless I pay them well. We do what we must. I expect word of the Tea Act will have reached Sir James by the time you return, but he will want to know my thoughts. I will provide you with a letter to take to him before you leave. Did he tell you I recruited him to work with us? I expect not. I saw his potential for this kind of work right away, so I find you interesting, since he has recruited you in turn. Well, welcome to the fight, Mr. Spence."

"Thank you, sir. I shall do my best. I am extremely concerned about the number of French ships I am seeing here in Boston. We saw a similar picture in Charleston. I believe Sir James would have told you by now about our encounter with Paul Allarde in Porto Bello? I intend to pay close attention to these French merchants before I leave for Bermuda."

"Very good. Yes, this man Allarde bears close attention every second you have him in sight. But you are off to Bermuda also?"

"Yes, Sir James has some concerns about the people in charge there. He wants me to have an eye on one fellow in particular."

"Yes, the esteemed Colonel Tucker. Actually, you need to pay attention to his whole family, for as near as I can tell most of them are hardcore sympathizers with this crowd of patriots, as they call themselves here in Boston. Whether it will all lead to more than talk, who knows? But I wouldn't be surprised if it does. Do write me if you learn anything of consequence. Come to think of it, I shall write a brief note to the Governor there too."

"Sir, I shall stop in before I leave tomorrow morning. It is a pleasure to meet you," said Owen, finishing his drink and rising to leave.

Owen was a block away from where *The Sea Trader* was tied up when he heard a distant commotion underway on the dock in front of his ship. Frowning, he picked up his pace as he tried to make out what was happening. He was dismayed to realize one of the groups were men from his own ship.

A crowd had gathered, forming a ring around two small knots of men shouting and pushing at each other. One of the combatants from the group facing off against Owen's men stepped forward and took a wild swing at his opponent, only to be blocked and pushed hard enough to fall to the ground. Owen shoved his way through the crowd, earning him a few curses and one wildly thrown punch he brushed off as he strode into the ring.

"What in God's name is going on here?" he

shouted, which made the struggling men pause.

He quickly saw four of his men were milling about, facing off against three sailors Owen had never seen before. One of his men spoke up on recognizing Owen's voice, without taking his eyes off his opponents.

"Captain, these are the bastard frogs who attacked us in Porto Bello."

Owen was left with no time to respond as Paul Allarde appeared on the far side of the crowd, having forced his way past the bystanders like Owen. He didn't get a chance to speak either as a file of British soldiers punched their own way through the crowd, smashing the butts of the weapons into spectators who didn't move fast enough. The officer in charge stepped into the middle of the ring and scowled.

"Right, I don't know what is bloody going on here, but you will all disperse, right now, or face the consequences. You've been told, so get on with it!"

The soldiers behind him fanned out and began shoving at stragglers to get them moving. Owen barked at his men to follow him and return to the ship. Making his way out of the range of the soldiers he stopped and turned to look back to watch what was happening. He was unsurprised to find Paul Allarde on the opposite side of the crowd doing exactly the same as he was. The two men locked eyes for a long moment before the Frenchman disappeared into the swirling throng. Owen was surprised at the look of frozen, naked hatred showing on the man's face.

His men were all back on *The Sea Trader* by the

time Owen arrived, where he learned what had happened. Owen hadn't realized the French ship Le Mystere had arrived the night before and was now docked further down the waterfront. The men involved in the fight in Porto Bello had unexpectedly run into their opponents and the fight renewed itself on the spot. Owen resolved to send word to Sir Ross Stanhope right away, for he knew it imperative he be aware of a rival in his domain. As he dismissed the men he turned to John.

"Damn it, I wish we had known these bastards were here. We could have gained a sense of what they are up to before we leave. Well, I will get a message to Sir Ross about this so he is informed. The plan is to head for Bermuda tomorrow and I think we will stick with it."

"Sir?" said Wilson, standing nearby. "Sorry to interrupt, but would it help to know the French ship just came from Bermuda?"

Both Owen and John turned in open mouthed surprise, but John found his voice first.

"Good God, how do you know?"

Wilson shrugged. "I asked the dock workers. I was dropping off the last shipment of rum, so I missed all the fun here. But I noticed Le Mystere and remembered her from Porto Bello, so I asked some questions. She is here trading more or less the same kind of goods we are, but they also confirmed she came in from Bermuda."

"Damn me, that is well done, Wilson. Please keep it up," said Owen, rubbing his chin. "But I wonder what these bastards were doing there? All the more reason to sail tomorrow so we can find out."

***

The town of St. George's on the island of the same name on the north-eastern tip of Bermuda proved to be a small, but bustling hive of activity despite the heat of a mid-July afternoon moderated only a little by an offshore breeze from the windward side of the island. When *The Sea Trader* arrived they discovered a host of different ships jockeying for space along the broad waterfront docks. *The Sea Trader* found a spot nonetheless and once again Owen was wrapped in a blur of activity as he worked to sell his wares to merchants who soon appeared to learn what he had on offer. Owen was surprised to find their primary interest was to purchase food and provisions. Although the rum, molasses, and sugar he had to offer was welcome, these men were looking for far more.

During it all Owen made time to have word sent of his arrival to the George Bruere, the Governor of Bermuda, along with a request for a meeting to introduce himself. By the end of the day a response arrived with an invitation to meet the Governor in his office in two days.

Owen was grateful for the delay, for it gave him time to organize the crew to offload their cargo and finalize arrangements for the sale of his remaining wares. He knew his uncle would be pleased, for the prices he was able to command would help defray the higher costs of the provisions he had purchased to take back to Barbados. As soon as he had time, he carefully walked the entire waterfront docks of St. George's to see who was in port, but he found no sign of any French traders.

***

Two days later Owen made his way to the Governor's office and after a short wait he was ushered in. Governor Bruere studied the brief general letter of introduction Sir James provided with interest, before taking longer to read a separate letter Owen had brought from Sir James along with the short note from Sir Ross Stanhope. Owen sipped politely at the French brandy the Governor had offered him as he waited, wondering idly if the French were succeeding in smuggling more than just their brandy around the world. As the Governor finished reading, he passed the letter of introduction back to Owen and regarded him with interest.

"Well, Captain Spence. The situation is not materially different now than it was the last time Sir James was here in February. I assume you are returning to Barbados after your stop? Hurricane season is on our doorstep. I will provide a letter for you to carry back to Sir James before you leave. Otherwise, is there anything I can do for you today?"

"Only one thing, Governor. I have a report there was a French ship named Le Mystere in Bermuda last month. Do you have any idea what she was doing here?"

"Le Mystere," said the Governor, a frown creasing his face. "Yes, I think there was a French flagged ship here not too long ago and I'm not sure if this was her name, but I have no details of what she did. Is this a ship of interest?"

Owen told him what he knew, and the

Governor's frown deepened.

"Hmm, I shall have a watch kept for it in future and pay more attention if she reappears. Since I can't help you with what she did this last visit I suggest you ask some of our leading citizens. I am hosting a little ball for them as a diversion from our cares two nights from now. You are welcome to attend and enjoy the ball. Making some contacts with our local people may prove beneficial. You may find this interesting. I personally think Bermudans are an obstinate bunch."

"Indeed?" said Owen, raising an eyebrow. "Well, this is a fine idea, Governor, and I thank you for the invitation. I shall certainly attend."

***

The Sea Trader was ready to depart by the day of the ball, so Owen gave the crew the day off. Most headed for the nearest tavern or brothel, but Owen hired a small cart to give himself a little tour of the island. Owen thoroughly enjoyed the little trip, for the coast of St. George's was dotted with numerous picturesque beaches. Owen stopped for a drink at a tavern overlooking one which was an obvious favourite with the locals called Tobacco Bay Beach, situated on a large cove with a fine sandy beach and shallow water with many children at play in it.

The Governor's home was filled with a small crowd of well-dressed men and women by the time Owen arrived later in the day. As his arrival was announced the Governor beckoned Owen over with a wave to join the group of people clustered around him. After ensuring his new guest had a drink and introducing Owen all around, the Governor turned to a grey-haired man who was clearly the oldest member of the group.

"Colonel Tucker, this is the fellow I was telling you about. Owen, permit me to introduce the Tucker family. They are all one of Bermuda's leading families."

Owen was instantly on guard, knowing this was the family Sir James had expressed serious concern about. What followed was a bewildering series of introductions to the various Tuckers attending which required focus to keep them all straight in his mind, for many bore similar names. The senior of the family was Colonel Henry Tucker, who had four sons and two daughters. With him was St. George Tucker, visiting from his home in Virginia, the oldest son who was also named Henry Tucker, and a third Henry Tucker who was also both cousin to and husband of the Colonel's daughter. To differentiate the two younger men the cousin was known as Somerset Henry, as he lived in Somerset on the western end of Bermuda.

On learning Owen was based out of Barbados the Tuckers began quizzing him about the situation on the island and what the businessmen there thought of what was happening in America. Owen did his best to be non-committal and provide no more than general information, while offering truthfully his honest opinion he desired to see a middle ground approach succeed. The reactions he got were different from all four men.

"The bloody government isn't going to give any ground, sir," said Somerset Henry, with the heat in his voice unmistakable. "They are interested in lining their own pockets and no more."

"My God, Somerset, we have been through this before," said the younger Henry Tucker. "It is not unreasonable to expect America to pay for what we have spent in her defence."

"Somerset is right, Henry," said St. George Tucker. "Even if they aren't as greedy as we all think they are, they simply don't understand the situation here and they aren't listening."

As the conversation went on Owen sensed it getting more and more heated. The Governor obviously saw it too and intervened.

"Gentlemen, this is not a new debate and I suspect our guest here has no idea of the nuances of what is going on."

All of them turned as one to look at Owen, who smiled ruefully.

"I do have some understanding, gentlemen, for I have been hearing of frustration everywhere I go. But I'm perhaps not familiar with the local circumstances here."

"What you need to know is simple enough, sir," said Colonel Tucker, pausing to shake his head for a moment before continuing.

"Bermuda is a lovely island, but we do not grow enough to feed our people here. The only real local product we export is the salt from Turk's Island, which we sell to the Americans. Yes, we do have fishing and whaling boats, but we make our living as traders, which means we must sail far and wide to earn our keep. The problem is our market is America. And what the government is doing to them is affecting our ability to survive. Mark my words, if these disruptions continue, we shall not be able to feed our people."

"I see," said Owen. "It is very similar to the concerns I hear in Barbados."

"I struggle with this, as Governor Bruere knows," said Colonel Tucker. "I am loyal to the Crown, you understand, but I am also a Bermudan now. If no one is going to look out for our interests, we must do so ourselves."

"Absolutely," said Somerset Henry, the heat in his voice apparent. "The government needs to pay attention or they will rue the missed opportunity. The settlers in the colonies are becoming very used to being dependent on no one but themselves. It won't be long before this boils over. The Americans are looking for friends to help them wherever they can find them."

"Indeed," said Owen, deciding to seize the opportunity provided. "I heard a rumour in Boston you even had a French ship here recently. Are you now turning to them for help?"

As before the reactions on the faces of the four men of the Tucker family were all vastly different. Both St. George and Somerset Henry had a shifty, startled look cross their faces before supplanting it with a bland, unsmiling appearance. Owen also saw the two men exchange a quick glance as they did. Colonel Tucker had a momentary look of what Owen thought was embarrassment appear on his face before he too masked his features. Only the younger Henry Tucker wore an initially puzzled look, before it turned to one of mild disgust.

"Good God, why would we turn to the bloody

frogs for help?" he said, staring at Owen as if he were a simpleton. "Bermudans would never stand for such nonsense."

"Well, I was just curious, sir. For myself, I think it prudent to pay attention to what our former foes are doing. I would like to think our fight with them is over, but one never knows what the future holds."

"Yes, I would like to know what they were doing here, too," said the Governor. "Would any of you know, by chance?"

A silence descended on the group as the men all looked back and forth at each other, before Colonel Tucker finally responded.

"As far as we know they just came to sell some wares. I believe I heard it was the usual sort of produce from them. I acquired a case of rather good French wine. You must share a bottle with me some day, Governor. Well, gentlemen, I see they have brought the food out, so I am going to fill a plate. Good day, sirs."

Owen was left standing with the Governor as the Tucker family all left to follow the Colonel. Once they were alone the Governor turned to Owen.

"Well, you see what I mean about this lot being obstinate now, I trust?"

"I think I do, sir."

"The people on the island are torn, sir. Badly. I would say half of the population is loyal and the other half are so disgusted with our government they want to be considered a part of the American colonies. You can see it in this one family, for some of Colonel Tucker's sons are obviously loyalist and others clearly are not. Of course, they all stay loyal to each other, despite their different political stands. Fascinating, isn't it? But the one thing I know for certain is if comes down to a choice between starving and being fed, I know what they will chose. I respect Sir James and his friends in the Foreign Office. I just hope they will find some way to make our masters back home see sense. Well, we won't solve any of this today, so let's go get some food too."

Owen agreed and followed the Governor. As he went, he mulled over the various reactions he had gotten and knew Sir James and his uncle would be most interested to hear of his conversation.

Chapter Eight
The Caribbean and America
August to December 1773

The weather in late August in Barbados was humid and hot, but nowhere near as bad as Charleston earlier in the summer. Owen and his uncle were sitting once again enjoying the view from The Boatyard Inn verandah while they awaited the arrival of Sir James Standish.

"I had a look at the numbers yesterday, Owen. You and the men did well overall, considering what is going on out there. To be honest I was expecting you would come back with a loss, but you managed a small profit. I would like to be optimistic, but the way things are going I will be keeping my expectations realistic. The other ships I have trading out there are encountering the same difficulties."

"I'm just glad I was able to bring back as much in the way of food and provisions as we did, Uncle Alan. I've heard rumours matters have not improved here?"

"They are not just rumours, and it is not only this island. We've had word Jamaica is beginning to run low as well. If every spare patch of ground wasn't dedicated to growing sugarcane it perhaps wouldn't be as bad, but then we wouldn't be making mountains of money, would we? In any case, I will be monitoring this. I may send you back to Porto Bello early in November to help out. Governor Sanchez needs to feed his people too, but he won't have the same issues we do, and he will be happy to trade food instead of his people's precious gold and silver for our wares. Ah, here is Sir James."

The two men rose to greet him as Sir James strode over to their table. The three men compared notes after ordering drinks. Owen was interested to learn Sir James had just returned himself from a trip to Martinique and Guadeloupe. On the surface he was attempting to sell British wares to the French, which were as in demand there as they were in ports along the Spanish Main, but his real purpose was otherwise.

"Reliable informants with good, solid information are worth a fortune in gold. The problem is finding them and actually being certain what you get for the gold you pay them isn't a load of horse manure. This is especially true on those two islands. Well, I shall keep trying. And how did you fare, Owen?"

After Owen finished detailing what he had learned both Sir James and his uncle turned to stare at each other in thought.

"What do you think, Alan? I'd say this justifies my concern about that lot in Bermuda, wouldn't you?"

"I have to agree, Sir James. But what would the French want with them? They certainly aren't there just to expand their trading horizons."

"Actually, I am not so much interested in the French as I am in this American First Mate of his. I don't know if they are plotting something, but I wouldn't be surprised. I think I shall plan a visit to Bermuda again right after hurricane season. In any case, you have done well done, Owen. If you chance upon this ship again, find a way to follow some of those Frenchmen and see what they are up to if you can."

"I shall try, Sir James."

***

By the middle of September the demands of offloading cargo, making small repairs, and doing maintenance on *The Sea Trader* had diminished to a point where Owen had plenty of free time on his hands. Elizabeth was waiting for exactly this to remind him of his promise to go riding about the island for a picnic.

Uncle Alan was too busy, but his wife Mary accompanied the two of them as they set out in the same small cart for a trip. With no threat of rain Elizabeth decided she wanted to find a spot on the eastern, windward side of the island. Mary wanted to visit a friend who worked at John Lord's plantation on Long Bay and claimed she knew of a place near it she was certain they would all enjoy, although the beach area would be much more rugged.

They stopped at the plantation on their way to the site for Mary to visit with her friend. The visit was mercifully brief. As Mary's friend worked in the kitchens, Owen and Elizabeth were left to explore the grounds around the building. For Owen it brought back memories of his time in Jamaica he would sooner forget, while Elizabeth simply stood frowning as she watched the slaves going about their business, with the always present overseers on guard. A hint of sorrow was in her voice as she spoke.

"This is wrong, Owen. They treat these people

like simple beasts, but they aren't beasts. They are as human as us."

Owen sighed and briefly rested his hand on her shoulder to console her.

"I know and I agree. One day this must end."

Elizabeth reached up to touch his hand on her shoulder for a moment.

"We must find a way to help, Owen."

They stepped back from each other as Mary appeared and came over to join them, but she made no comment about what they were doing. They left and soon arrived at the location she had told them of as it wasn't far from the plantation. Owen found the spot pleasant enough, although the afternoon wind off the water was strong enough to dispel any notion of going for a swim in the ocean.

The beach itself was long and beautiful, but Owen knew the reef offshore would be something every sailor would want to avoid. If there were too many lights on the shore ships would easily mistake it for Bridgetown and seal their doom on the reef, making it good there were so few settlements in the area. They ate lunch as Owen told them of his most recent trip, with Elizabeth listening intently to everything he said. As he finished, she stared wistfully out to the horizon.

"You know, I envy you. You can board your ship and visit all these exotic places and then come back. I've never been off this island, but I would like to take a trip away. Will you promise to take me someday?"

Owen smiled at the audacity of the request before responding.

"I would be happy to take you somewhere if your uncle approves, Elizabeth. I confess I rather like seeing different places."

"You could take me, too," said Mary, a smile playing across her face. "I've never been off the island either."

"Yes, I'll take both of you if Uncle Alan approves," said Owen with a laugh.

"My uncle won't always need to approve everything I do, you know," said Elizabeth, a hint of reproach in her voice. "And I wasn't expecting you to do so anytime soon."

Owen threw his hands up in mock surrender.

"You certainly know your own mind, don't you? Yes, Elizabeth, I solemnly promise I shall take you on a trip somewhere someday if the opportunity is there."

"Excellent," she replied, her face beaming with delight. "And now I have one more promise to extract from you."

"Oh?"

"I would like you to teach me how to dance."

***

The ball was being held on a plantation where the owner's home rightly deserved being called a mansion, for the place was massive. Owen judged the two-story building owned by another friend of his uncle had eight or nine large rooms on the main floor with the same upstairs. A huge verandah ran the entire length of the front of the mansion, which sat on a small hill overlooking the rolling landscape of the interior of the island. Numerous carriages with servants to care for them were pulled off to the side of the grand drive leading up to the well-manicured grounds.

Elizabeth's excitement was unmistakable. She somehow convinced Uncle Alan of her need to attend when she discovered he was invited to the ball, claiming she wanted to learn what being a real lady was all about. He finally agreed to bring her as he knew his friend would not object. He could only laugh when the full extent of her plot was revealed, as she casually mentioned she had already invited Owen in anticipation of gaining approval. Fortunately, Elizabeth had enough time to have a new ball gown made for her.

She was not alone in making a visit to the tailor. Owen assessed his meagre wardrobe and knew he had to treat himself to a set of new clothes to wear. With his steady pay from serving on *The Sea Trader* his financial situation was vastly improved. Being at sea as much as he was also helped, for it was impossible to spend money unless he was in port.

By the time they arrived many of the guests were already there. Elizabeth was clutching at Owen's arm and looking radiant as they entered. Until now Owen had thought of her as a child, but he was also aware she was soon to enter her teens. He admitted to himself she was growing fast and had changed even in the few short months he had known her. She was still far too young in his mind to warrant serious attention, but he knew someday she would be a woman worthy of it.

Owen was no expert at dancing, but he had done some. Many at the ball were dancing to the minuet, but the musicians were also playing waltzes which he was much more comfortable with. After Elizabeth studied the other dancers and they practiced a little away from everyone else on the dance floor, they soon gained enough confidence with each other to work their way further into the crowd. After several waltzes they both even ventured the minuet, once again well out of the way of the others. They both laughed helplessly as it became clear they were hopeless at it and would need far more practice.

Deciding they needed a break they mingled with the crowd. Several of the women complimented Elizabeth on her poise and her dress, bringing a gleaming smile to her face yet again. Owen soon got used to being of far less interest, although a few of the men greeted him amiably enough on learning he was the nephew of Alan Giles. Owen signalled he was going to get a plate of food from the buffet table set up in another room as Elizabeth continued talking with some of the women.

He saw the small knot of men in Navy uniforms near the table as he entered and headed for the food. Unable to resist, he glanced over to see who they were and was dismayed to recognize Harold Smithe turn to look at him at the same time. With an inward sigh, Owen decided he had to be civil with the man. He acknowledged him with a small wave of his hand as he took a plate and began to fill it.

"Captain Smithe, I wasn't aware you were in port. I heard you were given your own command, sir. Congratulations are in order. Are you still with Jamaica Station?"

The officer remained silent for a long moment before responding.

"No longer as of now, Mr. Spence. My ship and I are in transit to an assignment with this station, although we will be based out of Antigua. Thank you for your congratulations, sir. Good day."

Smithe turned his back on Owen in an obvious snub and began talking to the other three officers, but all three remained staring at Owen. Owen turned away and finished filling the plate. The other officers were all Lieutenants and Owen had never met them before. A look of recognition appeared on the face of one and he chuckled as he turned back to the others, speaking loud enough for Owen to hear.

"Yes, I remember now. He is the one court martialled for theft. Well, plenty of opportunity to practice his trade in the merchant class."

"How utterly rude! You should be ashamed of yourself," said Elizabeth.

Owen and the Navy officers all turned to find Elizabeth had come in and was standing with her hands on her hips, glaring at the officer who had spoken. From her reaction Owen surmised she had witnessed the entire exchange. The officer looked at her in shock, before scowling in response.

"Excuse me? What is this, a child speaking like this to an adult?"

"I may be a child, but I know right from wrong when I see and hear it, sir," said Elizabeth, the disgust obvious on her face. "What you said was uncalled for and, in fact, is based on a lie. Owen Spence is not a thief and someone in the Navy is a liar."

"Young lady," said Captain Smithe, frowning. "You do not know what you are saying."

"Oh, I certainly do. I am not saying you personally are a liar, sir, but someone who was on the ship where it happened certainly is. This someone has no honour, unlike my friend Owen. And since gentlemanly behaviour seems in short supply today, I have had enough of this conversation. Come Owen, let's go. Good day, sirs."

Elizabeth turned to Owen, still standing there holding a plate of food. Owen slowly smiled and offered his free arm. Without a backward glance the two of them left to find a place to eat. Outside on the verandah they made their way to a small empty table and sat down. Owen put his hand over hers and gave it a brief squeeze as they sat down.

"Thank you for that. You probably saved me from having to call him out."

"Well, he really was rude, speaking as if you weren't even in the room. If this is who we have defending us we are in trouble."

"Well, they are not all like that, Elizabeth. The Navy has its share of both fools and heroes."

As they were about to leave at the end of the evening one of the other Navy officers attending the ball with Captain Smithe came over to see them. As he strode over, he made a point of first carefully looking around to ensure none of the other Navy men were in sight. Once he was satisfied, he turned and to Owen's surprise, gave him a salute.

"Sir, it is a pleasure to meet you. I am Third Lieutenant Randall Miller. You do not know me, but you do know my former colleague Lieutenant

George Strand."

As Owen's face brightened in recognition, Lieutenant Miller smiled.

"Yes, you will be happy to know Lieutenant Strand has his own command of a small sloop now. I served with him a long time ago when we were midshipmen. He told me about you and what happened when he heard I was being assigned to serve with Captain Smithe here. I've had some experience with his father and the nephew who behaved so abominably. I do think my Captain Harold Smithe is different. He may be rather stern in his approach, but he at least I believe has honour."

"I am very glad to hear news of Lieutenant Strand. Please give him my warm regards if you see him again. And I agree with you about Harold."

"Indeed. But this wasn't the only reason I came to search you both out."

With a smile, he turned to Elizabeth to briefly take her hand and offer a quick bow.

"Madam, I just want to tell you how impressed I was with how you conducted yourself. You are clearly a formidable foe, and I can only hope to stand as firm as you if and when I am ever tested. Mr. Spence here is fortunate to have a friend like you. Well done."

Elizabeth nodded, smiling beatifically as if she was receiving only what was her due. Lieutenant Miller saluted briefly once more and left. When he was gone Owen turned to Elizabeth and grinned.

"And I certainly do feel fortunate. Let's go find your uncle and get out of here."

***

Both men looked to the eastern horizon by reflex almost as one as they touched on the subject of hurricane season yet again. Seeing no issues, Owen smiled ruefully at his uncle as they stood on the dock in front of *The Sea Trader*. What remained was for Owen to step on board and for the crew to cast off.

"I still have misgivings about sending you off this early in November, nephew."

"I know, uncle. Do not concern yourself, we will be fine. We will sail south first for a little before turning west. Hurricanes tracking so far southwest are rare. And we both know there is need for us to make this trip."

"There is. I suspect Sir John Dalling in Jamaica will want you to make a separate trip to Porto Bello for him too. If he does, please do so. You have the letter from Sir James Standish for him?"

"I do."

"Hmm, I expect the prices Governor Sanchez will charge will be outrageous, for he is not stupid, and he undoubtedly knows there are problems with supplies everywhere. Well, give it your best, Owen. Stay safe."

After clapping him on the shoulder he stepped away to watch the ship depart. Owen could see him still standing there as the sails filled with the wind and they rapidly headed out to sea, leaving Owen with the clear sense his uncle felt torn about his decision to retire from a life at sea.

***

During a whirlwind stop in Kingston over a

week later his uncle proved to be correct about the Jamaican Governor, for a grateful Sir James Dalling immediately took Owen up on the offer when told of it. After sorting out the details Owen agreed if sufficient provisions could be found at Porto Bello to help with both island's needs, Owen would make a trip back to Jamaica first. The Governor even provided him with a letter confirming he was making the trip with his approval should any questions arise.

Over a week later *The Sea Trader* docked in Porto Bello once again. This time there were no other merchant ships in port. After enduring the same formalities as last time Owen made his way to see the Spanish Governor, who was all too happy to see him yet again. As Owen explained his needs the Governor seemed unsurprised.

"I have been wondering when this was going to happen. Yes, we will be happy to work with you if you have items to trade as usual. We have some food we can supply you with, I believe, although we will have to be certain to keep enough for our own people. Corn, rice, potatoes, beans, and some fruit and vegetables. Maybe some timber if you need some. We can perhaps even sell you some cattle if you want. All for the usual premium, of course."

Owen smiled and brought out his bag of gold. "My uncle had confidence you would be helpful."

Two days later *The Sea Trader* was on its way back to Jamaica, fully laden with as much in the way of provisions as the Jamaican Governor's gold would buy. While it wasn't a full load, the amount was significant, and Owen had managed to acquire more than either of them had expected possible. Owen had arranged for a second load he would pick up on his return trip to take back to Barbados.

This time when they arrived in Jamaica Owen left the task of offloading the ship in John's hands after stopping to visit the grateful Jamaican Governor. John gave Owen a puzzled look when he told him he would be staying off the ship for the two days it would take before they could depart again.

"I am only going to stay with a friend for a couple of nights. I will be back the day after tomorrow."

"A friend?" said John, wearing a puzzled look on his face before understanding dawned and a grin appeared.

"Oh, I understand. This would be a female friend, wouldn't it? I didn't know you had one here. By all means, leave matters to me. Try to remember to at least get enough sleep the next two nights. I can't have you navigating us into a reef because you fell asleep on deck, can I?"

Owen smiled back at him. "Thank you, I shall return the favour for you some day."

***

The Spanish Rose Inn appeared unchanged except for a fresh coat of paint on the exterior of the building as Owen walked into the shade of the interior tavern area. With it not yet mid-day there were no customers for lunch yet. Isabella was standing with her back to the door talking to a serving girl Owen had not seen before as he came up behind her. Owen spoke as the serving girl's eyes shifted to acknowledge him, alerting Isabella to his presence.

"Any chance of getting a drink with a friend in this place?" said Owen, throwing his duffel bag to the side as Isabella turned and saw him.

Her face lit with joy and she flung her arms around his neck, crushing him to her as Owen did the same. After a minute Owen grinned and finally stepped back a little.

"Yes, I am happy to see you too, Isabella. So happy I thought I might stay a couple of nights if you have room?"

She laughed. "Oh, I will make room for you. In fact, why don't we go look at your choices right now?"

After leaving matters to her serving girl Isabella took him by the hand and they went upstairs. She began shedding her clothes the second she walked in the door of her room, as Owen did the same. Almost an hour later Isabella finally got out of bed to sponge herself clean of the sweat and to pull her dress back on. Owen admired her slim body as she went about her task and she saw his gaze.

"I must go downstairs and help out my new server, Owen. She isn't experienced enough yet to handle the entire lunch service if we get too many customers. And yes, I am almost a year older than the last time you were here, and it probably shows. You must tell me what you have been doing to keep you away for so long."

"Yes, it has been almost a year, hasn't it? But you still look young and wonderfully sexy to me, Isabella."

"You are a bad liar, Owen. But you can keep lying to me like this all you want."

She finished straightening her dress, combed her hair into a semblance of order, and made to leave, pausing in the doorway.

"I suspect you are hungry. If so, come downstairs and have some lunch."

As the door closed Owen felt his stomach grumble and he knew she was right. He also acknowledged to himself she indeed had yet more subtle signs of growing age he would never have noticed if he was seeing her every day. But they had both agreed this relationship was not forever and he knew this wouldn't change.

After making some quick arrangements Isabella managed to take the afternoon of the next day off and they went to their favourite beach once again. They exhausted themselves making love on the beach and fell asleep in each other's arms to the sound of the waves lapping on the shore. They ate the small picnic lunch Isabella had made for them when they awoke and finally made time to tell each other more of what they had done over the past year. Isabella listened to his story in silence before she spoke.

"There is little to tell for me. I am a year older, as is my daughter and my mother. Times are getting harder, Owen. Prices are going up for virtually everything, so my prices must go up too. More than anyone likes. So far it has not affected my business too much and I can only hope it stays this way."

"You have found no one else, Isabella?"

She shrugged. "No. You know, of course, if I do

this will end, right?"

"I do. Well, the way things are going I may be back in Jamaica more often. If getting basic food and provisions for Barbados and Jamaica continues to be a problem or gets even worse, who knows?"

Owen reached out to caress her face as he continued.

"If I am back here and I have enough time, I guarantee I will come to see you."

Isabella smiled and wrapped her arms around him, in a vain attempt to ensure he wouldn't see the single tear coursing down her face.

"I know you will. And I want you to."

***

The Sea Trader returned to a grateful welcome in Barbados in December after her second visit to Porto Bello. His uncle had gone over the manifest Owen had prepared of the goods he brought back and smiled at what he saw.

"Well, at least the people will find something on their tables to eat once we offload all of this. It is the slaves I fear for, Owen. If anyone is going to be short changed, it will be them. The other ships we have had out foraging for us have had limited success, but you have done somewhat better. But you say even Governor Sanchez was putting limits on what they would sell us?"

"Correct. Understandably, he wanted to make sure his own people are fed. Based on conversations I had with the various merchants in town, I think he did the best he could for us. He promised to continue to do so, but it will be limited out of necessity."

After ensuring the ship was offloaded Owen was able to give the men a few days off before their next voyage as Christmas was close at hand. Almost as soon as he had a free moment an invitation appeared from Elizabeth to visit her and he mentioned it to his uncle. On reading the message his uncle laughed.

"I did warn you, remember? It was her birthday last month and you were away. I'd say she is expecting you to visit to atone for having missed it."

The next day a light breeze was coming off the ocean, making the December weather in Barbados perfect. Owen was sitting with Elizabeth at the table on the bluff in front of his uncle's home enjoying a piece of cake she had made specially for him.

"Elizabeth, this is lovely. I didn't know you were such a good cook."

"I am learning from Mary. She is very good. Since you missed having cake on my birthday with me, I thought it would be nice to practice on you so you could have some anyway. So, Uncle has told me nothing. What did you do on your trip?"

Owen continued eating as he absentmindedly stared out to sea and began telling her what he had done. He missed seeing the frown appear on her face as he casually mentioned stopping in to stay at Isabella's for a visit. She spoke as he finally finished.

"I see. And who exactly is this woman Isabella you mentioned?"

"Eh?" said Owen, hearing an unmistakable edge to her voice. He turned to look at her face and realized at once he was in trouble. While she had managed to plant a mostly bland look on her face, the icy look in her eyes and the ever so slight narrowing of her eyebrows were impossible to miss. Owen took a sip of his drink to buy himself a moment to think of a response, but as rapidly as he thought of something to say he found himself instantly discarding it. After coughing into his hand to buy yet another millisecond, he finally blurted out a response.

"She is just a friend, Elizabeth. Someone I met when I was first set adrift in Kingston."

"A friend. I see. How did you meet her?"

"Um, well, she runs The Spanish Rose Inn. I stayed there until I found work, so I got to know the people running it."

"She is Spanish, is she?" said Elizabeth, now wearing a mild frown. "And she runs an Inn? Does she have a husband to help her with it?"

Owen sighed inwardly, feeling like he was digging himself deeper with every answer.

"She had a husband once, but he passed away. Look, she was extremely kind to me when I needed help, Elizabeth. This is why she is a very good friend."

Elizabeth remained silent for a long moment before she responded.

"I'll bet she is young and very pretty, isn't she?"

This time Owen knew for certain he had to be careful with how he responded. He offered Elizabeth what he hoped was a noncommittal, rueful smile as he spoke.

"Elizabeth, I would be a liar if I told you she isn't pretty. She is pretty. She is slim and petite and has inky black, curly hair. She is also in her late thirties in age. She is old enough to be my mother."

"And you'll be visiting her whenever you go to Jamaica, won't you?"

"Yes. Yes, I will. She is a very good friend."

Elizabeth sat silent for a moment, obviously considering what he had said. Owen sensed she came to an inner decision as she sat straighter and gave him a smile which seemed to reach into him, leaving his soul bare. He had no need to ask her what her thoughts were, for he knew she was now all too aware of exactly what kind of relationship he had with Isabella. With a look of serene confidence, she finally responded.

"I think a day will come when I shall be a very good friend to you, too."

Chapter Nine
America and The Caribbean
January 1774 to September 1774

In response to an urgent summons from Sir James Standish the three men met this time in the cabin of *The Sea Trader*. Owen was ashore dealing with a local merchant when one of his men tracked him down to request his presence immediately back at the ship. On arriving he discovered both Sir James and his uncle awaiting him. Both men looked grim.

"I'm sorry I was not available. What is happening?" said Owen, as he took a seat at the small meeting table in his cabin.

"It's Boston again, Owen," said Sir James. "Two merchants have just come into port with rumours of some sort of major upheaval happening in Boston. They were in other ports, so the rumours are second hand, and the reports are not clear as to exactly what happened. I confess I am extremely concerned and worse, I am not able to sail there to find out what is going on as my own ship is busy with repairs right now. Your uncle has therefore volunteered you, if you are willing, to drop your other plans and sail empty immediately to Boston to learn more."

"Of course, Sir James. Are we talking violence, do you know?"

"Given the current situation, anything is possible."

"Well, it is perhaps good we have finished adding a few cannons to *The Sea Trader* then. A trip to Boston will give me opportunity to give the men some practice with them."

"Excellent. I will provide you with a letter for Sir Ross Stanhope before the day is out. When can you sail?"

"Sir, we can sail with the dawn assuming I can round up all of the men. A few are off on shore leave right now. We will find them in whatever tavern or brothel they are holed up in."

"Owen?" said his uncle. "Do not concern yourself with the financial aspects of this. Depending on the situation, of course, if you can find a way to acquire the usual provisions we are always in need of here, then please do so, but understand this is a far less important secondary objective. I will give some thought to exactly how much I am prepared to pay for certain items and let you know. I will provide you with the appropriate funds before you leave."

A brief silence fell over the table as the three men looked at each other. Sir James sighed.

"Well, I fear this situation is going downhill and picking up speed as it goes. I hope we are not too late to find a way to stop this. We can only do our best, gentlemen. Thank you for this, Owen."

***

The weather was far colder than Owen was accustomed to in the northern waters off the coast of Boston in early February. Owen was forced to buy cold weather clothing he realized he no longer owned and pay the outrageous prices demanded in Barbados because of limited supplies on hand and the urgency of his need. By the time they finally arrived in port he was glad of his new and heavy winter cloak, for the wind carrying them ever further north was biting cold.

The first thing Owen noticed after tying up on the wharf beside other merchant ships in port were the number of soldiers standing guard and patrolling the nearby streets. As he stepped ashore after dealing with the usual customs men he couldn't miss the stiff, hard looks on the faces of dock workers and the people passing by. A small knot of men was lounging against the wall of a waterfront shop, catching his eye because every one of them looked as if they were straight out of the nearest jail.

One of them detached himself from the group and walked over to intercept the customs man who had just left *The Sea Trader*. The man stared hard at Owen as he questioned the customs man for a few moments before the two parted ways. The man lingered to glare at Owen for a few seconds longer before casually walking back to the others.

After warning John to be wary Owen made his way toward Sir Ross Stanhope's office, knowing this would be the best source of information. Fortunately, he was in his office, greeting Owen with a smile as he looked up from the letter he was writing. He waved at the chair in front of his desk and pointed to the brandy decanter nearby.

Owen helped himself as Sir Ross finished what he was doing with a sigh. He groaned as he got up and threw more logs on the fire, which Owen was immediately grateful for as the chill in the room was enough he had kept his cloak on. Sir Ross topped up his own glass and leaned back in his chair after sitting down.

"Well, Mr. Spence. I am not surprised to see you. I knew it would be either you or Sir James himself appearing at my door soon enough."

Owen passed over the letter from Sir James, which Sir Ross glanced at and put aside.

"I am afraid you have the advantage of both Sir James and I, Sir Ross. We had word there has been some sort of upheaval here, but we have no details. Something has clearly happened, though. From the moment we got here we have been under scrutiny."

Sir Ross raised an eyebrow to show his interest and Owen obliged by telling him what he saw at the wharf. Sir Ross seemed unsurprised by this too.

"Those fellows watching your ship were undoubtedly there to watch for more East India ships arriving. Your British flag automatically set you apart for scrutiny. I rather think the customs man was immediately asked what your cargo was, for that is what it is all about right now."

"Sir? What is going on?"

Sir Ross sighed again. "They are calling it the Boston Tea Party. Three ships carrying large cargos of East India Company tea came into port back in mid-December. One of these rabble rousers, a fellow called Samuel Adams, found out and gave a rather fiery speech about the injustice of it all to a huge crowd who gathered as word spread of what was happening. I am told it really was quite the rousing and inspiring speech. I have to give them credit where it is due. These patriots are excellent orators and know how to rouse the passions of people. Before all this the people were very divided.

A third was supportive of them, a third were not, and the rest were undecided. I don't know if this has now changed, but I fear it may have."

"It was just a speech?"

"Yes, but the speech led to actual deeds this time. A large number of men got dressed up pretending to look like Mohawk Indians. They boarded the three ships and heaved all of the tea overboard into the harbour. There was nothing the crews could do to stop them. I am told the Company lost 342 chests of valuable tea to the action, to the sum of somewhere around 18,000 pounds in value."

"My God, I begin to understand now, sir."

"Indeed. Of course, none of them were Mohawk Indians. I fear the arrogance of our masters and these tax policies are taking us down a dark path which is unlikely to end in a place where anyone wants to be. In any case, it has been impossible to identify exactly who the conspirators were. My local sources have begun to dry up. I think some of them fear the consequences if they are caught, while others have perhaps switched sides. Mr. Adams and his friends really are very persuasive."

"I see. Well, Sir James will wish to know all of this as soon as possible, sir. I assume you will have a letter for me to deliver to him?"

"I shall. What are your plans, Mr. Spence?"

Owen shrugged. "I was asked to come here to find out what is happening. If I can help in some way, I know Sir James would want me to. And lastly, if I can actually purchase provisions or food at a price which isn't completely ridiculous, I am to do so."

Sir Ross grimaced. "Well, right now the only thing I need is more intelligence about what their next moves may be. See here, the one thing I do know is the possible location where their quasi headquarters is sited. They are very much on their guard and I have not been able to infiltrate it. Would you be willing to see what you can learn there?"

"Certainly, sir. Command me, I shall do my best."

"Very well. There is an extremely vague rumour out there about The Green Dragon Tavern, which says this is where these patriots hold their meetings. Not surprisingly, it is on Green Dragon street, not far from the waterfront. I strongly suggest a passive approach. Pretend you are just a sailor on a brief stop, wondering what all the fuss is about. Try to soak up whatever information you can. Anything would help enormously."

"I shall do my best, Sir Ross. I will let you know if anything develops or, if not, when I will be leaving port again. Good day sir."

***

On returning to *The Sea Trader* Owen found John waiting for him with barely concealed excitement. Finding his normally taciturn First Mate so worked up was astonishing.

"Owen, the bloody French are here. Yes, it's Le Mystere. And even better, I don't think they know we are here yet."

Owen couldn't stop himself looking in both directions, but didn't see the French ship.

"She is much further down the wharf, Owen. I

risked a walk about and saw them. I made sure none of them saw me. I've been watching carefully and haven't seen any of them come near us."

"Well done, John. Hmm, this is a possibility I had not foreseen, but I think we are going to seize the moment."

Owen explained what Sir Ross had told him of the situation and explained he proposed for tonight to deviate from what Sir Ross had asked him to do.

"These goddamn Frenchmen are involved in this somehow, John. I can feel it and I am wondering what these bastards are doing here again. Well, in any case, I would like to spend some time watching them this evening and follow them if possible, see where they go. We have little to lose and something to gain. What do you think?"

John was silent for a moment before he nodded. "I agree with you. Are you proposing just the two of us?"

Owen rubbed his chin in thought. "I was. What are you thinking?"

"I think if they catch us, we may need help. I suggest we have Wilson as our backup. In fact, I'd like to bring Jack Hobart, too. I know for a fact he is a good man in a fight."

"I'll take your word for it. Hmm. Weapons? I suggest we don't want to look as if we are spoiling for a fight. Dirks and maybe some cudgels?"

"My fists work for me too, sir," said John with a smile. "I will round up the men."

"John? The question of what these bastards were up to before they got here really bothers me. Remind me later to see if we can find out if they were in Bermuda again."

An hour later the four men were seated in a rough waterfront tavern close enough to watch what was happening with the French ship through the frost covered windows. Owen explained what he wanted to John and the two sailors with them, emphasizing everyone was to pay close attention above all to the French Captain Paul Allarde and his First Mate William Bains.

Fortune shone on Owen, for less than twenty minutes after they had settled in both of their quarries stepped onto the shore. Two other sailors were with them and together the Frenchmen began making their way down the street. Once he was certain they were not coming to the tavern he was already in, Owen quickly paid the bill and the four men from *The Sea Trader* left, splitting into two parties.

Owen and John took the lead position, staying far enough behind their quarries as not to raise suspicion. With the weather so cold the task of keeping their faces mostly covered was easy. The French Captain looked around once but showed no suspicion as his glance passed over them. Other people were on the street going about their business in the dinner hour at the end of the day, making Owen's task even easier. As the four Frenchmen turned a corner onto another street a chill ran through Owen, which had nothing to do with the weather outside, for the street sign told him this was Green Dragon Street.

Sensing what they were about to do Owen pulled John to the side into a dark entrance. Once they were out of sight Owen looked around the doorframe with only one eye exposed to watch his quarries stop and peer carefully about. Appearing satisfied, they all entered The Green Dragon Tavern. Owen turned to John and ordered him to go back and find the other two men from *The Sea Trader* while he maintained a watch on the tavern. Moments later the four men were crowded into the small alcove of the entrance.

"Right, the men we are after went inside the tavern over there. Mr. Tate and I are going in to see what we can learn, but I have reason to believe we may get a less than pleasant welcome. I think it risky if we all go inside. I am not certain, but I think I recognized one of the sailors with them. It's hard to tell with everyone so bundled up from the cold. He may have been one of the Frenchmen who gave us a fight in Porto Bello. If so, it matters not who goes in. But if we keep our numbers small, they may not see us as a threat or even notice us. I hate to leave you out here in the cold, but I would like to have a surprise for them if we have to leave in a hurry. I suggest just keep walking about in sight of the entrance to stay warm. I don't think we are going to be in there long."

"If I may, this is probably a good plan, sir," said Wilson. "I haven't noticed any black men besides myself in this area of town. I might stand out if I walk in, so best we stay out here. We will keep a careful watch."

Owen and John left the two sailors where they were and made for the entrance. They were immediately greeted by the warm, smoky haze of the noisy interior as they stepped inside. A huge blazing fire to give warmth was in a massive hearth on the far side of the room, while the sheer number of men packed inside added their own heat. Many were smoking pipes, creating a dense, warm fog hanging almost motionless in the air. Although a few faces turned their way as they came in, no one challenged them.

Owen spotted two of the Frenchmen sitting at a table on the far side of the room, but neither was looking their direction. Seeing a free table close to the entrance, Owen made a beeline for it with John right behind him. A few of the patrons at nearby tables took sidelong looks at the newcomers as the two men ordered drinks. John ignored them and leaned closer to Owen to speak.

"Owen? I don't see the Captain and his bloody sidekick anywhere."

"Neither do I. The other two are on the far side over there. Let's keep talking as if we are minding our own business for now, but keep your eyes open."

As their drinks arrived Owen made a point of raising his voice a little and talking about having to make room for provisions on the ship. John responded in kind and as they carried on talking Owen noticed a steady parade of men leaving the room to go down a set of stairs with drinks in hand and others coming upstairs empty handed. As their server walked past once again Owen flagged him down and pretended to be intrigued, asking about what he was seeing.

"Say, I'm just curious. This is our first time here.

You seem to have a huge tavern here. Is business good enough you need to have tables downstairs too?"

The server's eyes narrowed for a moment, but he responded readily enough.

"Business could be better. We have a private room downstairs which is sometimes used for invited customers only. You can't go down there."

"Sure," said Owen as the man walked away. Once the man was gone Owen nodded to John.

"I'm going to keep an eye on that staircase. My money says this is where the other two are. And if I am right, it makes me wonder why they would be invited customers. I'd suggest we try just barging in on their little party, but I somehow don't think we would get very far. You see the big bastard sitting on a stool with his back to the wall near the stairs, all by himself and trying to look like he's just another customer? I think he's actually a guard. So maybe we should try another way to learn something."

"What did you have in mind?"

For answer Owen turned and looked over at two men sitting closest to them at the next table over. One of the men saw Owen from the corner of his eye and gave him a questioning look.

"Hello, mate. Say, we've never been to Boston before. We work for a Dutch master and just got in from Amsterdam. We heard there's been a deal of trouble here lately. What's it all about?"

Both men at the table were silent for a moment, before looking at each other. One of them finally stirred and shifted a little in his seat to raise his glass in their direction.

"Welcome to Boston. Yeah, you heard right. The damnable English government is trying to bleed us dry. Make us pay for their follies by taxing us so much it's impossible to make a living. So, a bunch of their damned tea got tossed in the harbour to show them what we think. And it's going to get much worse if these fools don't change their ways. You maybe work for the Dutch, but I expect you two are English and you maybe don't like what I just said. If you don't well, too bad. This is the way it is around here."

Owen shrugged. "We are English, but we are also just businessmen. We don't care about politics. You say it will get much worse, though? What does that mean? Our master was hoping to expand his trade to here."

"They aren't showing any signs of changing and the people are angry. If they don't change, we will make them change."

"Jonah, be careful," said the other man at the table, with an obvious look of warning on his face.

"I'm not telling them anything not already obvious, am I? Look, nobody around here wants a fight, but there will be one if this keeps up. People are arming themselves. There is talk. Read into it what you will."

"Hmm, perhaps we will have to tread carefully," said Owen. "Thank you for this, it is good to know the local situation if you want to make profits. And now I am wondering how well our competition is established here. The French are our competitors for selling goods from the continent. We noticed at least one of their ships in port already. Do you have many French ships come in often?"

The man called Jonah gave a tiny, almost imperceptible start when Owen mentioned the French. He gave his friend at the table a quick glance before planting a bland, frozen look on his face.

"I wouldn't know anything about the French. I don't think anyone around here would know more, either."

"Really? Well, they seem to enjoy it here, because I thought I saw a couple of the men from their ship on the other side of the room when we came in. Maybe just a coincidence."

"Yeah, maybe. You ask a lot of questions."

"Owen, we have company," said John.

Owen shifted his gaze to look in the same direction as John and immediately locked eyes with the American First Mate of Le Mystere, William Bains. He was standing at the top of the stairs with a drink in his hand and was now wearing a look of shocked surprise on his face. The look didn't last long, as he turned and began speaking to the guard sitting on the stool. Within seconds both turned to look at Owen. The guard nodded to the First Mate and slipped off the stool to make his way over to where Owen and John were sitting. The guard stopped at their table and glared at Owen.

"What are you doing in here?"

Owen shrugged and pointed at his mug of ale.

"We're just here to have a quiet drink."

"We don't want your business here. Finish it now and get out, both of you."

Owen and John looked at each other wordlessly and rose from their seats.

"I don't know what the problem with sitting and drinking is, but we aren't here to make trouble. I'll just leave some money to pay for our drinks and we will go."

As he pulled some coins out and left them on the table, the man Jonah rose from his seat and spoke up, raising his voice loud enough for men at the tables around them to stop what they were talking about and listen in.

"Elias, these bastards were asking all kinds of questions. I think they are goddamned English spies."

"I think you are dreaming, sir. Now if you will get out of our way, we will be off."

The man Jonah remained where he was, blocking their path to the door, and he jabbed a forefinger into Owen's chest.

"No, I don't think I'm dreaming, arsehole. I think you are a goddamn spy, and we should deal with you. I—"

Owen knew the situation was getting out of control and the time to leave was now. Stepping forward, he shoved the man hard enough he stumbled and fell backwards, crashing into a nearby table of men eating dinner and drinking. Knowing the guard would be reacting, Owen turned to meet his challenge only to watch the man drop heavily to the floor from a crushing blow to the head by John's cudgel.

Owen seized the opportunity presented by the momentary confusion to rush toward the door, with

John close on his heels. Men began rising from their seats on either side of their route to block their path as they realized what was happening. Owen pulled out his own cudgel and used it to smash at arms reaching out to stop him, drawing sharp cries of pain each time it landed. By the time they got to the door only one customer was left, but he was fully blocking the aisle. Owen kicked him hard in the groin and was exiting even as the man fell gasping to the floor.

As soon as he got outside Owen had to rush back to bash the head of another customer who had clutched at John's coat and wouldn't let go. John stumbled and fell out of the door onto the ground as he was released. Before he could get to his feet a small crowd of angry men filled the entrance. Owen was forced to try and keep them at bay while John recovered himself. By the time John was back on his feet Owen was already hard pressed and he yelled at John to run for it. After delivering one last blow with his cudgel Owen turned and ran to escape too.

A small group of three men boiled out of the now open entrance and charged after them, howling their anger. The man leading the three was fast on his feet and managed to catch up to John, forcing him to turn and fight. Owen heard him call out and did the same. John took a heavy punch from the man and gave his opponent one back in return. Owen found himself struggling against the other two men and feared they would soon overpower him, for both seemed strong and fit.

One of them pulled out a wicked looking knife,

but before he could use it Wilson appeared beside him, immobilizing the man's wrist in a grip impossible to break and delivering a crushing punch to his opponent's face. Wilson was left still holding the man's now limp wrist as his opponent dropped the knife and fell, bleeding profusely from his nose.

The third customer from the tavern was about to come to his friend's aid, but Jack Hobart stepped in front of him and hammered a devastating blow to his mid-section. The man clutched at his stomach and dropped on the ground beside his friend. The pursuer John was still struggling with realized what was happening and pulled away, running fast back to the safety of the tavern. As John rubbed his bruised face, Owen called to the four of them.

"Let's get out of here before they send more help."

***

Owen and John were both wary the next day, for the question was whether the men in the Green Dragon would leave matters where they were or come in search of them. Wilson proved his worth once again by nosing about on the waterfront, learning the French ship had indeed been in Bermuda once again. After making arrangements to purchase a small amount of food and provisions at rates appearing extortionate, Owen made his way back to the office of Sir Ross Stanhope and explained what had happened. Sir Ross shook his head in dismay.

"You did well, sir. At least now I know almost for certain the place is indeed a nest of rebels and the French are certainly sticking their bloody noses into this mess. I find it worrisome they were in Bermuda. I think they are playing the long game and cultivating relationships. Mr. Spence, you should be on your guard. These men may search you out."

"Yes, I am concerned about it. We had one particular fellow who seemed overly interested in our ship hanging around the waterfront today. Well, I have achieved what I came here for, at least to some extent. We will finish loading our cargo and make a little detour to Bermuda to speak to the Governor. I would like to know what the French were doing there. I may also stop in Charleston again to see if I can purchase more food. It is all becoming hideously expensive. Sir Ross, you should know almost half of what I purchased I am quite certain has been smuggled here."

"A sign of the times, sir."

Owen returned to the ship and found John standing on the deck staring at the waterfront. Owen raised an eyebrow and John pointed in the general direction of the dock.

"The number of men watching us has grown to a total of three at least. They seem to be rotating back and forth in the hope we wouldn't notice. There may be more we haven't spotted. No point getting in a fight I suppose, so I recommend we all stay aboard the ship tonight. Are we leaving tomorrow?"

"As soon as the rest of the cargo is loaded," replied Owen.

***

Three months later Owen sailed north for Boston once more. The weather in late May was far more pleasant than their last visit. *The Sea Trader* had stopped in Bermuda briefly on her return to Barbados earlier in the year, but the Governor had no news for him. He was unconcerned about the possibility the French might somehow be making trouble and once again preferred to spend more of his time worrying about the economic situation facing his people. Another brief stop in Charleston on their way back to Barbados had fortunately garnered more provisions, but they were at even more usurious prices.

Owen and John took careful note of their surroundings after finally docking once again in Boston, but no one seemed to be paying any attention to them. They had considered changing the name of the ship, but decided against it this time in order to see what would happen. Owen sent John and some of his sailors out to see what they could learn from the waterfront taverns while he went to see Sir Ross Stanhope once again. With two exceptions, Sir Ross had little more to offer than what he had back in February, emphasizing the only real change was matters were even worse. Local Royal Customs officers were now being harassed on a constant basis.

"Has it become so bad, sir?" said Owen.

"Oh my, yes," said Sir Ross. "The smuggling trade is booming, Mr. Spence. Why, just the other day I heard of two Customs men in Philadelphia who found a large shipment of wine being smuggled in. They attempted to seize it, of course. Word of the action leaked out and in the process a mob formed, beat the Customs men, and stole everything. Being a Customs officer may be a decent enough job, but I'm not sure I'd be applying to be one around here right now."

"Indeed. But you mention there is something afoot, sir?"

"There is. First of all, you are fortunate you got in before they close the port. I have no idea what the outcome will be, but it will likely end badly."

"Close the port?" said Owen, a look of shock on his face. "My God, why would they do this?"

"Because Parliament has passed the Boston Port Act. No one is to be allowed in until the East India Company is reimbursed for all of the tea dumped in the harbour back in December. Well, I gather they will let ships with food in, so no one will starve, but this is all. The Royal Navy will enforce a blockade and they are bringing more soldiers in to patrol the city. It is a way of establishing who is in charge here, of course."

"Good God, this is a recipe for disaster."

"It certainly is. The other concern I have is what I and my colleagues have feared for a long time seems to be coming to pass. The rumour is the colonies here have agreed to band together to discuss the situation in something they call a congress. I am actively trying to confirm whether this is true. If so, they will be much more difficult to deal with as one large entity than they currently are as a group of small ones with different interests. Come and see me before you leave for Barbados. I will have a letter for Sir James about this."

After agreeing Owen made his way back to the ship to debrief John and the rest of his men. While none of them had word of any tangible threats, they were unanimous Boston was a pot of seething anger bubbling under its surface. Owen confirmed it for himself as he talked with the various merchants to trade or purchase what he could to bring back to Barbados.

Despite the depth of ill feelings under the surface, the local merchants were not about to pass up opportunity to make a profit. Owen approached one fellow who he knew from prior experience was far less scrupulous than most about the rules. Owen decided to see what response he would get by asking him directly how it was possible to purchase such a wide array of goods. The man simply laughed in response.

"Mr. Spence, I have dealt with you and your uncle before you, so I am happy to keep doing business with you. Of course, if you don't ask me any difficult questions in the process, I won't have to give you an answer you might not like. Do we understand each other, sir?"

"I think we do," said Owen.

The man practically beamed as he reeled off a list of his wares. Wine and brandy from France, all manner of cheeses, olive oil, and other foodstuffs from everywhere on the European continent, and a huge array of manufactured goods from everywhere were available. Owen was astonished to find even British products which he knew should be subject to duties were on offer at prices low enough to make it clear no one had paid any tax whatsoever on the product. When the two men finished arrangements for Owen to purchase a large number of his wares

Owen couldn't help asking another question anyway.

"Purely out of curiosity, sir, does this blockade of the port concern you at all? What will you do to stay afloat?"

"The Port Act you mean? It doesn't bother me at all. In fact, it is good for my specific business. There is more than one way to bring my goods to market. Oh, it will make the job a little more complicated, but I have plenty of rather clever friends. You didn't hear this, of course."

Owen could only smile at the man's audacity. By using every source available to him Owen was able to purchase enough goods the trip would prove worthwhile for his uncle, although the profit would be minimal. Owen knew his uncle wouldn't care, for the provisions he would be bringing back would help stave off hunger on the island once more, at least for a time. By the time they finished loading the cargo Owen knew they would be ready to leave the next day, so he made his way back to see Sir Ross Stanhope. The man pulled an envelope out of a drawer of his desk on seeing Owen come in.

"Here is a letter for Sir James. Your timing is fortuitous, as I have only just learned what I needed to know and finished a letter to him. You remember this congress I was telling you about?"

"Yes, sir."

"Well, it is set to happen in Philadelphia in early September. There will indeed be delegates from most if not all of the colonies there to discuss making common cause against us. The main topic is going to be what they are calling The Intolerable

Acts and the plan is to propose a total boycott of British goods be implemented before the year is out if the government doesn't agree to their demands."

"What are these Intolerable Acts, Sir Ross? I believe Sir James mentioned a bunch of changes were afoot, but I have been at sea much of this year."

"They are in response to this Tea Party of late last year, as they call it. The big one which has the locals angered is an act taking away the self-governance and rights of Massachusetts. All of the colonies are fearful of this action, for they reason correctly if the government can do this to one colony, it could happen to all of them. Another is the Port Act you already know about. There are a few others I won't go into detail about. Suffice to say the locals all consider them infringements on their rights in one form or another."

"This all feels like I am on a ship with no sails about to smash into a reef and I am powerless to stop it, Sir Ross."

Sir Ross nodded sadly and went back to work at his desk as Owen took his leave.

***

By the time Owen reached Charleston in mid-June word of the coming congress involving all of the colonies had preceded him. He was unsurprised to find the atmosphere in the southern city was already coming to resemble the simmering cauldron of anger in Boston. Owen estimated the number of soldiers patrolling the area was double the year before. Despite this they managed to acquire yet more supplies as long as he wasn't asking too many questions about how it could be they were even available.

On finally reaching Barbados in early July both Sir James and his uncle were anxious to learn what he knew, for word of the looming congress had preceded him to Barbados as well. They both came at once after receiving Owen's message and met in Owen's cabin on *The Sea Trader*. As the two men finished reading the letter from Sir Ross Stanhope they sat back in their chairs and frowned in thought while remaining silent.

To break the silence Owen told them of his sense of the atmosphere in both Boston and Charleston. He also filled them in on the broad details of the cargo he had brought, noting the likelihood much of it had passed through smuggler's hands. Owen's uncle finally broke the silence.

"I gather from his letter Sir Ross told you this is what we have been fearing, Owen. I think we are now but a few steps away from acts of violence. Sir James?"

"I wish I could disagree with you, Alan. If these people begin to feel they have nothing to lose and something to gain by violence, it will start and be impossible to stop. I gather you have been drilling your men on use of the cannons installed on *The Sea Trader*? I suggest you keep them proficient, for I fear those skills will be necessary in future. Let us hope we still have time to influence our masters and avert this disaster."

Sir James rose from his chair. "I must be off to write a letter. There is a Royal Navy mail packet ship leaving for England in the morning and I need to make sure my letter is on it. Well done, Owen. Good day, gentlemen."

As the cabin door closed behind him Owen's uncle rose to leave as well.

"I agree, this was well done, Owen. You will have time on your hands for the next few months because of hurricane season. I think you may need to ensure *The Sea Trader* is as fast as she can be in future, so I am going to take advantage of hurricane season and have the ship's bottom cleaned. You won't have to sleep on shore for too long. You must join us at home for dinner once you have offloaded the cargo and the ship is in the careenage. Besides, Elizabeth will have my head if you don't come and see her soon. You have made a conquest there, I think."

Owen laughed. "I expect I have, Uncle Alan, but Elizabeth is far too young still. I don't take any of it seriously, although I do enjoy seeing her now and again. To be honest, we always do seem to have fun together when we see each other. I am away at sea and soon enough she will find other young men catching her fancy, I should think."

"I agree she is still quite young, but it isn't stopping her from taking you seriously, nephew. Perhaps you are right and this attention to you is just temporary in her adolescence. But don't be too sure about it. For whatever reason, she is more mature than her age would suggest."

"I will be sure to treat her as a gentleman would, Uncle Alan."

***

By the time Owen freed himself from his cares

over the cargo and maintenance of the ship it was close to the end of July. He made his availability known to his uncle and an invitation to dinner soon appeared. Elizabeth greeted him with arms folded and a mock frown on her face.

"And why has it taken you so long to come and see me? I was told you returned weeks ago."

"Owen has been busy on my behalf, my dear," said Uncle Alan, coming to his rescue. "But it is hurricane season now and he will be free for some time to come. And you have no right to complain, for I have already given in to you, haven't I?"

"Given in?" said Owen. "Given in to what?"

Uncle Alan laughed. "She has told me we are all far too boring. If I must confess, I actually agree with her. I haven't held a little ball and dinner for some of my local friends for a long time, so we are busy organizing one at the moment. And hopefully I will be far less boring in future."

Elizabeth beamed at Owen. "I'm going to be fourteen in November and every proper young lady has to know how to dance, you know. It has been so long since you danced with me, I have practically forgotten how to do it. You must make amends and help me, don't you think?"

Owen looked at his uncle and both men couldn't resist laughing.

Chapter Ten
America and The Caribbean
November 1774 to June 1775

Owen was both frustrated and worried, and he let the concerns show on his face. John came over to stand beside him unbidden, shoulder to shoulder with Owen as they watched the last of the meagre load of corn they were fortunate to be able to purchase in Charleston loaded. The trader was grudging and hesitant as he agreed the deal, but the lure of Owen's gold was too strong to pass up.

"We did the best we could here, Owen."

"I know. I'm just worried for the people in Barbados. I'm not sure if the problem is because we are English or if it is the locals here think they are going to need everything for themselves."

"I suspect it is both, Owen. So, what do we do now?"

"Well, no one in the taverns wants to talk to us either, even when we pretend to be someone else like we did in Boston. Sir James was hoping we might pick something up, but no one is talking. This congress the colonies held in September has hardened everyone's positions. Sooner or later, this is going to explode on us. Anyway, I see nothing for it but to sail back to Barbados. Damn me, the only good thing about this trip is the bloody weather in Charleston in November is almost civilized for a change. Anyway, we can try the Spanish Main again next after we offload this corn in Bridgetown."

"Owen? I have a suggestion, but we will have to

be real careful if we do what I have in mind. Are you aware we have some false flags in storage?"

Owen turned and looked at John. "Really? No, I did not know this."

John grinned. "Your uncle is a clever fellow. He never had cause to use them, but he always liked to be prepared. So how do you feel about sailing under a Dutch flag for a bit?"

"Sure. And sail where?"

"Well, this is the other reason we will need to be extremely careful. I know some—people in Norfolk. I haven't seen them for a long time, but they were friends once and I think one or two of them still would be, unlike some of the other bastards we used to know there. If I'm seen by any of them, we could be in for some trouble."

"Hmm. And these true friends of yours could maybe help us with some supplies, of course. Well, what are we waiting for?"

***

A week later *The Sea Trader* sailed into the Chesapeake Bay and made for the extensive waterfront docks along the Elizabeth River. A Customs official boarded the ship but took little note of the Dutch flag flying at the masthead. Owen made up a story about the ship having been recently sold to the Dutch in case the official recognized the ship and wanted to see her papers, but the man paid only cursory attention. A small pouch of gold coins was the only thing attracting his interest, and he was soon on his way somewhere to enjoy it. John carefully surveyed the people passing by, but no one else seemed to be paying attention to them either.

"So where do we go from here, John?" said Owen.

"Leave it with me. I will be back before nightfall. It may take a while to find the people I am after. I suggest being ready to leave in a hurry, just in case. If I am not back by then, you know where to find me."

To ensure he was as unrecognizable as possible John had remained unshaven for the last week and for added measure he put on a hat as he stepped ashore. John had left the details of where to find him in a tavern three blocks from the waterfront if he didn't return. Owen settled in to wait, but found no lack of things to do for the rest of the day, for to his surprise there were three French flagged merchant ships and a French Navy frigate in port.

Owen desperately wanted to know what they were all doing here, but he dared not leave the ship to scout for information, fearing he might draw unwanted attention to *The Sea Trader*. Owen was concerned there would be other Dutch flagged ships in port with Captains who might want to come calling, but fortunately none were in sight.

As the day wore on Owen became increasingly more anxious and even reached a point where he was organizing a party to go after John when his First Mate finally appeared and made his way back aboard the ship. John scanned the docks in all directions and appeared to be satisfied he was not followed. He pointed in the direction of Owen's cabin so they could talk as soon as he gained the deck. Once inside John slumped into the chair opposite Owen's desk. Owen poured them both glasses of brandy, which John took gratefully to down half of it in one gulp. He sighed in gratitude as the strong liquor took hold.

"God, that's better. Been a long day. Damn near got caught, Owen. Thank God I still have one actual friend in this godforsaken place. Between the bastards who almost saw me and all the bloody Frenchmen around here, this place is risky business."

Owen was alarmed. "Do we need to get out of here right now?"

"I don't think so, but we dare not linger long. I've arranged with my friend for a small load of corn, some local vegetables, and a little tobacco. We can buy all the tobacco we want, but I didn't think you would want much. Delivery will be at dawn tomorrow morning. We pay gold for it, load it, and get out. Prices are no better than we got in Charleston."

"This is excellent, John. How did you almost get caught?"

"I almost got caught because I'm an idiot. Well, it was an acceptable risk, I suppose. It took me a while to find the man I was after. He's an old friend from my childhood. He doesn't give a shit about politics and he always sat on the fence, but he's a good man. Anyway, I went into this one tavern and found him, but I completely forgot this particular place was also like a second home to one of the people I really needed to avoid. Of course, he showed up. He arrived while I was out at the johnny house. He was carrying a couple of mugs back to his table and I just about stumbled right into him. My luck was with me, though. I saw him first and did what I could to avert my face. I am fairly sure he didn't see me."

"Johnny house?" said Owen. "What is a johnny house?"

"A place where you do your business, of course. It's what they call a latrine in these parts. Anyway, fortunately there was a crowd of drunken Frenchmen in the bar and somehow a fight started between them and some of the locals. Guess they aren't as friendly as they make out to be when they've had a few, eh? It gave my friend and I opportunity to get out of there fast."

"Did you pick up any news about all these Frenchmen?"

"Just that it would be impossible for us to acquire anything were it not for my friend. The French are buying up everything they can get their hands on. The reason the frigate is here is allegedly to escort the goods back to Martinique and Guadeloupe. Apparently, they claim to be fearful of English pirates. A bunch of horse crap, of course. The word is there have been a lot of fancy dressed people back and forth between the local Governor's office and the frigate, and I'm not talking just naval officers either. The rumour I heard is a bunch of representatives from other colonies are in town. This would be many of the same lot who were in Philadelphia last September."

"God Almighty. Right, we are leaving the second we get the last of goods on board. Well done, John."
***

The load of goods John arranged to purchase was indeed small and with the crew working hard they had it almost fully loaded a little over an hour past dawn. But they weren't fast enough.

"Trouble, Owen," said John, as he grabbed a cudgel and made his way to the gangplank.

Owen was caught unaware, as he was supervising two of the men lowering a crate into the hold. He turned and saw a crowd of close to a dozen men making their way toward his crew on the dock. All of them were wearing strips of cloth tied around their faces to mask everything below their eyes and they were armed with both clubs and knives.

By the time Owen reached the dock the fight was already well underway. Although his men on the dock were outnumbered, Owen had quickly alerted his men on the ship and within seconds reinforcements were on the way. The scene quickly became one of chaotic struggle as punches were thrown and clubs smashed down, bringing screams of pain. Owen was grateful for the foresight to ensure his men were always armed with at least some kind of weapon in any of the American ports.

Some of the weapons were knives and they were soon in use. At least three men had already been cut and were bleeding from slash wounds while continuing to struggle, flinging blood in all directions. John hammered a blow from his cudgel to the side of the head of an opponent who was about to stab one of *The Sea Trader's* crew in the back. Owen arrived on the scene with his sword, and he brandished it at two men who turned to meet him.

"Right, who wants it first?"

The two men feigned backing away before both rushed at him at once trying to overwhelm him with their clubs. Owen easily blocked one of them and sidestepped the other, slashing at the back of the second man as he fell forward off balance. The man screamed and crashed to the ground, as Owen's blade had caught him in his side and laid him open badly. The other tried to smash the club on Owen's head, but he was stopped in mid swing by Wilson, who grabbed him by the throat from behind and flung him backwards to land awkwardly against the few remaining crates still to be loaded.

With the momentum of the fight turning away from them, the remaining attackers all fled. John came over to join Owen as he surveyed the scene. Three of *The Sea Trader's* crew were injured and were being helped on board the ship. The attackers had fared worse, for five men still lay senseless where they had fallen. Of them, only the one Owen had slashed was dead.

"What in God's name was all this about?" said Owen. "Someone here had it in for us."

"Apparently somebody did see me last night, Owen. Despite the mask he was wearing I can tell you one of this lot was the fellow I was trying to avoid last night. Must have been one of his friends who recognized me."

Owen looked around and was glad they had chosen a spot to dock in an out of the way location. Despite what had happened, the hour was still early enough few people were about and no one had noticed the melee. The problem was Army patrols would be along soon and would inevitably stumble on the scene of the fight.

"Right. Let's get the rest of this loaded and get out of here. We can hide these men in this alley here to buy us time. Don't think we'll be coming back to Norfolk anytime soon."

***

The pile of correspondence from diplomats around the Caribbean seemed to have grown exponentially since the last time Owen was in Sir James Standish's office. He simply groaned when told of the fight and what Owen and John learned in Norfolk. After a long moment to think, he muttered to himself about having to follow up on the meaning of it all. Owen was given little time to rest, as Sir James handed him a letter from the Governor of Barbados, identifying Owen as being in the employ of the government. The letter also specifically gave him protection from paying Customs duties on anything. Sir James saw the puzzled look on Owen's face as he read the letter.

"Yes, I know this is strange, Mr. Spence. Matters are getting worse by the day here in Barbados and elsewhere. In fact, your uncle has authorized me to send you off to Jamaica immediately. You are to attend the Governor there the second you arrive, and he will give you a similar letter. Both Governors desire you to find food anywhere you can. Your uncle recommends trying the Spanish Main once again. There are others out there looking for supplies elsewhere, but the thinking is because of your past relationship with the Governor in Porto Bello you might do well. If you can find a cargo for

Jamaica and one for Barbados as you did before, both men will be eternally grateful. I will continue trying to keep my finger on the pulse of what is going on out there."

"Sir James, why are these letters even necessary?"

"Because the Royal Navy was given orders earlier to stop and seize any ship with cargo they believed was smuggling goods into British ports without paying duties. Once the Governors learned of it word was put out to cease and desist, but who knows how long it will take to reach all of the ships out there."

"I understand, Sir James. We will leave right away."

***

Owen wasn't concerned on sighting the frigate, for his lookout quickly identified it as a Royal Navy warship. *The Sea Trader* simply stayed her course, but the warship changed hers and Owen knew they were coming to investigate. Owen was hoping to make Kingston before nightfall, but stopping dashed those hopes. He and his crew were tired, for they had no time to take shore leave since first departing Barbados back in November, even spending Christmas at sea. With it now nearing the end of January, the only possibility of a brief break on the horizon was Jamaica.

As he waited to see what the warship would do, he thought back over the last three months. *The Sea Trader* had dashed into Kingston only long enough to collect the letter from the Jamaican Governor before heading back to sea. Governor Sanchez in

Porto Bello was unsurprised to see Owen once again and seemed well aware of what was going on elsewhere in the Caribbean. The only surprise was the generous mood the Governor seemed to be in, for he promised Owen two full loads of desperately needed food.

"Yes, I know what you are thinking, Captain Spence. Why is this happening? The answer is yes, our French friends were here once again, and this time they annoyed me to no end. More veiled threats and demands for supplies. I gave them as little as possible and said we must look after ourselves first. Of course, the other reason is you continue to pay me well."

The bark of the warship's forward chase gun interrupted Owen's thoughts. He gave orders to heave to and await the boarding party he knew would follow. A half hour later a party of Marines led by a Lieutenant who Owen had never met before came aboard.

He saw the officer's eyes narrow when Owen introduced himself, but the man gave no other sign of recognition. He immediately pressed Owen for details of what he was doing, and he soon made it clear he thought *The Sea Trader* was engaged in smuggling. Owen showed the officer his letters, which only made him frown.

"I have no orders about this, Captain Spence. All I know is you admit you are returning from Porto Bello with a load of goods, and you even admit you will not be paying duties in Jamaica. For all I know you have already stopped in Black River or Old Harbour and sold some of your smuggled load there."

"But I'm telling you I won't because this is what the Governor wants, sir. Read the letter."

After five minutes of more back and forth on the issue the Lieutenant was still uncertain, so Owen lost his patience.

"Look, for God's sake, if you can't make up your bloody mind, why don't we row over to talk to your Captain? Maybe he can."

The two men glared at each other for a long moment, but the Lieutenant was the one to finally look away.

"Right, let's go."

Boarding a Royal Navy warship once again brought back a host of mixed feelings to Owen, but he had little time to dwell on them as they were ushered straight in to see the Captain. As with the Lieutenant, Owen had never seen this man either, but the Captain made no effort to hide the fact he knew the name Owen Spence. Owen acknowledged who he was, but steered the conversation around to the topic at hand, explaining once again why he had the letters. The Captain frowned and it soon became clear he was going to be as indecisive as his Lieutenant. Owen pressed him to make a decision and the Captain pushed back.

"Mr. Spence, I have no orders about you. My orders do say I am to deal with smugglers, which you acknowledge you are. And these letters—well, how do I know these aren't clever forgeries? Given your history, why should I think otherwise?"

"God Almighty," said Owen, feeling his temper rising. "Sir, the letters are clear, and they bear the seals of the Governors. Look, the last time I talked to the Governor in Jamaica I was given to understand he is very good friends with your Admiral. Perhaps it would be an unwise career move to hinder someone on a mission from your Admiral's very good friend. And as for my history, you should not believe everything you hear, sir. A liar is born every minute. It is hardly reasonable to expect the Royal Navy wouldn't have its share, however small it may be."

"Good God, I've never heard such back talk," said the Captain, the blood rising to his face. "What are you saying, sir?"

"You heard me. Through no fault of my own, I am no longer a Navy officer, and this means I can say whatever I want. And what I want is for you to make a bloody decision so I can get on with the business the Governor of Jamaica has asked me to undertake. Sir."

The Captain glared in barely stifled anger at Owen for a long moment before he glanced at the Lieutenant still standing beside Owen.

"We will escort this bastard into Kingston," he said, before turning back to Owen. "God help you if you are lying to me."

***

As the crew rushed to offload their supplies under the watchful eyes of the men on the nearby frigate which had stopped them, Owen made his way once again to attend to the Governor. The Governor frowned in dismay at the treatment Owen had received and promised to address the matter promptly with the Admiral.

"We live in difficult times, Captain Spence. This is perhaps a sign of it, but I shall do what I can. Please give my warm regards to Sir James in Barbados."

Despite the need to get on the with the job, Owen knew he had to stop in and see Isabella once again, for it was well over a year since he saw her last. She was the only one there as he walked into The Spanish Rose and a smile lit her face as she recognized him. They rushed into each other's arms and held each other without speaking for a long time. Owen told her how much he had missed her, but had to confess he was only in Kingston for a short time. Tears began to fall down her cheek as he spoke. Owen pulled back, sensing something was different.

"Isabella? Are you all right?"

"Oh, Owen, I missed you so much. I—"

Owen frowned as he sensed a momentary hesitation on her part, but she closed her eyes as if wrestling with something inside for a few seconds. Before he could speak, she finally smiled once again. Stepping back, she pulled at his hand and pointed upstairs. An hour later their desire was sated, and Isabella nestled herself into his arm as Owen stroked her shoulder, marvelling at how he had forgotten the softness of her skin. He felt her sigh and shift her position to look at him.

"Owen? I have a confession I must make. I am a bad woman and should not be doing this. But you must understand I simply could not resist you one last time."

"One last time? What does that—oh, of course.

You have found someone, haven't you?"

"I have. He is a good man, Owen. He is ten years older than me and a widower, also like me. He runs a successful business in Spanish Town. His wife passed away a year ago and he needs companionship, as do I. He wants me to sell The Spanish Rose and open a new business there. I—I have agreed, Owen. We are to be married in a few months. The opportunity to be closer to my daughter is there, too. I hope you understand."

"Understand? My God, I am so very happy for you. I've been hoping something like this would happen. Isabella, we both knew we were on different paths in life, didn't we? But I have loved every second of our time together and I will never forget you."

Isabella rolled over to straddle him, her breasts brushing across his chest as she leaned back to look at him. She bit her lip briefly before she smiled.

"You can still come and visit me, of course. But we won't have more time like this. As I said, he is older, and I expect he will not be anything like the man you are when he finally takes me to his bed. So, I will never forget you either. And now I think perhaps you should give me something else to remember, while you still have time?"

Owen laughed and pulled her closer.
***

The weather outside the port of Boston in early April was far less pleasant than the last time *The Sea Trader* made her way there. The reception they got was also different. One of a number of Royal Navy warships on blockade duty detached herself from the rest and came straight for her as soon as it became clear from their course she was making for the port. Owen reduced sail and ordered the ship to heave to while they awaited being boarded.

This time Owen was prepared with letters from both Sir James Standish and the Admiral on station in Barbados authorizing *The Sea Trader* to pass. The Lieutenant boarding her scrutinized both the letters and Owen carefully, but found no fault and he returned them. He peered about the deck, specifically looking at the cannons *The Sea Trader* now carried.

"Captain Spence, we will signal you are approved to pass. A word of advice, in case you are in the area again? You should ensure your men are trained and ready to use your weapons. These damned rebels have begun harassing us and it is getting worse. Their ships are small and no real challenge to a frigate, but they are fast and would pose a threat to you. We cannot be everywhere. Good day, sir."

The scene in the port itself was a stark contrast to what it normally was. Finding a spot to tie up wasn't a problem, for plenty of room was available despite a host of warships and troop transports of various sizes already being docked. Civilians were scarce ashore while soldiers were in abundance. Owen was stopped twice by patrols questioning him about who he was and what business he had being on the streets.

Although small mail packet ships criss-crossed the world on a regular basis between England and her colonies, there were only so many of them, and this was why Owen had recently found himself doing little more than delivering mail more and more frequently given the situation. In this case he was delivering yet more correspondence from Sir James to his counterpart Sir Ross Stanhope once again. Sir Ross bid Owen to wait while he read the letter and composed a quick reply for *The Sea Trader* to return. He sighed as he sealed the letter and gave it to Owen.

"There is no good news to report on the diplomatic front. Based on what I know, unless we have a miracle there will be a battle soon and maybe many more to follow. On the other hand, I have managed to find a couple of sources I am reasonably certain of. I think some kind of plot is in the wind, but I have no details yet. Please assure Sir James I will correspond the second I learn anything of consequence."

"I shall do so. Sir Ross? I am commanded to make brief stops to see if I can acquire any more provisions on our journey back to Barbados. We have had limited success in Charleston and Norfolk in past, but I fear we won't get very far this time. Do you think we might fare better in any of the other ports along the coast? New York perhaps?"

Sir Ross shook his head. "I highly doubt it. I've received reports the locals in New York and other settlements here in the north can best be described as boiling with anger. If you had luck in past further south, I suggest you stick with what worked. If it were not for supplies being brought in by sea, we would already be going hungry here in Boston. I've heard it's even worse for Bermuda, too. By the way,

I assume the Navy told you they are being harassed at sea near the port?"

"They did, sir."

"You should be wary wherever you go now. If this turns into a full-blown war, as I fear it is about to, this tactic of harassing our ships will not stay limited to the Boston area for long. Good day, sir."

***

Owen and John puzzled over their next move when Owen returned to the ship.

"Owen? What about trying North Carolina before Charleston. We haven't been to Wilmington yet. I don't know anyone there, but it might be worth a shot."

Owen frowned and they went to study charts of the area in his cabin, for they had not been there before. After doing so he shook his head.

"I don't like this. If there are unpleasant welcoming committees waiting for us along this coast, this would be a perfect place for it. Sailing up this Cape Fear River would be a mistake, too. Far too many places they could hide and wait for us, and limited room to escape if we needed to."

Given what happened in Norfolk on their last visit, Owen decided to bypass it too on their return journey.

"No, Charleston it is," he said. "It'll be late April by the time we get there. At least the bloody weather won't be as bad yet."

Sir Ross Stanhope's prediction proved prophetic far sooner than Owen expected. They were still well north of the entrance to Charleston harbour when a sloop similar in size to *The Sea Trader* came out from an offshore island straight for them. Owen was suspicious and had the men ready the cannons as he adjusted their course to meet the challenge. He knew for certain something was odd when his lookout called down in a puzzled voice.

"Captain? She is flying a flag I've never seen before. It looks to have a bunch of red and white stripes, with some sort of a white patch in the top corner."

As he finished speaking the ship fired her forward chase gun. Although the shot fell well short the message was clear, with it aimed directly at them.

"Owen?" said John. "Do we run, or do we fight?"

"Hmm. I'd say it was a four-pound chase gun. Well, we do both. Our mission isn't to be a combatant, but it doesn't mean we will let them off easily. As Sir Ross suspected, apparently sailing these waters is a bad idea now. I don't know if the military ashore know about this rogue, but it is no matter. We can deliver a friendly goodbye to them as our starboard side passes shortly and we will just keep sailing south."

The mystery ship fired their chase gun a second time a minute later as they came ever closer, but this time *The Sea Trader* responded. Four six-pounders and a small carronade were on each side of the ship, along with a four-pound gun forward, but it was the six pounders roaring out to engage their foe. As the smoke belching from the guns cleared Owen saw the shots fell just short of the bow of the mystery ship, almost exactly where he intended.

"Well shot!" he called, as their foe immediately changed course to one which would carry them out of range. Once satisfied they were in no further danger Owen stood the gun crews down. He turned to John and sighed.

"Let's hope the reception we get elsewhere is a little more pleasant."

***

Having to fight rough weather off the coast resulted in a much slower journey than Owen anticipated, making it the end of April when they finally reached Charleston. As he stepped ashore once again he saw the tension on the faces of people nearby was obvious. Army patrols were everywhere. Owen made his way to find a trader they had realized the most success with and found him in his office near the waterfront. The man sighed as he looked at Owen.

"You have not heard, have you? No, if you were caught at sea in the storm you wouldn't know, would you? Captain Spence, war is upon us. The British forces in Boston attempted to capture a store of weapons from the rebel forces, but they had intelligence of the move and they did not succeed. A significant engagement was fought as a result. They are calling them the Battles of Lexington and Concord, although I gather it was really just one big battle. Regardless, we are at war. I despair for the future, sir."

Owen was not surprised the man was despondent. Like many other men of business Owen dealt with in both the Caribbean and in America, he was being torn in ways he had not looked for. Like the others, this man still felt his loyalties to England strongly, but he was also a born American. On top of it all, he had to make a living. After commiserating with the man for a while longer Owen made his pitch, expecting to be rebuffed. The trader sighed and remained silent for a long time before he finally responded.

"Captain Spence, we have done business in the past and you know I have struggled to stay neutral in all of this madness. I just want to be able to run my business and feed my family. The day I feared is now here and I must make a choice. I have a small supply of corn people do not know about in one of my storehouses. Because we have done business before and I respect you, I will sell you a portion of it. Fortunately, it is not far from where your ship is docked. Your men will have to smuggle it to your ship at night. But Captain? Do me a favour and call upon me no more. This is my home. I will not consider doing this again."

***

Owen was appalled at the meagre the load of supplies he was forced to return to Barbados with, but nothing could be done. By the time they docked in Bridgetown once again it was the second week of May and the grim look on his uncle's face as he met them at the dock left no need for him to ask about the situation. They made their way to Sir James's office and Owen quickly debriefed both men. The dire looks remained when he was done. As they dismissed him, they thanked him for his efforts and told him to stand ready.

"We are having a meeting with the Governor and

his council shortly, Owen," said Sir James. "I fear drastic measures are needed to keep the population fed. Stand ready, for I may need you soon yet again."

The summons to attend Sir James came in early June. Owen found both Sir James and Owen's uncle awaiting him. The two men made no effort to hide the lines of worry on their faces. Both were clutching at full glasses of brandy as Owen came in. Sir James waved at the decanter on the nearby sideboard.

"Help yourself, Mr. Spence," said Sir James. "We both felt the need today and you will too."

"I am sorry we have not had time for you, Owen," said his uncle. "Barbados is on a war footing now and in such times there are no lack of matters to attend to. We are making efforts to increase the size of our fishing fleet. The plantation owners are also grudgingly doing the best they can to grow more foodstuffs and less sugarcane. Adding to their complaints is they are having to borrow money, and no one likes doing it."

"Well, they may have to get used to it, Alan," said Sir James, after downing a good portion of his drink. "Unfortunately, this rebellion is showing no signs of stopping and, in fact, I have heard rumours from both the Navy and other merchants it is getting worse. In any case, we did not call you here to fill you in on our sad situation, Mr. Spence."

"No," said Owen's uncle. "As much as it would be desirable to have you see if our friend Governor Sanchez can help us once again, we need you to go back to Boston. I've had word from others the

Governor in Porto Bello has become a little—stingy lately, so this time I am going myself with one of my other ships. We are not sure why this is happening, but we suspect the damn French. As I have always had an excellent relationship with him, it seems best I go in your stead. Sir James has concerns about Boston, you see."

"I do. Sir Ross Stanhope led me to believe something was afoot in his last communication. I am hearing rumour the rebel colonies may have held another of these damn congresses, as they call them. I simply must know more. The thing is, I have a contact in Wilmington who may have what I need, so I am going there to learn what I can. While I am at it, I will try to purchase some provisions, but I am not optimistic. So, this leaves you to sail to Boston, sir."

"Of course, Sir James. Aside from contacting Sir Ross, do you have any other orders for me?"

"No. There is no point in trying to find more provisions. We simply must find a way to survive on our own. I must warn you this may be a dangerous trip, Mr. Spence. The word from my Navy colleagues is matters have escalated since you were there. The blockade is still being maintained, but the rebels seem to be putting enormous pressure on. And it is not just pressure on our naval forces, sir. Boston is effectively under a full siege. The rebel forces encircled the city shortly after you were there last. I fear Boston is at the heart of all this."

"The men and I are not afraid, sirs. We will be underway with the dawn."

Chapter Eleven
America and The Caribbean
July 1775

By the time they were offshore of Boston once again it was the beginning of July, but Owen had little opportunity to enjoy the pleasant weather. Two rebel sloops lurking behind one of the Boston harbour islands dashed out hard after them as they tacked toward the harbour, forcing *The Sea Trader* to use every scrap of sail to try and outrun them.

Fortunately for Owen, a Royal Navy frigate guarding the harbour saw what was happening and came to the rescue, chasing the rebels away. When safe to do so Owen had *The Sea Trader* heave to so she could be boarded once again. The officer who appeared wore a sceptical look at Owen as he told him they wanted to enter the port, but he read Owen's authorization letters and agreed to escort them the rest of the way in.

As they drew closer the sound of occasional cannon fire on the horizon all around the city grew ever louder. After docking once again Owen soon realized this time the only other ships in the harbour were military. Soldiers were on guard on every street corner and no civilians were in sight. A pair of Army officers were waiting for them and boarded *The Sea Trader* the second they tied up, demanding to know their business. Once Owen explained who they were and showed them the letters, the officer in charge turned to the other.

"Go find an escort for this man. Captain Spence, deliver your message and do it fast. I know who Sir

Ross is. Please ask him to be quick about a response. I want you out of here as soon as possible. The situation here is—fluid. We have a host of civilians still in the city under our protection. Most will not be a problem, but some I think have rather suspect loyalties. I cannot guarantee your safety, so get on with it, please."

As Owen walked through the streets to Sir Ross Stanhope's office with two soldiers escorting him an occasional face peered out from behind drawn curtains, but he encountered no one other than more soldiers as he went. Sir Ross was fortunately in his office when Owen arrived. Owen was shocked at how tired and drawn the man looked. Sir Ross wordlessly waved him into the chair before his desk, poured him a brandy, and reached for the letter Owen had ready for him. He slumped back in his chair when he finished the letter and downed a portion of his own drink.

"Well, Mr. Spence, thank you for bringing this. Your arrival here at this juncture is fortunate timing. Yes, I must prepare my own letter in return for Sir James. You had difficulty entering the port, I expect?"

"It was a close affair, but the Navy interceded on our behalf, sir."

Sir Ross nodded. "Indeed. Matters have not improved since your last visit. While I am not a military man, I think even I can see we are in big trouble here. The city is under total siege now. The Army is doing what they can, but they are paying the price. You of course don't know there was a major battle at a place called Bunker Hill a little over two weeks ago. The Army wanted to establish control over some of the unoccupied hills surrounding the city in order to gain full control of the harbour, but our foes somehow learned of their manoeuvre. The Army believes they won the battle, but I question the notion. They achieved their objective, but it seems they lost far more men than the rebels and in particular they lost several senior officers."

"Good Lord, I can't believe it has come to this."

"Well, it has. And there is more. Sir James mentioned in his letter he heard rumour the rebels held another one of these congresses of theirs. I can confirm it is not rumour. They have not declared independence, but this congress has taken very large steps toward it. They are effectively a running a national government now. They've organized an army and have appointed leaders. I hear they have even nominated ambassadors. I shall detail all this in my letter, of course. But there is one other matter, and you may be able to help with this."

"Sir? I will do what I can."

"The few informants still willing to talk to me have picked up a very faint hint of something. Apparently there really may be some sort of plot being hatched and I have serious concerns about it. Absolutely nothing is certain, but the remote possibility exists it involves Bermuda. I cannot fathom why this would be. But the key point which perhaps lends this vague whisper some credence is if something is going on, it involves someone we already have questions about. You recall this man Colonel Tucker and his family? The rumour is he attended this congress in June, although exactly why is a mystery. I believe he has left and is on his way back to Bermuda, if he has not already long since returned."

"This does seem odd, Sir Ross. I met them and yes, it is clear at least some members of the Tucker family are very sympathetic to the rebels. But I got the impression the Colonel himself was very torn about it all, which makes it strange he would be the one in attendance. I wonder if they are trying to raise funds or even a levy of sympathizers from the island to support the rebels?"

"I expect anything is possible, Captain Spence. Perhaps he was trying to call for cooler heads to prevail. The problem is this situation has evolved to a point where you can no longer have it both ways. You are either a loyalist or a rebel now. People in the middle are going to get caught in the crossfire."

"Sir James wanted me to return as soon as possible, but I think he would understand if I were to divert to Bermuda on my way home. If there is anything to learn there, I can have word sent to you here or return myself."

"Excellent. It is good to see you again, Captain, but I must ask you to leave as getting sleep is difficult these days. Any sleep I will get tonight will only be after I get these letters prepared and sent to you. I will give you a letter to the Governor in Bermuda also. I think the man is a bit naive about the motivations of some of the people he leads, but this is his choice. All I can do is raise a flag if I see a concern. And Captain? I will ask for a naval escort at dawn to get you well out to sea. We cannot have you sunk or captured, can we?"

"I appreciate your consideration, Sir Ross. We will be alert for your messenger. Stay safe, sir."

Night had fallen by the time Owen left Sir Ross's office. All the way back to the ship Owen could hear the crackle of sporadic, distant musket fire from all different directions, some of which sounded near enough to make it clear why Sir Ross wasn't sleeping well at night. Owen found John standing in silence with arms folded on the deck of *The Sea Trader* staring out at the horizon. John remained silent as Owen joined him and looked around. The fires of both armies raised a flickering red light of varying intensity in a vast semi-circle which they knew encompassed the entire landward horizon. Haze from the smoke of cannon fire rose to meet the shifting clouds of the night sky above it all, with the garish fire light reflecting off it all.

Both men were startled when a number of distant cannons all barked out within seconds of each other from one spot on the horizon. A crackle of musket fire reached a crescendo from the same location following the cannon fire. Five minutes later the fighting died down almost as quickly as it began, but over the next hour the scene repeated itself in several different locations.

"John? This is going to go on all night. You may as well try and get some sleep. I'll stand watch and wait for a bit longer for Sir Ross's letters. I'd like to get out of here by dawn."

The letters were delivered by an Army officer close to midnight, along with an ominous verbal message.

"Captain Spence? Sir Ross advises he requested a naval escort for you, but I'm afraid your departure may be delayed. The rebels have made a push against us, as you have undoubtedly noticed. They have apparently done so on the water as well and I gather the Navy is a bit stretched. You are to remain docked until further notice."

***

Sir Ross Stanhope was looking no less haggard than the last time Owen saw him when he appeared on the dock looking for permission to board *The Sea Trader* almost a week later. Within moments the two men were alone in Owen's cabin sharing a glass of wine each.

"Apologies, Mr. Spence. I'm sure you thought everyone had forgotten you. Maybe everyone else did, but I did not. Nothing to do with you. It turns out the Navy had issues with a couple of their frigates on station, requiring them to seek the attention of the Halifax Naval Dockyard. As you might expect, this was a rather inopportune time. I don't know if the rebels decided to seize the moment seeing how thin the blockade was. In any case, we now have reinforcements at hand. A frigate is being detached to come inshore and escort you far enough out to sea to ensure your safety. It is now the third week of July, sir. I am not a sailor, but even I know hurricane season is a concern. Are you still willing to undertake the trip to Bermuda?"

"Sir, you need not fear for us. If we discover anything of consequence to communicate to you, I will consider the situation at the time. One way or another I will get the news to you, though."

"Excellent. Everything I have put in the letter I have also shared with you. The Governor may want to quiz you about your own experience here. Safe travels, Captain Spence."

***

The weather in Bermuda in late July was perfect as they sailed into St. George's harbour once again. Owen saw no one warranting attention as he scanned the ships tied up along the docks. Aside from perhaps a few extra soldiers about the town of St. George's, nothing was there to alert anyone a fierce war was underway not far from their shores. Leaving John and the rest of the crew to look to the ship Owen took the message from Sir Ross and made his way to the Governor's offices. After identifying himself and announcing his purpose he waited for ten minutes before being ushered in to the see him.

Owen found the Governor was not alone. A Royal Navy Captain Owen did not know was with him. The Governor introduced the two men, but the Captain didn't smile and only returned the briefest handshake after hesitating for an obvious moment to think about doing it. The Governor noticed and tried to smooth it over by moving the conversation on.

"Captain Spence, I was just finishing a meeting with Captain Sanders here. When I heard you bore a message from Sir Ross, I asked him to stay. Captain Sanders is the senior Royal Navy officer in Bermuda and is aware of the role Sir Ross plays for us. I expect the message could be of interest to him as well."

"Of course, Governor," said Owen as he passed the envelope across.

"Thank you. Please stay, I think we might also both like to hear your thoughts on how matters stand in Boston."

Silence descended as the Governor slit the envelope open and began reading. The message wasn't long and after two minutes the Governor finished reading it, but he frowned and went back to reread one part. He was still frowning and looking thoughtful as he finally passed it over to the Navy officer.

"Oh dear, this is a surprise. Hmm, I'd like to hear what you make of this, Captain Sanders."

The officer raised an eyebrow as he took the letter and began reading. A minute later he made an inarticulate choking noise before shaking his head to recover himself. He peered up momentarily at the Governor with a look of disbelief on his face before carrying on reading. When he finally finished the letter, he threw it on the desk in front of the Governor.

"Well, the situation in Boston is about what we feared it might be, so there is no surprise there. The rest of it is a load of bloody rot. I don't know where this kind of utter nonsense comes from."

"Captain Spence," said the Governor. "Are you aware of the contents of this letter?"

"Sir Ross said he had told me everything, yes."

"And have you had anything to do with this beyond being the messenger, sir?" said Captain Sanders.

Owen was caught off guard by the question and

stared in surprise at Captain Sanders, who was wearing a suspicious look on his face. Owen felt his blood rising as he realized the implications, but he strove to be civil as he grated out a careful response.

"Sir, I have no idea if you are suggesting something untoward. Sir Ross confided his message to me. I carried it here. If you have concerns beyond this, you need to be clearer about it."

"Captain Spence," said the Governor, hastily interrupting. "I think Captain Sanders may have concerns about what Sir Ross has mentioned about Colonel Tucker."

"I certainly bloody do," said Captain Sanders. "Colonel Tucker is a fine gentleman and one of the leading citizens of Bermuda. This is a load of scurrilous nonsense. The members of the Smithe family I know are all fine gentlemen. And this is all I am saying, Mr. Spence. Governor, I have other matters to attend to. If you have no further need of me, I should like to depart."

"Yes, of course, Captain. Please understand what you read in the letter is highly confidential, sir. Thank you for coming today."

The Captain nodded stiffly, ignoring Owen as he rose from his seat, and wished the Governor good day before departing in silence. The Governor sighed as the door closed behind him, turning to see the obvious anger suffusing Owen's face.

"I am sorry about this, Captain Spence. I wouldn't have asked him to stay if I had realized the message was going to contain this reference to Colonel Tucker."

"It is not your fault the man is a rude buffoon,

sir. But help me understand, please. I assume the reference to the Smithe family relates to my history, of course. Does this link with something I am not aware of?"

"It does. Captain Sanders is married to a cousin of the Captain Smithe who you once reported to. And you are likely not aware the Tucker family are also closely related by marriage to the Smithe family. This is why you may have noticed I was somewhat dismayed when I read the message. Unfortunately, I was already committed to showing it to him."

"I see. Well, this makes it all clearer. Governor, I have no idea whether the intelligence Sir Ross has come up with is valid, but I can assure you he seemed very concerned about it. Matters are not good in Boston, sir. I think he fears that if there is indeed some nefarious plot underway, it could be enough to turn the tide away from us."

The Governor was silent for several long moments, before finally throwing his hands wide in obvious frustration.

"I don't know what to say, Captain Spence. I know Sir Ross well and respect his opinion. The problem is I have nothing to go on here. There are innumerable reasons Colonel Tucker may have been present at this congress of theirs. You must understand their family established themselves on this island long, long ago and their ties to the colonies on the continent are deep. Maybe he just went there to ensure he understood their thinking and the overall situation? Captain, I can and will talk to him about this, but I don't know what else I can do. If the man is involved in something, he is obviously not about to tell me."

"This is true, sir. I think Sir Ross was hoping you may have picked up some intelligence of your own and this might help to lay bare what is going on. Well, I have a little time. I will remain here for a bit before I return to Barbados. We will nose about and see if we hear anything of interest. If we do, I shall certainly bring it to your attention."

"Thank you for bringing this message, Captain. I confess the only thing which might support this concern is I haven't seen the Colonel around the island for some time, but this isn't really unusual. To be completely honest with you, I doubt this intelligence very much. The people on this island have always looked out for themselves first, sir. They have no choice, because we would starve if we didn't. Speaking of which, have you brought any stores for us?"

"Unfortunately, no. It is nigh impossible to find food anywhere now."

The Governor sighed. "Well, I'm afraid this is still the real problem as far as I am concerned. It is weighing on me so much I find I am dreaming about it at night. Good day, sir."

Although he had done his best not to show it, Owen's anger and frustration at his treatment by the Navy officer had not abated and he found himself stewing over it as he made his way back to the ship. He was so lost in thought he wasn't paying close attention to his surroundings and he almost stumbled into a small group of men walking off a ship onto the dock. With a start Owen realized the ship was Le Mystere and the three men now standing and talking were Paul Allarde, William Bains, and Colonel Tucker. The Colonel was carrying a small luggage case.

Owen ducked into a nearby doorway as none of the men had noticed him as yet. Peering around the corner he saw them finish their conversation and shake hands. The Colonel left and began walking away down the street while the others went back on board Le Mystere. To Owen's surprise the crew freed the ship from her tethers to the shore and made sail. Within minutes she was underway, heading for the harbour entrance and open sea.

Owen made his way slowly back along the waterfront to where *The Sea Trader* was tied up. The ship was far enough away he thought it unlikely anyone aboard would have noticed Le Mystere, but he was wrong. John was waiting for him as Owen reached the deck.

"Owen? You won't believe who I just saw—"

"You just saw Le Mystere, I know. I saw them too."

"I don't understand. We would have seen them when we came into port. I happened to see them leaving a few minutes ago, though. Owen, what is going on here?"

Owen signalled to make for his cabin so they could talk in private. Once there he told John what he had learned from the Governor.

"I don't think we are going anywhere for a while, John," said Owen as he finished. "I have the same question as you, but if I had to guess about Le Mystere I'd say the reason we didn't see her originally is she actually wasn't here then. I think she stopped to simply drop off a passenger, who just happened to be Colonel Tucker. So yes, if we do nothing else, we really need to find out what is going on."

***

Colonel Henry Tucker was tired from having endured his second trip to the continent in less than three months. His first visit to attend the second continental congress in Philadelphia was a less hurried affair, for the discussions were long and there were many delegates from the colonies who all needed to be heard. His latest trip was the opposite, for the situation in America was evolving far quicker than he anticipated.

On reaching his home he had word sent to his son in law of his return and for him to attend him as soon as possible. After washing up, the Colonel slumped into his desk chair. He poured himself a brandy and downed a good portion as he sat back to await his visitor. Although all he wanted was to take to his bed for a long rest, he knew he had little choice but to set in motion the plan he had agreed to. William Bains and the other men of the committee of correspondence made it clear there was no time to waste.

A knock on the door announced his visitor and the Colonel called for him to enter. Somerset Henry entered and sat in the chair before the desk as the Colonel poured him a drink without bothering to ask whether he wanted one. Somerset remained politely silent, waiting for the old man to begin. The Colonel sighed.

"Well, God knows I tried, Somerset. The Americans drive a hard bargain, and they are not budging one bit. You know I don't want us to be involved in this, but I do not see other options. I assume the situation has not improved since I left?"

"It has not, Colonel. They weren't even interested in larger quantities of the salt?"

"I tried arguing this yet again. Salt in great quantities is not what they need. And since all we can offer in trade is salt from Turk's Island, we have little choice. And yes, I tried the last resort of gold. The gold would be useful to them, but they aren't interested. The problem is they know they have us in a corner with little choice. I appealed to their sensibilities about our long friendship with them, but this didn't work either. I had not thought true friends would behave this way."

"Colonel, they are true friends of ours. The issue here is they are in a corner, too. This is why we need to work with them and find a solution which gets both of us out of our respective corners. We must have the food and supplies only they can provide. So is our course of action from here on agreed?"

The Colonel sighed once again. "It is. The date is set for August 14th, just under two weeks from now. I am hoping this is enough time for you to make the arrangements."

"Plenty of time, Colonel. All we really need do is find enough men for the job, which I do not foresee is a problem. I need to talk to some people and work it out. I will send word when we are ready. What about the location? Is it where we agreed?"

"It is."

"Very good, Colonel," said Somerset Henry, downing the remainder of his drink and rising to leave. "I know you fret about the consequences of this, but I am certain with every part of my being this is the right path for us. We must stay true to our friends. Good day, Colonel."

As the door closed behind him the Colonel sighed one more time and downed the remainder of his drink. He shook his head in dismay as he spoke aloud to himself.

"We will be true to our friends, but what about allegiance to our homeland? What will the cost of losing it be?"

Colonel Tucker needed no one to respond to his question, for he already knew what the answer was. Wearily rising from his chair, he shuffled off to his bed.

***

Owen was increasingly torn as the days passed. All the signs pointed to something being afoot, but he saw no easy way to learn more. Both he and John had taken to slowly making friends along the docks and spending time in the local taverns to try and learn what they could. Frustrated at their lack of progress they enlisted the entire crew in the job, even providing them money to spend in the taverns. The men couldn't believe their good fortune and needed no further encouragement.

Owen seized the opportunity presented by a mail packet ship from England which briefly came into port to prepare a report to send onward to Sir Ross in Boston. He also sent a letter to Sir James in

Barbados, but he knew he might reach the island long before his letter.

Both his uncle and Sir James would grow concerned the later the days stretched into August and Owen shared the worry. But if a plot really was underway, solving the mystery of what was happening was critically important. The problem of bringing his ship and crew safely back to Barbados was also a responsibility not to be ignored. With every passing day the possibility of sailing south straight into the path of a hurricane grew exponentially.

If something was going on, however, it was not obvious. The people of Bermuda went about their normal daily business while giving no sign of anything untoward. The talk in the taverns was mostly about the food shortages, for the Governor had instituted a rudimentary form of rationing. The expectation was it would be getting much worse before it got better.

Owen knew he faced the same challenge. He was carefully monitoring his own supplies on the ship and was already contemplating his own rationing plan for whenever the journey back to Barbados began. He knew he had little time left by the middle of August and with little to show for his efforts, he would have to depart soon.

He kept convincing himself they would find something. Two members of his crew were in a tavern one evening and overheard part of a conversation at a nearby table between three local men talking about being recruited for work. After casually signalling they had overheard mention of recruitment, Owen's men pretended to be on the lookout for different work and asked about it. The locals quickly rebuffed them and refused to talk. Owen knew he had little enough to go on, but the incident gave him hope they would learn something sooner or later. But with it now being mid-August, his hopes were virtually gone.

"Well, another night with nothing to show for it, Owen," said John, after finishing the last of the ale in his mug. "What do you think, is it time to leave for Barbados?"

"I fear we can't delay any longer. I think we leave tomorrow morning," said Owen, peering about the tavern.

Earlier in the evening the room was packed with people, but most were long gone to their beds by this time. The owner of the tavern waiting patiently behind the bar yawned and looked bored enough to fall asleep where he stood. Owen reached into his pocket and threw enough coins on the table to pay for their drinks.

He was about to rise from his chair when he saw John give a small start and look toward the door. Owen turned and saw Wilson Jones coming over to their table in a rush. Owen's heart soared as he sensed from the sailor's look he was bringing news. Wilson peered about to ensure they were alone, before slipping into a chair beside Owen.

"Sirs, I have a possibility for you. You must come now. I will explain on our way."

As soon as they got outside Wilson once again looked around to ensure they weren't being observed before he pointed down the street, continuing his story as he waved for them to follow him. He set off walking at a fast pace with the two men following close behind.

"Sir, I was in Madam Sweet's with a girl tonight and we got to talking. She claims to have information, but it will cost you and we must swear to forget we ever saw her once the deal is done. She has agreed to wait for us behind Madam Sweet's, but she won't stay long. We must hurry. I hope you have some gold on you, Captain?"

The flicker of hope in Owen's heart flamed brighter as he struggled to keep pace, for he knew Madam Sweet's was one of two popular local brothels in St. George's.

"I do, but perhaps not as much as she maybe wants. But what does she claim to have? And why the urgency?"

"She would not tell me what exactly she knows, sir. But she claimed what will happen is set for tonight."

Within minutes they reached the brothel located near the edge of town and worked their way around to the rear of the building. With little to light their way beyond the dim moonlight struggling to penetrate a high layer of night clouds they were forced to pick their way with care. Wilson slowed his pace and called out in a low voice as he peered about in the gloom.

"Minnie? Where are you? I am back and I have my friends."

A dark figure detached herself from behind a nearby tree she was hiding behind and came over to where the three men stood. As she came closer

Owen saw she was a young black woman. She peered about to satisfy herself they weren't being watched before she spoke.

"Have you brought the gold?"

"Ah—Minnie is your name?" said Owen. "I have some with me. I am this man's Captain. What do you have for us?"

"Show me the gold."

"We have not negotiated a price."

"I have information you want, and you need it now, because tomorrow is too late," said the woman, before finally relenting and naming a sum.

"My God, I do not have that much on me. I would be insane to carry such a large amount of gold around."

The woman groaned in frustration. "Show me what you have, or I will leave."

Owen sighed and pulled out his coin pouch and emptied the contents into his palm. As heavy as his pouch was with coins, it wasn't enough to satisfy her.

"Not good enough," she said. "I am leaving."

"Wait," said John. "Captain, let me add what I have."

After he did so the woman wavered, but Wilson pulled another small fistful of coins from his pocket. The final sum needed both of Owen's hands to hold.

"Madam, this is the best we can do right now. I would have to return to my ship to get more, but you have still not convinced me whatever you have is worth this. What we have here is substantial."

Owen could see the struggle between greed and

desire to leave on her face. She finally gave an exasperated sigh and reached for the money, stuffing it all into the pockets of her dress.

"It will have to do. I cannot linger here any longer. Madam Sweet must not find out I am no longer in my room with this man. You seek to know what is happening tonight? Do you know the storehouse the Army has near Retreat Hill Road, not far from Tobacco Bay? Make your way there now and you will find what you are after."

"A storehouse?" said John, looking puzzled. "What does this have to do with anything? Are you certain about this?"

Even in the dim light Owen could see the look of scorn on her face as she responded.

"Of course I am certain, you fool. Do you think me an idiot? Men talk to whores when they shouldn't all the time. They all think I have no ears and no brain, either. But I am not going to be a whore forever and this will help free me sooner than later. I must go."

As she took a step back a wicked looking dirk appeared in her hand from wherever she had secreted it on her body. She brandished it at each of them in turn.

"You did not hear this from me, and I will deny ever having met any of you. If you expose me, I swear I will find a way to kill all of you."

With this she was gone, leaving the three men looking at each other. John grunted as he watched her disappear into the night, before turning to Wilson.

"You have an interesting taste in women. Well,

do either of you know what she is talking about?"

Owen was rubbing his chin and furiously searching his memory of past sojourns about the island when a flash of insight finally struck, and he groaned aloud.

"What?" said both Wilson and John in unison.

"There are a couple of forts on the hills on the other side of the island here, but now I think on it, I recall the military has a number of storehouses for all manner of goods in the area, too. But consider it, gentlemen. If you accept the notion a military storehouse is the target, now give thought to what it is that the rebels are probably most in need of?"

A momentary silence descended before John groaned aloud too.

"Oh, shit. It's gunpowder they are after, isn't it?"

Chapter Twelve
Bermuda
August 1775

Owen remained standing with arms folded, deep in thought as he stared into space. John finally broke the silence, a worried tone to his voice.

"My God, what are we going to do, Owen?"

"Do you want me to go back to the ship and rouse the crew, sir?" said Wilson.

Owen sighed as he made his decision. "No, let's go see what is happening. I need more information here. It's already well past midnight and I can't go disturbing the Governor with something this vague. The woman has no reason to lie to us, but she has our money and may already be on the run to escape if she was indeed lying. Are you two armed?"

Both men had small dirks, as did Owen, while he was the only one with a sword.

"It will have to do. Let's go. It won't take more than twenty minutes to walk there."

The route Owen chose was a winding road hugging the contours of the land taking them past Tobacco Bay first. As they crested the final small hill blocking their view the three men all stopped in their tracks. The moonlight was still dimmed, but enough was there to see a sight none of them were expecting. Two small warships were not far offshore of the bay, while pulled up on the beach of Tobacco Bay itself were three of the thirty-foot whaling boats commonly in use in Bermuda. A crowd of close to forty men were lounging by the boats doing nothing.

"Well, I don't know what business these ships have out there at this time of night, but I'd say this is a sign she wasn't lying to us," said John. "Where to from here, Owen?"

"We carry on. Just being out there isn't a crime. Let's go. I'm going to hug the side of the road and the treeline, so they hopefully won't spot us. Single file and keep your eyes and ears open."

The road began to wind eastward as it rounded the crest of a smaller hill leading down to the Tobacco Bay beach. After a few minutes walking Owen heard the unmistakable sound of distant voices further up the road in the direction they were going. He raised a hand to call a halt near an intersection with a small side road.

"They don't seem to be hiding their presence, do they? I am fairly certain Retreat Hill road is a short distance ahead. I think we are in danger of being discovered if we carry on further on this route. If they are doing what I think they are doing, they will be coming this way with their stolen goods."

"What do we do, Owen?"

"Let's work our way around to the flank. I'm not sure where this side road leads to, but let's try it."

The side road proved to be a dead-end street, but a well-used foot path led into the trees in the direction Owen wanted to go in, so they carried on. As they carefully worked their way closer the sound of voices grew ever nearer as well. The high clouds obscuring the half-moon were now being pushed away by the light wind, making it much easier to see where they were going.

Owen finally raised his hand to signal a halt as a

large stone building loomed into sight through the thin foliage surrounding it. Owen whispered to the others to slow their pace and move forward crouching low to remain in cover. They carried on until they reached a low stone wall surrounding the structure and he led them along it to get closer to the street they had originally been on.

As they did, they saw another large group of men all talking excitedly as they clustered about the entrance to the building. To the side of the entrance Owen made out a guard in uniform lying on the ground with hands tied behind him and a gag in his mouth. Oddly, none of the men were trying to gain access through the door, but were instead all looking upwards at the wooden roof of the structure. Owen followed their gaze and as he did the sound of wood being cut with an axe came from above. After several more blows, a crashing sound was heard and a few seconds later the door to the storehouse was opened from the inside.

The men poured through the doorway into the storehouse, leaving only one man standing outside. Owen frowned, for despite the poor light the dark profile of the man seemed oddly familiar. Owen slithered even closer down on his hands and knees to get a better look and see if he could hear what they were saying. As he did the first of the barrels of gunpowder was rolled out the door by two men. They stopped and one of them saluted the man as he spoke.

"These seem sturdy enough, Captain Bains. What do you think, can we just roll them down the hill?"

"Yes, but be careful. Two men to each barrel. We need every grain of it."

The American Captain clapped the man on his shoulder and sent them on their way, turning to give the same instructions to the next pair of men with a barrel. Chilled by the implications of hearing the American referred to as a Captain, Owen decided he had seen enough and he slunk back to where John and Wilson were waiting for him.

"It's the bloody American Bains again and I shouldn't be surprised. They are rolling the barrels down the hill to those whaleboats. Now I think on it, someone told me Tobacco Bay is too shallow for anything large to sail into, so this is why the rebels have their ships further offshore. The whaleboats are obviously there to move it from the shore to the ships and unfortunately the seas are calm tonight. It is obvious what they are doing and it's time to find some help. There is a fort a little further up the hill. Let's make for it and rouse the garrison."

Retracing their route to a point further from the storehouse the three men began to skirt the perimeter, following the stone wall around until it met with yet another path through the foliage. They moved as fast as they could while trying to keep the noise of their passage to a minimum, but Wilson stumbled on an unseen root and fell cursing with a crash into a bush. Owen knew they were still some distance from the fort and hoped no one was about to notice, but a voice hailed them out of the gloom. The suspicious tone in the voice was obvious.

"Who goes there?"

Owen sighed, for he had no simple answer to the

question which wouldn't raise even more questions and suspicions. He took a few more desperate moments trying to come up with something better than what he had in mind, but nothing did. While it seemed clear the man was a guard, the question was whether he was part of the garrison or a member of the raiders stealing the gunpowder. Owen motioned to John to circle around to the side before he walked into an open patch of ground where he could be seen as he spoke.

"A friend."

"A friend? What is the password?" said the guard with a wary tone to his voice, as he stepped into the light himself. As soon as he did Owen saw clearly he was not in uniform and the only weapon he carried was a cudgel.

"I'm sorry, I don't know any password, but I am a friend."

"You need to explain yourself now, or I am going to beat—"

John's hand appeared covering the man's mouth, preventing him from saying anything else. The two men crashed to the ground with John on top of him. John ripped the cudgel from the startled guard's hand and hammered him with it hard on the head. The man grunted inarticulately before falling silent, but as Owen feared, the guard was not alone. More alarmed sounding voices came from nearby and the sound of men hurtling through the foliage to reach them came from three different directions.

John met the first to appear with the cudgel, smashing the man in the face as another tackled him from the side. Owen came to his rescue and pulled the attacker off John as two more men came running into the clearing. Wilson barrelled into the fray using his fists. The fight rapidly became mass confusion in the dark, as meaty sounding punches landed hard and men cried out in pain at being struck. Owen knew time was not on their side, for their foes might already be bringing more reinforcements to the fight. With their path toward the still distant fort blocked, they had little choice.

"Back the way we came!" he roared out, knowing Wilson and John would recognize his voice.

With one last hard shove he sent the man he was struggling with stumbling into another trying to join the fray and the two of them fell hard into the low stone wall. Owen saw his way was now clear to the path he had come on and he ran fast for it.

"To me!" he called, to give Wilson and John another signal of where he was and the direction he was going.

The three men had the advantage of knowing where they were going. Owen sensed John and Wilson were with him, but he also heard a pursuer. Wilson was the last in line and he stopped to meet the man, who wasn't expecting him to turn back. The guard groaned as a heavy punch to his midsection took him and he crumpled to the ground.

As no one else seemed to be following them Owen quickly ordered a double time march and best efforts to stay out of sight. The cacophony of distant voices they left behind them grew once again as they neared the storehouse, where the scene was now frenzied. Several men were brandishing weapons and milling about looking in the direction of the fort further up the hill, while barrels were still being rolled steadily down to the beach.

Owen kept his men moving back down the path, knowing pursuit might soon be after them. He had no illusions about the treatment they would get if they were caught. Their way was blocked when the path intersected the road they originally came up, for a steady stream of men rolling barrels down the hill were being met by an equal number trudging back up the hill for more. With little choice they were forced to plunge into the thick foliage away from the road in order not to be seen. While it solved the immediate problem, it also slowed them enough the mosquitos and other insects had time to feast on the three struggling men.

When they finally reached the top of the hill where the road turned back toward St. George's the men paused to gather their wind and rest for a moment. All three were sore from injuries sustained in the melee. Wilson had a large bruise on the side of his face, while John was still bleeding from a minor cut on his left hand. Owen had taken a glancing blow to the side of his head which he knew would ache for a few days.

As they looked out over Tobacco Bay it was obvious Owen's original assessment was correct. Two whaling boats were almost fully loaded while the now empty third one was already being rowed back from the ships offshore to collect another load. Owen sighed.

"Well, I fear by the time we get some help the storehouse will be empty, but perhaps we can get someone to go after those two ships out there. John, do you remember seeing any Navy ships in port?"

John frowned. "No. There was one a few days earlier, but they left. Unless someone has just showed up, I think we are out of luck."

"Right, double time back to town. We can stop at the Navy's dock since it is on the way to the Governor's residence in case there is actually a ship in the harbour."

A half hour later they reached the port, but Owen's hope was crushed as there were no Royal Navy ships anywhere in sight. A sleepy Navy guard confirmed what Owen was seeing and told him none were expected for several days. When told of the problem the man shrugged.

"What would you have me do, sir? My orders are to stand guard."

"Are there more men at hand in St. George's? Perhaps we can take the whaleboats and prevent them from escaping."

"Sir, there are two others who serve in the port here with me and they are sleeping. I say again, my orders are to stand guard. I would take you to an officer you could speak to if there was one here, but there are none here."

Owen saw no help for it but to carry on to the Governor's residence. By the time they reached it Owen sensed the night was waning and with it their opportunity to put a stop to what was happening, but he knew he had to try. A lone soldier slumped against the door stood guard at the entrance to the Governor's residence. The man shook himself fully awake on seeing the three men appear and advance to the entrance. He called out a warning and brandished his weapon.

"Halt. What is your business here, sirs?"

Owen hurriedly explained the situation and requested the man wake the Governor. The soldier frowned and looked dubious.

"My orders are the Governor is not to be disturbed. Can this not wait till morning? The dawn is perhaps a little more than an hour or two away now at most. I suggest you come back later."

Owen groaned. "Do you not see it will be too late by then, you fool? They will escape with the gunpowder."

The man became obstinate and refused, continuing to argue with Owen. The guard was so focused on Owen he failed to react in time when John and Wilson appeared on either side of him and pinned his arms, pulling him to the side. John nodded in the direction of the door.

"Perhaps you should let the Governor know we are here, Captain."

Owen pulled out his sword and used the butt of the grip to pound hard several times on the door. After waiting what he thought was long enough for someone to come to the door he used his sword twice more to demand attention. The door abruptly opened after the third such effort to reveal the Governor himself standing in the doorway in his nightshirt. He was brandishing a sword in his hand, waving the point back and forth at the men outside. He glared about at all of them before a look of recognition appeared and his gaze settled back on Owen.

"Captain Spence? What in God's name is going on here? I hope you have a very good reason for this disturbance."

"I apologize for this, but we certainly do have reason, Governor. Time is critical and we would not have disturbed you otherwise."

Owen quickly detailed the situation for the Governor. As the implications of what Owen was telling him became clear, the man lowered his sword and his face fell. A look of total shock slowly came over him and he held his free hand to his forehead.

"My God, this is a disaster. You could not stop them?"

"Governor, as you can see from our various injuries, we were lucky to escape. There are far too many of them. We need help and a lot of it."

"Yes, yes, of course," said the Governor, still looking flustered. "Come in and sit. I must get ready and come. Give me some time, please."

A half hour later the Governor reappeared fully dressed and ready to go. Despite the urgency Owen had tried to convey, the man had roused his household to brew a quick cup of tea for everyone and he had his groom ready his carriage for him. Owen downed his tea gratefully to help shrug off his weariness and decided to simply give up fretting about it, for he knew they had done what they could. Owen and his men joined the Governor in his carriage, and they set off heading north at a brisk pace toward the storeroom. The first bare hint of the coming dawn was showing on the eastern horizon as they set out.

By the time they arrived at the storehouse no one was about. The raiders had left the door wide open and the guard lying still trussed on the ground near the entrance. The Governor stopped the carriage, and they quickly untied the grateful guard, who was sporting a vicious looking bruise on the side of his head. Owen peered into the storehouse, but it was empty of barrels and all that remained was the sulphurous, metallic smell of the gunpowder. Owen feared the worst as the four men jumped back onto the carriage and headed for Tobacco Bay.

As the carriage drew close and the scene before them became clear his heart soared once again. To Owen's utter surprise the two American ships were still there. The reason was immediately clear even in the now dim light of pre-dawn, for the ocean surface was like glass. John looked about in all directions and turned to Owen.

"There's no wind, Owen. Look at the trees, there isn't even a single leaf moving. They are becalmed."

"Governor, there is still time to stop this," said Owen. "They aren't going anywhere until the wind picks up. We must find some men and ships."

"Yes, yes, I agree, but where? I thought you said they were using whaleboats, Mr. Spence."

Owen looked down at the beach and saw he the three boats used to ferry the gunpowder out were nowhere in sight.

"Governor, they must have left as soon as they finished the job. The whaleboats harbour in St. George's. They must be rowing them back there. Can we commandeer them if they have returned and go after the gunpowder? Maybe get some others? I recall seeing several whaleboats in the harbour."

The Governor chewed his lip briefly before responding. "We can but try. Let's go back to St. George's. We will need men."

Twenty minutes later they were back in St. George's and as soon as they arrived the Governor launched into a frenzy of activity in the port. The three whaleboats could be seen silhouetted against the eastern horizon only now coming around the eastern headland of the harbour. Many men were already working around other whaleboats docked in port.

Owen was suspicious about the sheer number of men in the area and surmised many had simply walked back from Tobacco Bay, while others were returning by rowing the boats to the harbour. Other fishermen and sailors were also in the area, working on their own boats in preparation for the coming day. The sun was now a golden, molten line shimmering on the eastern horizon helping them to see what they were doing.

The Governor stopped his carriage on the dock and began calling loudly for the men to gather around him. Several looked at each other wordlessly before slowly shuffling over to gather in a semi-circle around him. Standing on his carriage, the Governor began by quickly explaining what was happening and asking for their help to row out and recapture the stolen gunpowder. None of the men stepped forward as it became clear what he wanted and to Owen's dismay, several turned away and went back to doing what they were before the Governor had interrupted them.

The Governor looked incredulous as more and more men drifted away. He climbed down, reaching out to grasp the sleeve of one who was in the act of leaving. The man stopped and scowled down at the Governor's hand. The Governor let go and pleaded with him to help. The man's reply was direct.

"We don't want to do that, Governor. Find someone else. Good day."

The Governor appeared stunned and stood watching them all leave before turning back to Owen.

"Good God, Mr. Spence. I don't know what to do."

"Sir, what about the Navy or the Army? Can they supply us with men? They could take these boats whether any of them like it or not. I will offer up my men off *The Sea Trader* if I must. But we must have more boats and more men."

"Yes, of course. We'll take the carriage back to my residence, quickly."

"John, Wilson, go to *The Sea Trader* and rouse the men," said Owen. "Get them armed and ready to seize some whaleboats once enough men arrive. I will remain with the Governor. Those two American warships will be far stronger than we are, but if we can round up some men and perhaps get more boats, we can row out together and overwhelm them with our numbers."

Minutes later Owen and the Governor were back at his residence where his aides were wide awake and awaiting orders. The Governor decided the best course was to have the local Army and Navy commanders meet them at Tobacco Bay, for he thought it likely they would want to assess the situation before taking action. Owen chafed at the notion of yet more delay, but saw no other course. Aides were dispatched to find both officers and ask them to meet the Governor back at Tobacco Bay after beginning a muster of their men.

The sun was fully over the horizon and dispelling the remaining night shadows fast by the time they arrived back at the bay. To Owen's amazement their luck had held, for the two warships were still becalmed offshore. On seeing the ships still there it became the Governor's turn to fret.

"What do you think, Mr. Spence? Will the wind come up?"

"I'd like to be optimistic, Governor. The problem with weather conditions such as this is it almost always changes soon, especially as the heat of the day begins. It is unusual to have a calm sea for very long."

Ten worrisome minutes later the Governor finally cried out as he spied an Army officer riding a horse come down the hill from the direction of the raided storehouse. As the man came to a halt and dismounted in front of them Owen saw Captain Sanders in his Royal Navy uniform also coming from the direction of St. George's and making for their position. When they were all present a hurried conference began between the four men, with the Governor filling the two officers in on what had happened from the beginning.

As he finished, he looked back and forth at the two men, obviously expecting a reaction he wasn't seeing from them. The two officers remained silently staring out to sea at the warships, with both men obviously deep in thought. The Governor had an edge to his voice as he drew their attention back.

"Well, sirs? We have a serious problem here. We must act, because those ships won't stay becalmed forever. What are we going to do?"

The Army officer was the first to respond. He shrugged and waved a hand in the general direction of the ships.

"Governor, I will help with a specific request if one is presented, but when it comes to action on the water I must defer to the Navy. I have men being rousted and they will join us soon, but this is not my domain."

The Governor immediately turned to Captain Sanders, who responded with a shrug of his own.

"Governor, I would be happy to help also, but I have no ships or men close at hand. They are all at sea. In fact, the only reason I am in port just now is my own frigate is in for repairs at the Dockyard over on the west island. With the exception of a few people to service the port here in St. George's, I have no other men to command. There is nothing to be done here."

"Good God, man," said Owen, unable to contain himself any longer. "We have to do something."

Captain Sanders scowled at Owen.

"What would you have me do, for God's sake? Swim out to the warships with a sword in my teeth and have at them? Even from here I can see the crews on their decks. Those ships likely have at least thirty or more men on each one."

Owen glowered back at him. "What I would

have you do is get off your arse. You don't have ships? Find some men, commandeer whatever ships you can find, and let's get after these bastards even if we must row out to do it. I have already offered my own ship's men for the effort. This stolen gunpowder will be used to kill our soldiers and sailors if we don't find a way to stop this."

"I just told you, you fool, I have nowhere near enough men to command here. Are you deaf?"

"My God. What about the Army?" said Owen, turning to the Army officer, who rubbed his chin in thought.

"Sirs, I have perhaps twenty or so men on the way to the port as the Governor requested."

"You are mad," said Captain Sanders, still glaring at Owen. "You would have me use soldiers to board those ships? They would be cut to pieces even if we had some magical way to get them alongside those two frigates. Soldiers wouldn't know the first thing about how to conduct a boarding action."

"Perhaps not, but if they know they could be saving the lives of many of their comrades, I think they would learn fast. Look, if you aren't bloody willing to deal with this, I will."

Owen turned back to the Governor.

"Governor, I volunteer to lead a party to take those ships. We must act. If we delay any longer, men will die."

"Governor," said Captain Sanders, making no effort to hide the note of scorn in his voice. "As much as I agree our men are at risk, I cannot support the notion of putting a man dismissed from the Navy in charge of an effort to retake those ships. I guarantee men will die if you do. Leave it with me. I will send word to my squadron as soon as possible to be on the lookout for these two warships."

"Look, sirs," said Owen, unable to keep a hopeful tone from his voice, as he pointed up the hill to where John was now coming toward them with a half dozen of their crew.

"Some of my men are arriving from St. Georges. Perhaps we can find other boats nearby to use?"

The Governor cursed aloud in response and let his head fall to his chest for a moment before he looked up. When he did, the other three men realized as one the man was not looking at any of them. Owen was puzzled for a moment until the sickening realization the wind had finally risen came to him.

All four men turned to look out to sea and saw growing ripples on the water of the bay. Both of the frigates had let their sails out and the wind was even now filling them. Although the breeze was still light, Owen could see the tell-tale signs of the wind strengthening even more.

"Thank you for your time, gentlemen. It seems the weather has made a decision for us. Captain Sanders, please do your best to get the word out. We can but hope your squadron finds them in time. I must return to my office and write some letters about this. Captain Spence, I will ensure Sir Ross is made aware of what has happened as soon as possible."

"Thank you, Governor. That will allow me to

return to Barbados sooner. I will be departing within the hour."

The two officers mounted their horses and left in silence. Owen remained staring out to sea for a long moment, watching the two ships sailing east to disappear past the headland and make for open ocean. The Governor called to him from his perch on the carriage, impatience to be away in his voice. Owen didn't care, for he knew it was far, far too late. With a sigh, he waved the Governor away and told him he would walk back to St. Georges with his men.

"I couldn't bear waiting any longer, Owen," said John as he walked up. "We came to see if anything could be done here."

Owen only shook his head and pointed back in the direction of St. Georges. All he had left was an overwhelming desire to go home.

Epilogue
Barbados
September 1775

The weather mid-September in Bridgetown could usually be counted on to be easing from the blazing heat and humidity of the summer. Despite that Owen found his clothes sticking to him a bit more than expected as he walked along the docks, for it hadn't lessened much on this particular day.

Relief would be at hand soon enough, for he was on his way to a shady table on the upper deck of The Boatyard Inn to meet his uncle and Sir James Standish for lunch once again. The two men were already there, nursing drinks while waiting for Owen. A server appeared as Owen sat down and he gratefully ordered his own drink.

"I've already taken the liberty of ordering for us, nephew," said Owen's uncle. "Turtle soup, a spicy flying fish sandwich with rice for the main, and the usual array of desserts on special."

"Perfect, uncle. I am amazed they have managed to provide all of this with the food shortages we have."

"The owners of this establishment have friends everywhere, but even they may not be able to provide for us this well in future, so enjoy it while you can," said Sir James. "We asked you here to give you a full update, Owen. We didn't have much time when you first returned, but we do now. I'd like to thank you for your efforts. It is sad they were in vain, but you personally did well and if anyone deserves some credit here, it is you."

"Thank you. You know I was angry about this, and I confess I still am, although I am calmer about it now. But do we have news, sir?"

"I'm afraid we do. The Navy was not able to locate the two American ships and they delivered their cargo to the rebels. One ship apparently went to Charleston in South Carolina and the other went to Philadelphia. What you also may not know yet is the Americans sent a message they are calling the Olive Branch Petition to the King in July, while issuing a document the next day which justifies for their own purposes the taking up of arms. We have just received word the King was so angered he wouldn't even look at their Petition. He has issued his own Proclamation of Rebellion and is declaring them to be traitors."

"The die is cast, then," said Owen, letting his frustration boil to the surface once again. "Damn it, just damn it all."

The two older men regarded him in silence. Owen knew they could say little to allay his anger, but he finally spoke once again.

"Sir James? What about those bastards in Bermuda who helped them with the raid on the storehouse? I hope the Governor has tracked them all down and is making them pay for their treason. Good men are going to die because of it."

Sir James and Owen's uncle both grimaced in unison and stared at each other for a moment, before Sir James responded.

"I'm afraid it isn't happening and won't be happening, Owen."

Owen was incredulous. "Good God, why not?

Those men manning the whaleboats they used had to be local people. It couldn't be hard to track them down. And whoever owns those three whaleboats should be taken out and shot, because I have no doubt they were involved too."

"Owen, the three whaleboats are owned by the Tucker family and the men who sail them all work for the family. The thought of holding them or any of those men to account is not likely to cross the Governor's mind. I suspect the Governor may not have mentioned to you he is related by marriage to the Tucker family, did he? Hmm, I see by the look on your face he did not. Yes, he has a daughter married to the oldest son of St. George Tucker."

Owen shook his head in disbelief. "I see. And no one is going to pursue this issue with the Governor? This is treason we are talking about."

Owen's uncle grimaced again. "Owen, as with many things in life, what is going to happen and what should happen sometimes end up being very different. You can be assured there are many people seriously unhappy about this, but it has been deemed expedient to simply move on."

"There is no benefit to making this an even larger issue than it already is," said Sir James. "Exposing incompetence and treason at a time when the nation is badly torn and on the brink of an escalating war will not serve the greater purpose. In point of fact, the only people coming out of this affair not looking like buffoons are those of us in the employ of the Foreign Office and you in particular. It's not like we didn't warn them all, you understand."

The conversation lapsed into silence as their main course began arriving and Owen used the interruption to think about what they had said. In between sips of his soup, he finally spoke up.

"I see I have much to learn still. I do not like this, but I understand and agree you are right. I guess I still haven't given up on a world where there is right and there is wrong, with nothing in between."

"I wouldn't lose sight of the notion yet, Owen," said Sir James. "We all know this is wrong, but we just have to take the long view and deal with it. As I said, note has been taken of the people responsible for this, including the goddamned French. They are mixed up in this. If some other opportunity to hold any of these people to account arises, you can rest assured it will be seized."

"You know, Sir James, I agree with you about the French in particular. I think sometimes the best way to deal with a problem might be the convenient solution of a knife in the back. Please don't think I'm bloodthirsty or anything, but I try to be a realist. I just don't like the fact their treachery will result in many good men dying. So I'm not opposed to expediency as an option if it is necessary in future."

"Who knows, Mr. Spence. It may well be. Our job is to simply carry on and find a way to bring this madness to an end as soon as possible. Sadly, I fear it may be a long way off now. We simply must get down to business."

"This would all be a lot easier if it weren't for the reality we all have some sympathy for the Americans," said Owen's uncle. "We have spoken of this before. Many are torn in their loyalties and it is getting worse."

Owen was busy working on his sandwich, but he paused to sip at his drink and respond.

"Well, I just hope people start listening to you gentlemen. I think they need you more than ever now."

"It would be good if they were paying attention to you as well, Owen," said Sir James. "I have had a long conversation with the Admiral here in Barbados and I plan to do the same with his colleague in Jamaica. It seems clear to me your former Captain and his family have spread their poison far and wide in the Navy about you. This nonsense has to be stopped and the Admiral here agrees. He is a very good friend of mine, so you know. He is not beholden to Captain Smithe in any way, although the fellow in Jamaica may be another matter."

Sir James paused to shrug before continuing.

"In any case, I have made it clear you and your crew are a valuable asset to the Foreign Office and are doing good service. I have asked him to discreetly impress this point on all Captains under his command in the Caribbean. He can't change what happened, but he will be emphasizing obliquely your dismissal may have had—issues. It will be left at this and I don't know if it will change the minds of any of these fools, but we shall see."

Owen was silent for a long moment as he considered Sir James's words. While grateful for everything his uncle and Sir James had done for him in giving him a new life, the notion this was even necessary in the first place still rankled. The

Smithe family had impacted his life and his family far too much.

Somehow, Sir James's use of the word poison seemed entirely apt, and their malign influence was being felt by many others too. Owen vowed to himself if an opportunity ever came his way to curb it, he would seize it without hesitation. Recalling himself from his thoughts, Owen nodded to Sir James.

"Thank you for this, Sir James. It is good to know I am appreciated."

"You deserve it. I am sorry it took me so long to address this issue. I should have done this much sooner."

"No matter, sir. I will ensure the crew knows our work has been favourably noticed as well."

"Well, we need you to be effective at what you do, because I fear there will be no lack of Foreign Office tasks coming your way in future."

"This is not all others have noticed, Owen," said his uncle with a laugh. "My niece is most unhappy you have not come to pay court to her yet. I would remedy this before you really end up in trouble if I were you."

"Pay her court?" said Owen with a rueful smile. "Uncle, she is still—what, only thirteen or fourteen? You know I like her as a friend, you understand, but she really is still a little young for this, don't you think? She still seems a child to me."

"She is fifteen this coming November. And need I remind you of when I first introduced you two? I recall telling you she behaves as if she is ten years older than she is. Consider yourself warned."

Both Sir James and Owen's uncle laughed.

***

The day Elizabeth agreed to go riding with him arrived with a brilliant, clear blue, cloudless sky. The sticky heat of the summer had finally eased, but it remained pleasantly warm. Elizabeth's aunt had packed them a small snack to stop and eat, along with a blanket to spread on the ground.

Elizabeth and Mary knew the area far better than he, so they gave him directions to a secluded spot on a little bluff overlooking the ocean. He took Elizabeth's hand to help her down from the carriage and helped her unpack what Aunt Mary had given them. They spread a blanket and sat on the ground looking at the ocean as they all ate their small snack. Afterwards Elizabeth wanted to walk the beach and Owen agreed. Owen was surprised Mary was not going to join them, but she waved his concern away.

"Oh, I know I decorum says I should be along as a chaperone, but I would rather stay here. I've had my share of walks on the beach in my time. Besides, you are a gentleman, are you not, Mr. Spence?"

Owen stood straight and looked her in the eye as he responded.

"Mary, I am very much a gentleman. You may rest assured nothing untoward will happen."

"I know," she replied with a smile. "Have a good time."

Owen and Elizabeth removed their shoes and walked off barefoot along the beach. Owen once again marvelled at how soft the sand was. Elizabeth reached out to steady herself on his arm as she almost lost her balance. Somehow her arm stayed entwined with his as they carried on and she smiled up at him.

"You will be happy to know I have almost forgiven you for so cruelly ignoring me until now."

"A ship is a demanding mistress, Elizabeth. It needs care and attention. I had reports to do, paperwork to deal with, make sure the men get paid. The tasks are endless. And I can assure you, this is the soonest I could free myself from my duties."

"I trust you, Owen. I expect I am just being greedy."

"I do enjoy my time with you, you know. I am not pretending, Elizabeth."

"I know," she said, giving him a blazing smile once again, before turning serious.

"And what of your friend in Jamaica? Did you stop to see her again?"

Owen laughed. "Yes, yes I did. I told you I would. But you will be happy to know she has found someone since my last visit. They are to be married."

"Married? So, you won't be seeing her again?"

"Well, I expect I will. She is a friend, remember? But if you mean seeing her in the way I think you mean, the answer is no. I wouldn't do anything so untoward. But I would like to know she is doing well, for she really is a wonderful person."

Elizabeth glanced at Owen, a searching look on her face, before she stopped and stepped away, looking out to sea. She reached down to pick up a seashell from beach and spent a few long moments examining it. When she finally spoke, she took Owen by surprise.

"I know, you think I am still far too young, and in some ways, I expect I am. But in other ways I feel much, much older. I don't know why this is, but it is who I am. Aunt Mary and I have had many long talks, you know. I am well aware men have—needs. You are away at sea and are on different islands for long periods of time. There are many beautiful women out there and I expect there are many who would want you. I cannot expect you to ignore them. I would just prefer not to know about it. So please don't break my heart, Owen. Does this make sense?"

Owen smiled. "It does."

She bit her lip briefly and hesitated a moment. She took a deep breath before finally getting out what Owen knew she really wanted to say.

"What I would very much like to know is you will promise to give me a chance one day too? Will you do that, Owen?"

Owen reached out to grasp both her hands and she shivered ever so slightly as he took them, looking into her eyes.

"Elizabeth, I guarantee I will give you a chance, and I hope you will do the same for me. I look forward to it. But let's just see what the future holds, shall we?"

Her fierce smile matched the light of the sun all around them and Owen knew he somehow was both wanting and waiting to see it. Elizabeth simply laughed with joy.

The End

Author Notes

Many others before me have made the observation the oldest profession in the world is prostitution. In other books I have written I noted spying on your foes and enslaving other people are likely competition vying for this distinction. As these three activities continue to flourish to varying degrees to this day, I shall leave it to you to decide what this says about humanity. I personally find it especially appalling to know slavery is still alive and well.

Another thought to consider is around the dawn of time someone decided it would be a good idea to make people pay part of their hard-earned money to the government on a regular basis. In the course of writing this work the idea of perhaps adding this activity to the list crossed my mind.

Over the millennia these payments have been called levies, tolls, fees, and heaven knows what else for whatever purpose, but in reality, they are all just forms of taxation. I am quite certain protests clamouring about how unfair it all was appeared a millisecond or so after the first such tax was applied. While it is certainly true governments on occasion spend these monies for sometimes dubious reasons, it is also fair to note much of it is spent on positive purposes, and this is what perhaps distinguishes this from the other three activities.

I hope my portrayal of the desperation, anger, and mixed feelings people had about the whole situation in this era has done justice to those who experienced it all. Times were hard in the colonies of America, the people were badly torn, and taxes were the flashpoint. The inhabitants of the British Caribbean islands felt much the same way.

In places like Barbados the slaves really were coming to face starvation, as most of the arable lands of these islands were given over to producing the incredibly profitable sugar cane. Growing crops and catching fish to feed everyone was left to the American colonies. When this was disrupted there were problems everywhere in the Caribbean, and not just in the British colonies, because the countries involved in sugar production were all using the same approach.

The divide between the loyalist and rebel causes was stark in America. The people were forced to make a decision and sometimes families were torn apart as a result. As the rebel cause gained momentum those who chose to support the loyalist side were forced to either fight or flee.

Those who fled were often leaving the place of their birth for distant shores they had never been to, and many departed with little or nothing to their name. Some went to England and some to the Caribbean if they had family who could help, while many came to Canada. The United Empire Loyalists, as they came to be known, settled in Nova Scotia and in what are now called the provinces of Quebec and Ontario. I suspect the large, free grants of crown land available to them made the proposition of having to endure our cold winters a more palatable choice to these settlers.

I have attempted to ensure the historical framework of this work is as close to the reality of what happened as possible. The court case Granville Sharp won, the earthquake which devastated Port Royal, the history of Porto Bello, the Boston Massacre, the use of the Green Dragon Inn to plot revolution, the crisis brought about by the bad behaviour of The East India Company, the Boston Tea Party, the siege of Boston, and the battle of Bunker Hill are all well documented, real events.

As for the Bermuda gunpowder plot, everything about the raid on the storehouse was real, as was the local support provided via the men and whaleboats to convey the gunpowder out to the waiting American ships. The Governor's attempts to convince the locals to row out to the becalmed ships and retake the powder fell on deaf ears, for many Bermudans very much wanted the raid to succeed.

The characters in this book for the most part came out of my imagination, with a few exceptions. The Governor of Bermuda and the various Tucker family members with confusingly similar names were all real and behaved as portrayed. Of the imaginary characters all are new, except for Sir James Standish.

For those of you who may not be aware, I have six books of already published historical fiction entitled The Evan Ross Series, which spans the period 1783 to 1805. This is also set in the Caribbean and Sir James Standish is featured in the series as a spymaster. As I needed one for The Owen Spence Series too, I decided it made no sense to create a new one when I already had a perfectly good character at the ready. He is naturally a bit younger in this work.

As for the French and American spymasters, they are of course imaginary too, although the committees of correspondence were real. One of these was indeed dedicated to intelligence activities. I have no historical record to point to in support of the notion the French were somehow involved as I have portrayed them in this work. Given their reputation and relationship with the British over the years, I submit it is not farfetched to depict them as I have. And if they weren't as involved in events as described, this certainly changed fast not long after.

In all of the books I've written involving the Caribbean, slavery is a constant element impacting the people and events of the time massively and it underlies the metaphor I keep using for my book titles. If one were somehow able to count all the grains of sugar sand on the beaches of the Caribbean and convert them to pennies, I suspect the total might be close to the staggering sum of money people made from using slavery to support the sugar trade in this era. Perhaps this is a stretch, but maybe the image is not so far off either.

I love the Caribbean and its history, with its fascinating characters and amazing islands. There are so many I couldn't resist inserting a small reference to an example of one such character in this work. In Chapter Eight, Owen and Elizabeth have lunch at a location owned by a fellow named John Lord, who was in fact real. A few decades after this the owner's also real son, a man named Sam Lord, earned himself enduring notoriety in Barbados.

Because his estate was situated on the eastern

shore of Barbados, ships arriving from England with the trade winds would have to sail past his land. The story is he hung several lanterns from the palm trees at night to fool ships into thinking they were the lights of Bridgetown. When they smashed onto the reef offshore, Sam Lord would have his men scavenge for goods to recover and sell.

In this way he managed to accumulate a fortune large enough to build what was known as Sam Lord's Castle. This was turned into a tourist attraction with a hotel on the property, which I visited long before the Castle burned down in 2010. In this case, his form of piracy paid well, for his Castle was indeed an amazing mansion when I toured it.

If you enjoyed this work, you have more interesting stories on your horizon. The entire era from the beginning of the American Revolution through to the Battle of Trafalgar is fascinating and the Caribbean was in the thick of many of the tumultuous events of the time. If you have interest, please do take a look at *The Evan Ross Series* if you haven't already done so.

You can also look forward to more in *The Owen Spence Series*. This consists of three works, in the following order:

The Sugar Sands
The Sugar Storm
The Sugar Winds

The Sugar Storm will take you to a couple of small Caribbean islands most readers likely know little about, if you have even heard of them before. The first of these is St. Eustatius, which in our times has lapsed into obscurity, but for a few brief years in the late 1770's it was quite the opposite.

You will also visit the little-known island of Dominica and enjoy its rich history in The Sugar Storm. For those of you who may not know, the fascinating island of Dominica is not to be confused with The Dominican Republic, a popular vacation destination with plenty of all-inclusive beach resorts occupying half of the nearby island of Hispaniola.

Both St. Eustatius and Dominica were very much worthy of the attention of the world powers involved in the Caribbean in this era. To find out why, watch for *The Sugar Storm*, coming in 2022. I hope you have enjoyed *The Sugar Sands*.

Made in the USA
Monee, IL
13 June 2021